the
last best
kiss

Also by Claire LaZebnik

The Trouble with Flirting

Epic Fail

If You Lived Here, You'd Be Home Now

The Smart One and the Pretty One

Knitting Under the Influence

Same As It Never Was

Claire LaZebnik

the last best kiss

An Imprint of HarperCollinsPublishers

HarperTeen is an imprint of HarperCollins Publishers.

The Last Best Kiss
For information address HarperCollins Children's Books, a
division of HarperCollins Publishers, 10 East 53rd Street, New
York, NY 10022.
www.epicreads.com

Library of Congress Cataloging-in-Publication Data
LaZebnik, Claire Scovell.
The last best kiss / Claire LaZebnik. — First edition.
    pages cm
Summary: In this modern take on Jane Austen's "Persuasion,"
Anna Eliot tries to win back Finn Westbrook, the boy whose
heart she broke three years ago.
    ISBN 978-0-06-225228-9 (pbk. bdg.)
    [1. Dating (Social customs)—Fiction. 2. Interpersonal
relations—Fiction.] I. Title.
PZ7.L4496Las 2014   2013021524
[Fic]—dc23   CIP
                                                              AC

    14 15 16 17 18   CG/RRDH   10 9 8 7 6 5 4 3 2 1
                                ❖
                          First Edition

For Will, my *Doctor Who*—*Buffy*—*Merlin*—
Sherlock—junky-'80s-sci-fi-movie companion.
If there's a greater joy than curling up with you to
binge-watch something fun, I haven't found it yet.

prologue

freshman year

On nights when I'm honest with myself, I can admit that Finn Westbrook was the best thing about my ninth-grade year.

But it hurts to think about him, so I try not to be honest with myself too often.

That was my first year at Sterling Woods High, but I had a group of friends who were all moving on from the same middle school together, so it wasn't a crazy-scary move. Just the normal amount of scary.

I came in feeling pretty confident: by the time I had finished up middle school, I *owned* the place. I spent eighth grade strutting around elbow-in-elbow with my best friend, Lucy; greeting everyone I knew—and I knew everyone; raising my hand a lot in class; and hanging out with friends after school. I worked on both the yearbook and the school newspaper and started an art-and-literary magazine that made my English teacher cry tears of joy when she held the first issue in her hands.

My home life wasn't so great, though. My parents had divorced back when I was in fifth grade, which didn't exactly make me special—a lot of my friends had parents who'd been divorced once or twice. I was, however, the only girl I knew whose mother had given full-time custody to her ex-husband. And not because he had fought her for it. Because she wanted it even less than he did.

"I'm just not good at being a mother" was how she explained the decision to her three daughters. "You can't really disagree with that."

She was right: we really couldn't.

Anyway, so long as Marta was our nanny, we basically had a mom: she was the one who had doled out the hugs and cupcakes over the years, not my parents, who both went off to work until it was way past dinner every weekday and then argued for the right to isolate themselves from the kids on the weekends. (Marta's sister Rosa solved that problem by becoming our weekend nanny.)

About three years after my mother moved out, my dad celebrated my thirteenth birthday by taking me and my sisters to Benihana, where, over fried rice and sautéed shrimp, he informed us that he had fired both Marta and Rosa. "You're too old for nannies now," he said. "Molly has her license already, and Lizzie will get hers soon, and"—a nod toward me—"Anna's old enough to be home alone. See how much faith I have in my responsible girls?" He smiled and ran his fingers through his thick brown hair that was still free of any trace of gray. (Later I learned to be suspicious of that, but back then I was proud that my father wasn't gray and balding like a lot of the other dads.) "Now who wants green-tea ice cream?"

I shook my head, my appetite gone. Molly did the same. Lizzie said she'd have some, then shifted closer to Dad on her stool and said, "You're all we need, Daddy." He smiled back down at her.

"What about Marta and Rosa?" Molly said in a dull voice. "Do they have other jobs?"

"I've been asking around," Dad said. "I'll help them find something—don't worry. I gave them both good references and very generous severance checks, so they're going to be fine."

I think that was when Molly got quiet.

She'd never been a big talker, but she used to like to sit with me and Marta and share stories about her day. After Dad fired Marta, though, she barely said a word around him. He called her a "typical sullen teenager" and laughed it off.

When Marta and Rosa still worked for us, we three girls usually ate meals with them, but that pretty much fell apart after they left. When we got hungry, we made ourselves meals from whatever food Dad picked up on his way home from work or we ordered in pizzas and ate slices over our computers. I spent most of my time when I was home connected to my laptop by earbuds, watching movies or video-chatting with friends. My sisters did the same thing, but sometimes Molly would bring her homework into my room at night, and we'd sit side by side, not really talking, just sharing the space companionably.

We always got along well, but the age gap between us was big—four years—and we were pretty different: I liked to see friends and draw pictures of horses, and she was a hardworking student who ran track and listened to music. But we clung together. Lizzie sometimes hung out with us, but we bored her. She was my father's daughter in every way: they both loved gourmet food and exercising and dishing about other people—and not much else. Molly and I disappointed them by having other interests. So the family usually split in half. When Dad wasn't home, Lizzie visited with friends or stayed in her room.

About once a month until she left for college (and during vacations after that), Molly would drive us out to see Marta in her small apartment in Glendale. Lizzie went the first couple of times and then stopped. I didn't blame her: we didn't have much to say to Marta, now that she wasn't part of our daily lives and was working for another family. We loved her because she had taken care of us, and that was enough to make us want to keep seeing her, but it wasn't enough to make those visits not feel awkward.

By the time I was fourteen, my interest in drawing had become more of an obsession. I took classes at the local art school, experimented with different media, and moved beyond just drawing horses. I discovered I could get lost in making art: it gave me something to do when I was feeling bored and lonely—which I was most of the time at home after Molly went off to college.

Molly left the fall I entered high school, which meant Lizzie was in charge of driving us both to school. That first morning she told me I had to sit in the back because she was picking up her friend Cameron and they wanted to be able to talk together. She was also going to be driving another kid, whose name and address she had found in the school directory and whose body in the car meant she had a carpool of four and could therefore get a space in the best student parking lot at school, right near the entrance.

After Cameron had gotten in and the two of them had gossiped and ignored me for several blocks, Lizzie pulled over in front of a small house with an unkempt front yard and honked the horn. A boy emerged from the front door and flew down the walkway, a backpack slung over one shoulder.

I figured it was the freshman's little brother on his way to the bus stop or something, but then he came up to the car and opened the door, and I realized he was older than he looked from a distance and might actually be my age. He had brown eyes behind bulky tortoiseshell glasses, a narrow face, curly brown hair that needed a trim, and stooped shoulders. He couldn't have weighed more than ninety pounds.

He slid onto the seat next to me, closed his car door, introduced himself as Finn Westbrook, and pulled out a phone from his pocket. "Here," he said. "Look at this. How cool is that?"

The photo was of the aurora borealis over an icy landscape in Norway. It was startling and beautiful, with green water flowing under spiky ice floes. He hadn't taken the photo, he quickly explained—he just liked it. I liked it too and told him so. He beamed, his smile broad in his thin face, and flicked through the photos on his phone to find some more treasures to show me.

Many more photos followed, not just that day but every morning from then on. Finn loved the natural world, loved the way cameras and telescopes and microscopes and rovers and submarines could show us things we'd otherwise never even know existed. Sometimes he'd make me try to guess what I was looking at. I almost always guessed wrong, assuming a photo was of a planet's surface when it was really just some parched area of

Asia or something, and every time he'd say something like "That's what I thought at first too," which couldn't possibly have been true but was kind.

The other thing he said a lot those first few days was: "I know—I'm a total nerd." He always said it with a shrug and a smile. He wasn't apologizing for it, just acknowledging it.

"Me too," I told him a few days into the carpool.

He shook his head. "No, you're not. You may be smart and like science, but you're not a nerd." Then he ducked his head and mumbled something I couldn't entirely hear.

"What?" I said.

He flushed. "Just . . . you don't look like a nerd. Too cute."

"That's not fair," I said with mock outrage. I liked the compliment—a lot—but didn't know how to respond to it. It seemed easier to ignore it. "I can be a nerd if I want to be."

"Okay," he said. "You're right."

Finn and I turned out to have one class together—Spanish—but we didn't sit together there, because I had a couple of friends in that class and they always saved me a seat. I wished I had science with him. Science with Finn Westbrook seemed like it would be a fun thing. He knew the coolest facts about the natural world.

There was no overlap between his friends and mine.

He hung out with two boys—Josh Starr and Otis Chan—who were both undeniably brilliant, undeniably focused, and undeniably nerdy. Not unlike Finn. The three of them were lucky to be at a prep school like ours, where most of us were focused on getting into a top college, so good grades and intelligence were admired.

Although . . . no one really wants to make out with good grades and intelligence, so these kids were more popular in the classroom than they were after school let out.

I never saw them at the parties I went to that year, parties that were pale imitations of the ones the upperclassmen threw, because none of us could drive yet, and our dependence on our parents for lifts back and forth meant we couldn't get away with drinking alcohol or dressing as skimpily as we'd have liked to. We *could*, however, make out with the guys we thought were hot—as far as we knew, parents couldn't detect recent tongue kissing.

Being free to make out and *wanting* to make out were two different things, though. The sad truth was that the list of hot guys in our class was extremely short. My friends and I were discriminating. Sam Richards was broad-shouldered but had acne. Eric Manolo was cheerful and likable but too chubby. Jackson Levy was a good athlete but had body odor. Oscar Green was perfect and almost definitely gay.

Tiny, nerdy Finn Westbrook never even made the discussion, let alone the actual list.

When I waved to him one day in the hallway, Lucy said, "Who's that guy again?" and I said I knew him from carpool.

"Well, he can't take up too much space in the car" was her shrugged response. And that was as much interest as Finn inspired in any of my friends.

We all wanted to fit in so badly. That was the thing. We'd left middle school filled with confidence, but this new school, with its hulking athletes and seniors who looked more like adults than like *us*, was intimidating. There were a few kids in our grade who had the guts to dress weirdly or go off and read by themselves during lunchtime, but for most of us, the survival strategy was to cling together. We dressed alike (in skinny jeans that year, with short leather boots and wide-necked, silky tops that floated over tighter tanks) and grew our hair as long as it would go and coveted or bought the same iPhones, the same messenger bags, the same necklaces. It made us a tribe. It made us safe. It made us bonded. Alone we were vulnerable. As a group we were strong and safe. I needed my friends and knew how lucky I was to have them. The last thing I wanted to do was risk alienating or losing them.

My life compartmentalized that fall. There was home, where I stayed quiet and worked hard and practiced drawing and painting and tried not to mind that Dad preferred Lizzie's inane conversation about designer clothing and expensive restaurants to anything I could say. There was my life with my friends—at school and at parties—where I laughed a lot at things that weren't always funny and spent a lot of time shopping for the same shoes and dresses my friends were buying. And there was the car ride in the morning, when my world was four feet wide, and where, for about twenty minutes every day, I felt totally relaxed and entertained and even sort of happy. In the backseat, I didn't have to figure out who to be. I just was.

Sometimes I stayed up late surfing the web just to find something interesting to download onto my phone—a photo or website that Finn might not yet have seen—and once or twice I did manage to surprise him. But even when he hadn't seen a photo before, he always knew more about it than I did. His mind was like the Google search engine—he could instantly produce information on any subject and then connect it all to other equally fascinating facts.

He liked when I showed him my drawings. He told me I was good, and I told him he was just saying that. "I *would* just say that to be polite, but I'm not," he insisted. "You really are good."

"But you just admitted you'd say that even if I weren't."

"But I wouldn't have admitted *that* if I hadn't been sincere in the first place," he said calmly, and shoved his glasses back up his nose. They were always sliding down. The nose bridge was too big, and his nose was too thin. I don't know why he'd bought that pair in the first place. They didn't fit, and they were ugly, the colors weird and muddy, the shape too round. It was like he'd just grabbed the first pair he spotted at the optometrist's. It was like he just didn't care how he looked. Sometimes I wished he did. Just a little.

We used carpool time to quiz each other before tests. Finn always came up with mnemonic devices to help me remember information, and my grades—already pretty good—got even better because of him. I wanted to return the favor, but the truth was that whenever I tried to quiz him, he already knew all the answers. He had a ridiculously good memory.

When Cameron was sick one week, I had to sit up front with Lizzie for a few days. I tried talking to Finn over my shoulder, but it wasn't the same, not with Lizzie sitting next to me, rolling her eyes and snickering at everything we said.

"King Nerd totally has a crush on you," she said to me one day that week, after we'd gotten out of the car and Finn had slipped away with a quick wave.

"We're just friends."

"Don't be so narrow-minded," she said. "He's perfect

boyfriend material—you could carry him around in your pocket. He could be your little pocket boyfriend, and you could take him out whenever you felt like it and then stuff him back in when you got bored." I stalked away from her, upset mostly because she was right: Finn liked me.

I knew it, even though I pretended I didn't. His scrawny face lit up whenever our paths crossed at school. Sometimes in the car, when we were studying pictures on one of our phones and our heads were close together, I'd realize he wasn't looking at the screen at all. He was looking at me. But if I glanced up, he'd quickly lower his eyes, his cheeks reddening.

One day he asked me if I wanted to do something with him after school, like get frozen yogurt or something.

I hesitated. And then I said yes.

I wasn't sure if I liked him as much as he liked me, but I did like him a lot. I liked his big brown eyes, I liked his enthusiasm for the natural world, I liked his brilliance and his cheerfulness, and I liked the fact that he liked me. Those were all reasons to say yes, and the only reason to say no was a sort of fear that our friendship couldn't last outside of a car—that the real world would make it seem wrong and ridiculous.

Four feet of leather interior expanded to a couple of vinyl chairs at Yogurtland, which we could walk to from school.

We went once and then again.

And then again.

There was also a Starbucks nearby; when we got sick of yogurt, we went there and got icy, thick drinks that were even sweeter than the froyo.

Without Lizzie and Cameron a couple of feet away from us, our conversation expanded—became more personal. We talked about our families. I told him about Mom's leaving and how that didn't hurt nearly so much as Dad's letting Marta and Rosa go, and about losing Molly to college, and about how Dad and Lizzie were a party of two and I was the odd man out in my own home.

He told me about his parents, who were both scientists: his father taught; his mother worked in a lab. He had a much older brother who was already out of college. His parents were nice, just a little old and a little distracted. "We move around a lot," he said one day, when we were at the frozen-yogurt place. "I've lived in five different cities. Every time one of my parents gets offered a more interesting job, we hop."

"Is it hard?" I asked. "Starting over again every time?"

"I don't know," he said. "I have nothing to compare it to." He dug his spoon into his chocolate-vanilla swirl, then glanced up again. "I like it *here*," he said.

I didn't tell Lucy and my other friends about going out with Finn; I only went on days when they wouldn't notice. A couple of times I had to cancel with him at the last minute, because my friends asked me to do something after school, and I didn't want to explain to them why I couldn't. I told myself it was because my friendship with Finn was no big deal—not worth even bringing up.

But I'd had less intense flirtations with other guys that I'd talked about endlessly to my friends in middle school. And Phoebe had pretty much driven us nuts over the last month or so, obsessing about some guy who had never even said hello to her. But still I never mentioned Finn to them.

My friend Camille ran into us at Starbucks one day and came over to say hi. The next day she asked me at lunch why I was getting Frappuccinos with Finn Westbrook, and I just said, "Carpool," and all my friends nodded.

No one bugged me about it, for one simple reason:

It never occurred to any of my friends that I could actually be romantically interested in Finn. Like I said, he wasn't on the radar.

I could have put him there with just a few words, but I didn't.

Finn kissed me one day after winter break.

No, that's not true.

We kissed each other. I wanted to as much as he did.

We had gotten frozen yogurt and were walking back to school, where I was supposed to meet up with Lizzie for a ride home, when he suddenly took my hand and tugged me down around the corner into a quiet alleyway where no one could see us.

It was the first time we had touched, other than by accident.

His hand was warm and dry and—a nice surprise—larger than mine.

He looked at me, and I knew he wanted to kiss me and I smiled to let him know I knew and it was okay. My heart was beating fast. Which seemed so silly—I mean, it was only Finn, right? But apparently my circulatory system thought it was a bigger deal than my brain did.

Our faces were about level, because I was wearing flip-flops. I briefly thought about how I was glad I wasn't wearing heels and also that Finn was noticeably taller than he had been in the fall. He'd grown.

It was a good kiss. I'd kissed three other guys by that point in my life, and this was the best one so far. One guy had shoved his tongue into my mouth way too fast, and another had tried to suck my lips, and the third one had pecked me quickly and uncomfortably.

Finn did it right. His lips were warm and gentle, and I didn't want him to stop. I think he was new to the whole thing, but his instincts—to be patient and go slowly—were good ones.

For a while I completely forgot that Lizzie wasn't the kind of sister who was willing to wait.

It was the vibration that brought me back to reality—the one from my phone, I mean. "Hold on," I said, and pulled away.

Finn stepped back and waited, shoving his glasses up his nose.

Lizzie's text:

Get here in five or you're on the bus.

"I have to go," I said.

"Because you want to?"

I slipped my hand in his, smiled, and shook my head. We walked back to campus together, but I let go of his hand when we were within sight of it.

After that, when I slid over in the backseat to make room for him, we let our legs and shoulders press against each other, and at school, when we passed in the hall or spotted each other across the room, we shared a secret, happy glance.

After school we met each other and found places to be alone.

"I don't understand people who are all over each other in front of everyone," I said to him once, when we were alone. "It's better like this."

He didn't say he agreed with me, but he didn't argue either.

I had a sleepover with Lucy and Phoebe, and of course we talked about the guys we liked, and I swear I was just on the verge of telling them all about Finn when Phoebe said something about Carlos Mercado—about how she knew the nerds would one day be all rich and famous and everything, but who cares when they looked the way they did *now*?

And Lucy laughed and said, "And what if you start going out with some ninety-eight-pound nerdling now, and then he *doesn't* get all rich and famous? And you could have been with, like, Sawyer Thomas all that time?"

"Sawyer Thomas has backne," Phoebe said.

"Stay in front of him, and it won't be a problem," Lucy said. "His shoulders are like ten feet wide."

And so I didn't say anything about Finn and me.

I should have. But I didn't.

We were all taking Modern Civilization that year, and between Christmas break and spring break, we did a unit on Nazi Germany. I remember wondering if I would have been one of the people who stood up to the Nazis—and got myself sent to a concentration camp—or if I would have kept my head down and done whatever heinous, evil thing I was ordered to do.

It's the kind of thing you think about when you start doubting your own integrity.

Spring break, Finn and I spent a lot of time together. We'd meet between our houses and walk to the nearby bluffs, where we'd watch the waves roll in below us, and our profound awareness of both the enormity of the ocean and our own deeply meaningless insignificance usually led to a lot of kissing.

The more time I spent with Finn, the more I liked him. He was nice—not just to me but to stray cats and jumping spiders and little kids. He listened intently and responded thoughtfully to anything I said. His kissing only got better, and it had started out pretty good. His face had grown handsome to me now. I could see beyond those stupid ugly glasses to the beautiful brown eyes behind them. Maybe it was just because my feelings about him had changed, but it seemed to me he was growing stronger and more manly as the year went by.

Break ended. The first lunch back at school, he came over to my table with his tray and sat down next to me. He'd never done that before. I turned to my friends and said, too brightly, "You know Finn, right? He's in my carpool."

He didn't add anything to that, just kind of nodded politely to my friends' brief hellos and then listened quietly to our conversation without joining in, but later, when we were alone, instead of kissing me as soon as he had the chance, he stepped back—away from me—and said, "'He's in my carpool'?"

I laughed an artificial laugh. "What? You are."

Sometimes things don't feel like a big deal when they happen, and it's only later that you look back and think, Maybe that was *it*, the moment when things could have gone in one direction, but they didn't—they went in a different one.

Maybe that was one of those moments, and maybe it wasn't. Finn got quiet for a little while, but before the afternoon was over, we were kissing again. It wasn't hard for me to cajole him into being okay with whatever I did. I knew I had a lot of power over him, and I may even have thought it was infinite.

A few days later, a school email went out about semiformal, and Finn asked me to go with him.

I said, "I'd better check with my friends. If they don't have dates, it would be weird for me to go with you."

"Would it?" was all he said.

I did ask Lucy and the other girls what our semiformal plans were—without mentioning that I'd been asked to it already—and Lucy said she was thinking we should all go as one big group with some guys we were friendly with, not pairing up or anything, just sharing a limo and hanging together at the dance. "I think Justin's planning to ask me to go with him," Phoebe said, and Lucy made a face and shook her head. "That would be weird," she said. "The only people who go in couples to this are, like, *real* boyfriends and girlfriends. If you go to semiformal with a guy, you're basically publicly committing to him for *life*."

I slept over her house that night, and in the dim, sleepy moments right before we both drifted off—the best time for confiding in someone—I told her that Finn had asked me to go with him to the dance.

"Oh, god," Lucy said. "I hate when stuff like that happens and you have to hurt someone's feelings. Especially since you have to sit next to him every day for the rest of the year. It's like he *wanted* to put you in an awkward position." A yawn thickened her last couple of words. We were lying side by side on the queen bed in her room, which I knew almost as well as my own, since I'd been sleeping over there pretty much every weekend since seventh grade. Her mother made pancakes in the morning, and her dad cuffed us both affectionately on the shoulders as he passed by. I liked staying at her house. "He knows you're never actually going to go with him," she added. "So it's just mean."

"Finn isn't mean," I said. "He's not like that."

"But he *knows* there's just no way. . . . I mean, come on. You're like totally gorgeous, and half the guys in our class are in love with you." Part of the reason Lucy was my best friend was because she said these kinds of things and even seemed to believe them. Maybe she did—I certainly thought *she* was gorgeous, even though Lizzie and my dad were always tut-tutting about how

Lucy needed to lose a few pounds. But they were crazy. She was adorable with her big eyes and round face. "And he's . . . you know. Not in your league."

"He's really smart," I said. "And nice."

"If he were really nice, he wouldn't have put you in this position."

"Yeah." I stared up at the ceiling, which I couldn't actually see in the dark but was reasonably certain was still there. "I guess you're right."

Maybe *that* was the moment when I went so far down one path, I couldn't find my way back.

Because I could have said, *Finn and I have secretly been going out for the last three months.*

I could have said, *I actually want to go to semiformal with him.*

I could have said, *You don't understand. He's wonderful, and I'm kind of in love with him.*

But it was only later that it felt like I could have said any of those things. At that time, in that moment, it felt like I couldn't say anything but "I guess you're right."

The Saturday morning of the dance, Finn and I met at one of our favorite semideserted bluffs, and as we stood there looking at the ocean, he took my hand and said, "So are we going together to the dance tonight?"

A simple question. Too bad my answer was a babbled mess.

I told him that of course I wanted to go with him—it would be a lot of fun—but all of my friends had agreed to stick together and go in one big group, and it would be mean to the girls who couldn't get dates for the girls who could to just *abandon* them, and I had to go along with what everyone else wanted, since these were my closest friends, and, anyway, semiformal was pretty lame, everyone knew that, and no one went in couples, no one except people who were, like, really going out seriously and . . .

That's when I stopped, suddenly deeply uncomfortable. All the talking I'd done made my abrupt silence all the more obvious. It also made me aware that Finn had let go of my hand at some point during my speech.

"So," he said lightly, "it's a no." He turned toward the ocean. "Waves are big today."

I glanced at the side of his face, saw how suddenly rigid all the muscles in it were, and part of me wanted to say, *Screw my friends—let's go together*, but the other part of me was relieved to have ended the conversation. So I joked about how I should learn to surf, because with my gracefulness and agility, I'd just totally rule at it, and then I laughed too loudly while he didn't laugh at all, and eventually he walked me back to my house.

We said good-bye at the front door, and he hesitated, then abruptly leaned toward me. He had been so quiet since our conversation that, when I tilted my face up to his, I expected a quick, dismissive peck. Instead his arms went around me and tightened hard as his lips crushed mine in a way that was hungrier and more demanding—and more wonderful—than any kiss we'd had before. I was glad his arms were pinning me against him, because it felt like my legs were dissolving underneath me.

Then, just as suddenly, he released me and stepped back. I wasn't ready for that: I swayed and caught at the door handle to steady myself.

"I'll see you," he said, and walked away.

Maybe I should have realized there was a hint of something desperate in that good-bye kiss, but I didn't. I felt slightly dizzy as I watched him go, and I pressed my fingers against my mouth to try to hold the exciting warmth in for a while longer.

I was convinced all that passion was proof that Finn wasn't angry at me. I walked into the house smiling and humming.

Was he deliberately testing me that night at the dance? I don't know.

I was definitely tested, and I definitely failed, but whether it was deliberate on Finn's part—that's the part I can't decide.

Not that it matters.

We went to the dance separately, me with my group, Finn by himself.

He showed up late and alone, in a suit that was too big for him. It looked like his father's. It probably *was* his father's, and probably was from the nineties.

The guys in my group were all in slim black tuxes, rented for the occasion, which made Finn's boxy orange-brown suit look even weirder.

When Finn spotted me and headed toward us, Camille started giggling and couldn't stop. I wasn't all that close to Camille, but Phoebe had invited her to join our limo since she lived in our neighborhood, and she'd stuck with us once we arrived at the dance. Camille had smuggled a water bottle filled with vodka into the limo we'd all shared and drunk a lot of it on the way. "My god," she said as Finn came near us, "he looks like an Oompa Loompa." And Jordan, who was her best friend and had just wandered over to our group, called out to Finn, "Where's Willy Wonka?"

Finn said, "What?" and the two of them snorted with laughter.

He flushed. He may not have heard what they said, but he knew he was being made fun of. He turned away from them, toward me. "Hey."

"Hey," I said. I was wearing five-inch platform heels and a super-tight bandage dress. We were all wearing bandage dresses that year, not because we had made a pact or anything, but because they were in. Mine wove together diagonal stripes of purple and pink spandex. Lucy and I had gotten our hair done together at a blow-dry bar, and mine was pinned up with a couple of tiny braids woven in. I felt very sophisticated.

Finn said, "Do you want to dance?"

In those heels I towered over him, and I knew we'd look ridiculous dancing together. People would laugh at the sight of us. I didn't want to hurt him by saying no without a reason, but I couldn't think of one that would sound genuine. I opened and closed my mouth without saying a word and glanced desperately at Lucy, who instantly knew I needed help. She took me by the elbow and said, "Hey, Anna, remember that thing we were going to do over on the other side of the room?"

"What?" I said stupidly.

"That *thing*," she said, and dragged me away.

And I let her.

I even thanked her for it.

The rest doesn't really matter, does it? That Finn left the dance, or that I felt sick to my stomach for the rest of it, or that he dropped out of the carpool and stopped going out for frozen yogurt and coffee with me—stopped kissing me—stopped talking to me other than a grave nod and an occasional distracted "hi" in the hallway . . .

You rip a seam, the thread pulls out.

If I had apologized, would it have changed anything?

That's the kind of question that can keep you up at night.

Anyway, I didn't. I'm not even sure I could have. What are the right words to say after you've made someone feel like his attention is an embarrassment to you?

I hung out with my friends at school and at parties, and I worked hard at home on my schoolwork and my art, and I sat alone in the backseat during carpool while Lizzie and Cameron gossiped and complained to each other up front, and I felt lonelier that spring than I ever had before.

And then it was summer vacation. I'd gone to the same sleepaway art camp in northern California for eight weeks every year since I was eleven. Lucy always said, "How can you stand to be away from home for so long?" but her parents totally adored her, so of course she didn't get it.

Anyway, off I went, and by the time I came back, there were only two weeks left until school started again. Lizzie was packing for her freshman year at UC Santa Cruz, which meant she wouldn't be driving me that fall, and I didn't have my license yet, but Phoebe knew a senior named Natalie who was putting together a carpool in our neighborhood. "We just need one more person to get in the good lot," Phoebe told me on the phone.

"Finn Westbrook lives nearby," I said, and wondered if he'd agree to share a backseat with me again. I hoped so. I'd been thinking about him a lot that summer and was pretty sure that if I just had some time with him, I could convince him to forgive me.

"Who?"

"The guy who was in my old carpool."

"Oh, him," Phoebe said. "I'll tell Natalie."

Later she called me back and said, "That kid Finn is gone. His family moved. To Portland. Or was it Seattle? Whatever. Somewhere in Oregon."

"Seattle's not in Oregon," I said. "Are you sure?"

"About Oregon? Clearly not."

"No, I mean about Finn's family moving away."

"That's what Natalie said. She got his number out of the directory and called him. You didn't know?"

"It's not like we've kept in touch," I said.

Natalie's information turned out to be accurate: Finn's house had a new For Lease sign out front, and when I went back to school, there was no Finn Westbrook in the hallways; no small, thin guy with glasses and big brown eyes to look up and smile at the sight of me; no one to show me pictures of the latest photos from outer space or Outer Mongolia; no one to meet me for frozen yogurt and sweet, stolen kisses.

I shared the backseat of Natalie's small Mazda with a freshman named Helena whose one great dream was to be on the cheerleading squad and who first told us all every detail of the tryouts and then, after she didn't make the cut, devoted herself to shredding the reputation of every girl on the team.

I sent Finn a text a week or so after school started. It was late one night and I was sick of doing homework and I suddenly really wanted to talk to him. I missed him so much it hurt.

I spent a long time figuring out what to write and decided—hoped—that simple and casual was the way to go.

Hey! You're really not coming back?

He didn't respond that night, but when I woke up, I found he had sent a text at two in the morning.

Nope.

The fact that he had responded at all made me decide to try one last time.

Carpool's not the same without you.

Again, no response for hours. But that evening one came in:

LOL.

We used to joke about how much we hated when people wrote *LOL*—that no one ever means it literally, and it's really just a lazy way to get yourself out of an exchange you want to end as quickly as possible.

So. That. Was. That.

one

'm walking past Molly's room when she calls out
to me, so I go in. She's home for a couple of weeks
between her summer internship at a San Francisco legal
aid office and her final year of college, and she's made
it pretty clear this will be the last time she'll ever live at
home. It makes me sad: I like having her around. Lizzie's
been home this summer, but she and Dad mostly talk
about the restaurants they want to go to and how badly
most of the world dresses and stuff like that. I just can't
get into their conversations, and when I try to switch
it to something more meaningful, like movies or cur-
rent politics or . . . you know . . . the relative merits
of small versus big dogs, they don't have much to say
and just murmur some empty response before returning
to subjects that interest them. Which are usually food,
exercise, and how much classier they are than anyone
else in the world.

In a year I'll leave for college myself. I can't wait. Neither can Dad, who's already talking to Realtors about putting our house on the market. He wants to move into a Century City high-rise. He says he'll have a guest room for whenever we girls visit, and he told Lizzie she could decorate it, since she has such a "good eye for these things."

Whatever.

I go into Molly's room, and she's lying on her bed with a book and she looks up at me and says, "I heard you walking by. Come talk to me."

I'm happy to comply. I sit down on her desk chair and swivel it around so I can face her. There's something effortlessly cool about the way Molly looks, with her honey-colored hair that she wears chin-length and usually tucked behind her ears. She always wears jeans and T-shirts, but they look good on her because she's tall and thin. I wish I looked more like her, but I'm shorter and curvier, and my hair is thick and dark and wavy, which isn't completely awful, but I've always wanted straight, fine hair like hers. We have the same hazel eyes and arched eyebrows, though.

"You started packing," I say, because her suitcase is open in the corner, pants and bras spilling out of it.

"I never unpacked."

"I don't blame you. A quick getaway from here should always be an option."

30

She smiles briefly, and then she's silent for a moment. "Anna," she says, suddenly pushing herself up to a higher sitting position on the bed.

"Yeah?"

"You know I'm gay, right?"

I stare at her. "What?"

"Then again," she says, her lips twitching like something's funny, "maybe you didn't."

"Why would I know? You've never said anything."

She raises the book in her hand. "Well, there's this, for one thing."

"*Rubyfruit Jungle*? I just assumed you were reading it for school."

"Not everything is assigned reading, Anna."

"I guess not. Wow. I mean . . . You know. Wow. So . . . you're really gay? Definitely?" She just tilts her head at me with a *Come on* kind of look. "Okay. Fine. Good. That's cool, Mol. Do you have a girlfriend? Like a steady one?"

She nods. "Her name's Wally."

"Seriously?"

"I know. It's ridiculous, but it's not her fault. Her parents named her Wallis, after the Duchess of Windsor, but that Wallis was a Nazi sympathizer douche bag, and she hates the name. So . . . Wally. And, yes, that makes us 'Molly and Wally,' which is pretty awful, but there's not a lot we can do about that."

"But, I mean, do you . . . um, are you guys like a real couple? Or just dating?" That's not really what I want to ask. What I want to ask is far more complicated— something about whether they have sex and how they have sex and whether she thinks about girls the way I think about guys and a million other things. But this is what comes out.

"We're a real couple," Molly says. "Whatever that means."

"How long have you known?"

"That I like Wally?"

"That you were gay."

"For a while." She puts the book down and pulls her knees into her chest, hugging them with her arms. "I mean, I didn't wake up one day and think, Oh, look, I like girls. It was more that I just knew I reacted to stuff differently than my friends—they were all excited about dating and the guys in our class, and I just didn't care. It took a while for me to realize why, but by junior year of high school, I was pretty sure."

"That was so long ago."

"Four years."

She's known for four years. I feel left out. And hurt. "Did you tell anyone?"

"Not until I got to college."

"Were you afraid people would be mean to you?

Because there's a gay guy in my class and he's totally popular. People can be cooler than you think." *I would have been cool about it. If you'd just told me. Why didn't you tell me?*

She shakes her head. "I wasn't worried about being bullied or anything like that. More that my friends wouldn't be as comfortable with me anymore—that they would start to act weird and think I was staring at them and not want to have sleepovers and stupid stuff like that. It didn't seem worth it."

"Yeah," I say, trying to be understanding, even though it still stings me that my own sister waited four years—*four years*—before telling me something this important about herself. I know I'm the member of the family she trusts the most. But not enough, apparently. "I get that."

"Well, you shouldn't," she says, almost irritably, and my head snaps up with surprise. "I was a wimp. I should have come out."

"But you just said—"

"I wasn't that comfortable around them, anyway. I might as well have been honest. I'd have been more comfortable with *myself*, at least."

"Do Mom and Dad know? Or Lizzie?"

"Not yet. I thought maybe they'd notice the lack of boyfriends or something."

I feel better: at least she told me first. "You could wait a long time around here for anyone to notice anything," I say.

"I know. I was hoping . . ." Her voice trails off. She looks sad. Then she shifts with a shrug. "But I invited Wally to come visit before we go back to school, and she's going to take the train down next week. I thought I should probably tell you guys before then."

"Don't tell Dad and Lizzie ahead of time," I say.

She tilts her head at me. "Yeah? You think?"

"Definitely. I want to see if they figure it out."

She bobs her head. "All right, then. Why shouldn't we have some fun with this?"

I'm starting to feel kind of excited. This is big news. I want to tell all my friends, only I'll be super casual about it. *So my sister's home . . . my oldest sister . . . the gay one.* "You know I think it's great, right?"

"Do you?" Molly says, picking up her book. "Thanks, Anna."

All right. She's done with this conversation. I stand up. "I can't wait to meet Wally."

"She's pretty wonderful," Molly says with a smile as she opens the book. She glances up. "You have anyone in your life, Anna?"

"Not in the boyfriend sense." I'd had a few brief hookups at parties . . . but nothing that mattered. Not since Finn. If that even counted.

"Wait until college," she says. "The people are more interesting in college."

All Molly tells Dad and Lizzie is that a friend is coming to visit and she's picking her up at the train station, so when she and Wally walk in holding hands, I swear Dad's eyes almost come out of his skull. But he's polite and doesn't say anything embarrassing. He's very civilized that way. I've never seen him treat a guest rudely or say the wrong thing in public. He and I might not have much in common, but at least I can introduce him to people without any embarrassment or fear.

After Molly and Wally head out for dinner together, Dad closes the door behind them and says, "I'm a little confused. . . ."

"She's obviously a lesbian," Lizzie says. I'm surprised she says it so calmly, but then I realize she's talking about Wally, not Molly. "And she clearly has a crush on Molly. I can't tell if Molly realizes it."

"They're both gay," I say.

Two pairs of light blue eyes swivel to stare at me. Dad and Lizzie look the most alike out of all of us: big, steel-blue eyes; straight noses; and thin lips. "Are you joking?" Lizzie says.

"Molly told me."

There's a pause. Then: "Molly *is* a terrible dresser," Lizzie says to Dad. "She always has been. And I don't think I've ever seen her in a dress. Except for prom. And she's never had a boyfriend."

"I suppose it makes sense," he says thoughtfully. "But even so—" He shakes his head. "She could do so much better. I've seen the girls at her school, and some of them are very attractive. Even some of the lesbians. And I've always said that Molly could be beautiful if she just put some effort into her looks. But this girl—"

Lizzie's already nodding in agreement. "That nose! And the short hair . . . Could she be any more of a cliché?"

"I think she's pretty," I say. "And she seemed really nice."

They both shrug.

"I should probably tell your mother." Dad smooths the front of his shirt, a tailored pinstripe made out of crisp cotton. He has beautiful clothing, all of which he gets professionally laundered and ironed. He prides himself on always looking good, and he does. With his thick, dark hair (which I now know is carefully and regularly dyed) and his well-maintained, slender figure, he looks a decade younger than his fifty-three years, and women at restaurants often turn to stare at him. Sometimes I see my friends' dads with their ballooning stomachs and balding heads—and overprotecting devotion to their daughters—and wonder what it would be like to have a father like that.

Lizzie says, "Maybe wait to be sure. It's really hip right now for college girls to pretend to be gay."

"Really?" Dad says. "Times certainly have changed."

"I don't think that's what's going on here," I say. "Molly told me she's known since high school."

"Well, of course that's what she'd *say*," says Lizzie with a toss of her impeccably blow-dried mane of hair. She's highlighted it so many times, it looks blond now, lighter even than Molly's natural honey color, but she started with dark brown hair like mine. "It's possible she just couldn't get a boyfriend, and this seemed like an easy out."

"Seriously?" I say.

"Oh, grow up, Anna," she says. "People do stuff like that all the time. You'll see when you're older." Lizzie always likes to act like she knows a lot more than me, but most of her "wisdom" makes me stare at her in disbelief.

Wally stays with us for three days, but she and Molly are almost never home. I go with them once, to see Grauman's Chinese Theatre. We have fun, but I get the sense Wally and Molly would rather be alone. They share Molly's room at night, and no one says anything about that.

The last day of vacation, they load up Molly's car so they can drive to school together. Wally gives me a quick hug good-bye and then thanks Dad and Lizzie for letting her stay there. They tell her she should come back and visit again—a little too politely. Molly whispers to me to call her whenever I need someone to talk to, and then the two of them are gone.

Mom calls that same night to say she'll be in town tomorrow and wants to have dinner with us all. She does this periodically: swoops in and reminds us all why she stays away most of the time. I think she actually comes to LA on business much more often than we know, so I guess I should be grateful these reunions are as rare as they are. She says she's disappointed that she missed Molly by a day—probably because it's easier to see us all at once and just get the family obligation over with.

Anyway, it's bad enough we have to go meet her at Katsuya—restaurant of the rich and spoiled, where a few scraps of raw fish will run you a hundred bucks a person—but that afternoon Lucy calls to say that Jackson Levy (who's moved up her list from "has potential" to "we could have a future together") is taking advantage of his parents' trip to take his sister to college to throw an end-of-summer party.

"I don't know if I can make it," I say glumly. "My mom wants to have dinner, and she has this whole *I'm so cosmopolitan, I can't think about eating before nine at night* thing."

"Can't you just tell her you have something more important to do?"

"I haven't seen her in almost a year."

"Well, whose fault is that?"

"Hers—but I still have to go to dinner."

"Why?"

"I don't know. I guess because she's my *mother*."

"Fine. Just come to Jackson's as soon as you're done."

I promise and hang up. Now that Lucy's questioned it, I do wonder why I feel like I have to make time for Mom whenever she asks. I guess it's because I don't know when or even *if* she'll ever ask again. And there's part of me that thinks maybe we'll connect more as I get older—maybe she'll see something in the adult me that she didn't see in the kid me and will actually show some interest in being part of my life. It hasn't happened yet, but it could, right?

In the car I ask Lizzie if she knows why we always meet up with Mom when she wants us to, and she says, "Because Mom makes a lot of money, and we might need some of it one day."

Dad isn't with us, of course. He and Mom don't have much of a relationship. I can't remember them ever talking much, even when they were still married—usually they were just playing parent tag, each trying to pass the kids on to the other as quickly as possible so they could get work done. They communicated mostly by email, even back then. Neither of them is the type to get all nostalgic about the past, so I don't really know why they got married in the first place, but Molly once said she figured it was because they were both ambitious, high-earning attorneys who liked the idea of being married and having kids and respected each other's genetic makeup. The difference between them, she added, is that Dad felt a real sense of responsibility to the kids he'd brought into the world, and Mom didn't. The reality of having a family wasn't what she thought it would be—more work and less glory—and so she moved on. But he stuck it out. Which is definitely to his credit, and I should remember that when I get impatient with him.

At dinner tonight both Lizzie and I have trouble knowing what to say to Mom, who looks healthy and self-satisfied and much younger than her age, which is somewhere around fifty-five—I'm not sure exactly. After the divorce, she gained some weight, and I think the extra roundness in her face is part of why she looks so good. She once said to me, "Your father was obsessed with my being thin. I realized it was his issue, not mine. I eat what I want now and enjoy every bite." She added, with a cackle, "And I'm still ahead—after all, I lost a hundred and sixty-five pounds of ugly fat just by divorcing him."

She asks me whether I think I'll get into a good college, and I tell her I'm mostly considering art schools. She makes a face and says, "I had higher hopes for you than that."

Lizzie distracts her by saying, "Molly brought her girlfriend home for a visit," and Mom says, "Girlfriend?" and Lizzie says, "Yes, didn't you know? Molly's a lesbian." "Good for her," Mom says, and Lizzie says casually, "I wonder if it has something to do with the absence of a maternal influence."

Mom just shrugs and says, "Sexual orientation is hardwired, Lizzie."

We're stuck there for a little longer while Mom asks us questions about our lives and then seems uninterested—or at least unimpressed—with our answers.

Dinner is endless—since we're all three fidgety, I can't figure out why Mom orders an after-dinner drink, which forces us to sit for another ten minutes—and it's almost eleven by the time we say good-bye to her in the restaurant parking lot. I text Lucy from the car to say *I'm coming*, but she texts me back: *Don't bother. Cops already shut it down. Come to my house and I'll give you the deets.*

When I get to Lucy's house, the twins' Audi is parked in front. Hilary and Lily Diamond came to Sterling Woods in tenth grade. I've gotten to be good friends with them over the last year or so. I'm probably closer to Hilary, who's incredibly smart and in a lot of my classes, but it's impossible not to like Lily. She's the kind of girl who'll start a conversation with the strangers at the table next to you in a restaurant, and by the end of the meal, you're all exchanging phone numbers and life stories, and the strangers will be hugging Lily like she's their long lost sister or granddaughter or whatever.

They're not identical twins, but they still look a lot alike: they both have stick-straight brown hair and the same pointy chins; dark eyes with a mildly exotic tilt to them (their mother was born in Korea); and small, straight noses. But Hilary's hair is very long right now, and Lily cut hers last year, so it's asymmetrical, chin-length on one side, midway up her cheek on the other. She changes the way she wears it every day—sometimes she pins it up at the sides; sometimes she lets it swing forward; sometimes she makes these tiny braids in front—and she changes her makeup to suit her hair, so you never know what she's going to look like, only that she's going to make everyone else look boring and predictable. Especially her own sister, who has pretty classic taste in general.

Right now, though, all three of them are in their pajamas, because the twins are sleeping over at Lucy's. I join them at the kitchen table, and Lucy offers me hot chocolate. They've already got three steaming mugs in front of them, each one blanketed with marshmallows. I'm still stuffed from dinner, so I pass on the cocoa and beg them to hurry up and tell me what I missed.

"It was an amazing party," Lily says. She's wearing

a pair of tiny plaid boxers and a tank top. She's pulled her hair into a ridiculous, small ponytail on the crown of her head and it bobs while she talks. "There must have been, like, five hundred kids there before the cops came."

"More like seventy," Hilary says.

Her sister shakes her head. "Way more than that. And then the cops saw someone drinking out front—I don't know the guy; he doesn't go to our school—and they handcuffed him and arrested him—"

"No, they didn't," her sister says.

"Yes, they did! I heard they shoved him into the back of their car without even reading him his rights."

"I was *there*," Hilary says. "I saw the whole thing, and none of that's true. They just made him pour out his drink and gave him a warning—they didn't even call his parents. People exaggerate so much." She tugs on the thick braid that's hanging over her right shoulder. She's wearing Harvard sweatpants and a Princeton T-shirt, souvenirs from our junior year East Coast college tour.

"Why'd they shut down the party?" I ask.

"Too noisy." Lucy is cozy and adorable in old-fashioned lace pj's, her hair piled on top of her head. With her thick light hair, big blue eyes, round face, and curvy figure, she sometimes looks like she's stepped out of a nineteenth-century painting. "I think the neighbors were complaining. Probably because a couple of guys were peeing on people's lawns."

Hilary wrinkles her nose. "May I just say—boys are gross."

"Oh, like you wouldn't pee on a lawn now and then if you could," I say jovially.

"I *have*," says Lily.

"I don't even want to think about that," says Lucy.

"Ignore her," says Hilary. "She says things like that for the shock value."

"I do," Lily agrees. "But it's also true."

I push off my short leather boots and curl up in the chair, hugging my knees to my chest. "Moving right along . . . Any juicy hookups? Who's going to be embarrassed when school starts on Tuesday?"

"Dylan and Dylan!" says Lucy, and the others nod.

"Boy Dylan and girl Dylan?" I say. "Or the two boy Dylans? Which would be way more interesting."

"Coed Dylans. Dylan Ryan and Dylan Britton."

"I totally want them to become a couple," Lily says. "Just so we can say things like, 'I hate when Dylan tongues Dylan in front of everyone.'"

"And think about their couple name," Hilary says. "I mean, if you put the first half of one of their names together with the second half of the other one's name, you get—"

"Dylan!" we all cry out together.

"It would be weird dating someone with the same name as you," Lucy says.

"It would certainly be weird if you dated a boy named Lucy," I say. "Speaking of which, what happened with you and Jackson tonight? Anything?"

"Nothing," Lucy says. "Well, maybe a little flirting. But the wheels turn slowly." She sighs. "I don't know why—we're made for each other. He's the captain of the lacrosse team, and I'm the captain of the field hockey team; he coaches little kids' soccer on the weekends, and I teach dance at Fresh Feet. We both take AP French and AP bio and—" She stops abruptly. "Oh my god—I can't believe I forgot to tell you, Anna! Guess who was at the party?"

"Lady Gaga? Was she pissed I didn't show?"

"Seriously." She leans forward. "Remember that kid you carpooled with in ninth grade? Finn Westbrook?"

"You know that guy?" Hilary asks, turning to me.

"Wait, what?" I sit up straight, suddenly very alert. "Finn Westbrook? He was at the party? Why? How? Did you talk to him?"

"He moved back!" Lucy says. "They're living in that same house, and he's going to be in our class again."

I blink. Then I blink again. "Wow," I say. "I haven't thought about Finn Westbrook in ages." This is a lie. I've thought about him a lot. And right now I'm thinking especially furiously about him—everything from He probably still hates me, to Maybe he doesn't hate me anymore, to a whole bunch of points in between, like, Maybe he only hates me a little bit.

"I can't believe he was in your carpool!" Hilary says. "I had three stuck-up seniors in my freshman year carpool, and not one of them would even talk to me. You got so lucky, Anna."

"You think? I mean, he was—is—a great guy, but—" I stop before I say what I'm thinking, which is that I wouldn't expect a girl like Hilary—who's been asked out by a lot of guys and has found fault with almost all of them—to get excited about a guy like Finn. Unless . . . "Has he changed a lot?" I ask Lucy.

"A ton. He's a lot taller, for one thing. He was really short in ninth grade," she tells the twins. "You know how some guys still look like little kids when they're fourteen? He was one of those."

"Late to the puberty buffet," says Lily.

Her sister stares at her. "Sometimes I don't know who you are."

I'm impatient to get back to the subject of Finn. "Is he tall now? I mean, like actually *tall*?" That seems impossible. That has to be impossible. Although . . . it's been two years. And he was growing quickly back when I knew him.

"Tall-ish," says Lucy. "Like maybe five eleven?"

46

"Not that tall," Hilary says. "I saw him standing next to Jackson, and he was at least three inches shorter. So probably more like five nine, five ten."

Lucy shrugs. "All I know is he's not a shrimp anymore. He's totally in the right *range*. And he's cute now, Anna. Seriously cute."

"He was always kind of cute," I say, even though I had never said I thought so back when I should have.

She gives me a skeptical look. "I guess, maybe . . . but not the right kind of cute. He was cute like a little brother. Like a little cute nerd brother. Now he's hot-cute. And did you know he invented an iPhone app?"

"Which means he's rich," says Lily.

Hilary shakes her head. "People don't make money off of apps."

"They do if enough people buy them."

"Then Apple makes a ton of money, not the designer."

I look to Lucy for clarity, since I have no idea which one of them's right, if either.

"All I know," she says, "is that someone at the party already had his app on their phone without knowing it was his. Which is pretty cool."

"What is it?"

"I don't completely understand it, but you know how you can't see stars in big cities because of all the light pollution? With his app you can take a photo of someone against the night sky, and it figures out which stars

47

should be there based on the location and angle and fills them in. So you end up with this amazing starry-night sky in your photos. You can also just use it to see what constellations are above you."

"I really don't think it's made him rich," Hilary says. "He didn't *feel* rich."

"How does rich feel?" I ask.

"Fabulous, darling," says Lucy with a laugh.

"I mean, he wasn't driving a solid gold Ferrari or anything like that," Hil says.

"He drives an electric car," Lily says. "I talked to him about it. It's not a Tesla or anything crazy expensive, but it's still pretty cool. He's a super big environmentalist. He said he's going to talk to the school's board of directors about installing solar panels in the main building—he said the roof is perfect for it, and he can't believe they haven't done it yet."

"When did you talk to him?" Hilary asks her, almost accusingly. "I didn't see you guys together."

"Right at the end. The cops came, and things got a little crazy, and I lost track of him. But we talked for, like, fifteen minutes before then."

"Where was I?"

"How should I know? Oh, wait," Lily says, turning to me with sudden excitement. "If you carpooled with him, does that mean you have his number? Could we text him? Maybe he'd come over and hang with us."

Hilary quickly seconds the idea.

I shake my head. "I can't text him."

"His number's probably in the school directory," Hilary says, already pulling her phone toward her. "You could use that."

"I seriously can't text him," I say. "It would be too weird."

"Oh, right." Lucy hits herself in the head with the palm of her hand. "I can't believe I forgot about semi-formal and all that."

"What are you talking about?" Hilary asks.

"Anna totally blew him off. In front of everyone." Lucy plucks a dripping marshmallow out of her mug of cocoa and drops it into her mouth.

"Why?" Lily asks.

"She wasn't into him," Lucy says. "But he liked her. So it was a pretty awkward situation. It wasn't her fault. She handled it as well as she could."

"Why didn't you like him?" Hilary asks me.

"I did," I say. "He was a great guy."

"But you blew him off?" Lily says, her brow wrinkled like she's trying to figure this out.

"Yeah," I say, and stare at the marshmallows turning into goo in her mug. "I blew him off."

I spend most of the rest of the weekend wondering whether I should try to get in touch with Finn before school starts. I could try texting him. . . . Or calling . . . Or dropping by . . . But it would be so awkward to try to pretend we're just old friends—we were so much more than that. And then we weren't even that.

Maybe he's forgotten what happened at semiformal.

Yeah, right. The guy has a photographic memory.

But maybe it no longer feels like such a big deal to him. We were only stupid little ninth graders, right? He's probably moved on.

Although . . . the fact that I'm sitting around obsessing about all this means I haven't exactly put it behind me, so why should I expect him to have?

I decide to wait to see him at school—he doesn't know that I know he's in town, anyway, and this way I can gauge how he feels about me and react accordingly. If he seems angry or distant, I'll try to find a time to apologize and explain what happened. If he seems relaxed and friendly, I'll meet him willingly as a friend. And if he seems *really* happy to see me again . . .

I'll explode with relief and joy. Because I still miss him, and I want a second chance.

two

This is how my reunion with Finn Westbrook goes:

I walk into English class and I'm looking for a friend to sit near, when I notice a thin guy with dark, wavy hair already tucked into a desk next to the wall, and I'm just thinking, Wait—could that be—? when he looks up and spots me and I can tell it *is*, even though he's changed a lot. He studies me for a brief moment and then he says, "Hi, Anna."

That's it.

"Hi, Anna."

Totally calm and relaxed.

He's wearing contacts, or at least I assume he is, since the glasses are gone, and he has shoulders now—decent ones too, not sloping at all—but it's definitely Finn.

It's definitely Finn saying that completely indifferent "Hi, Anna."

This is not what I expected from our first reunion

in over three years. Not that my expectations were particularly definite or anything—sometimes I pictured him deliberately turning his back on me, and sometimes I pictured him throwing his arms around me. But I thought it would be some kind of a *Moment*. I didn't think it would be this: a flap of the fingers and a lazy "Hi, Anna."

"Finn!" I say. "Wow." I step closer, wondering if we should hug—I mean, we should, shouldn't we?—but he doesn't get up or hold out his hand or anything, so I halt and adjust the strap of my book bag on my shoulder. "Hey, how are you? I heard you were back in LA."

"Yeah," he says. "My parents like to keep moving."

"I remember that," I say. "They go where the jobs are."

He just nods and smiles up at me. Blandly. Like we're two people who once carpooled together and haven't seen each other in a while. Like he never pulled a phone out of his pocket and said with almost delirious delight, "You have to see this photo of Mars—how amazing is that?" Like he never met me at the bluffs for private kisses and stupid jokes. Like he never looked at me as if I were the most important thing in the world to him.

My throat suddenly feels too big to fit inside my neck.

I manage to swallow and try to think of something else to say. He's got a pleasant enough expression on his face, but his eyes keep shifting away and darting around the room, as if he wouldn't mind finding someone more interesting to talk to.

"My sister's in college now," I say. "Lizzie—the one who used to drive us."

"Huh," he says politely, and then he shifts and waves with sudden enthusiasm at someone who comes running up and dives into the seat in front of him, twisting her body so she can talk to us while simultaneously plunking an enormous turquoise-and-silver tote bag on the desk.

Lily.

Her hair is curled today, little banana ringlets all over her head, with a fat, bouncy one hanging down over her right eye. She's wearing pink eye shadow and pink blush and pink lipstick. She looks like a cross between a four-year-old and a geisha. It's an odd look but undeniably eye-catching.

Finn's eyes are caught.

"I know you!" he says. "We're basically best friends, except I can't remember how I met you or what your name is."

"We talked at Jackson's party," she says with a pleased wriggle. She's wearing a flowered spaghetti-strap summer dress with cherry-colored Doc Martens.

"Right," he says. "We talked until the cops came."

"Stupid cops," she says. "They ruin everything."

His brow puckers. "Lily? Lila? Lucy?"

"Lily," she says. "Lucy's another girl."

"Yeah," he says, and glances briefly at me. "Your friend, right?" Before I can even respond, he turns back to Lily and gestures at the top of her tote bag, where you can see the neck of a sparkling green ukulele peeking out. "What's up with that? You going to serenade us in class?"

"I might," Lily says with a little smile. "If I feel inspired."

"She actually does sometimes," I say, because it's true: Lily takes the ukulele to classes and sometimes picks it up and strums a little song and sings and gets away with it, because she's Lily and everyone adores her.

"Don't the teachers mind?" Finn asks her.

"As if I care."

He grins at her. "That's the spirit."

"They *don't* mind," I say. "Everyone likes it when Lily plays."

"I bet," he says, still looking at her.

The teacher calls for class to start, so I have to find a place to sit in a rush, and end up next to Samantha Gutterson, which I hate—I've hated sitting next to her since sixth grade—because she has this habit of whispering to me when the teacher's saying something important, and then going, "Wait, what did she say?

Did we miss something?" which makes me miss even more.

Lily actually does play her ukulele during class: Mrs. Reese says something about conjunctions, and Lily calls out, "'Conjunction Junction'!" and launches into the song from *Schoolhouse Rock!* Everyone joins in, including Mrs. Reese. Lily gives a self-satisfied glance back at Finn when she's done, and he gives her an enthusiastic thumbs-up. He knew all the lyrics to the song. So did I, but no one was looking at me when I sang.

At lunch Lily hauls Finn over to our table. "He's going to eat with us," she says, and pushes him down on the bench.

"That will be much more successful if I'm allowed to get myself some food first," he says meekly.

"You can feast on our beauty," Lily says as she sits down next to him.

"Then I'm already full." Wow. He's definitely gotten slicker since ninth grade. He didn't know how to do the flirty-teasing thing back then, but I guess he's learned. His voice is different too: deeper, of course—no surprise—but also slower, like he's trained himself to sound less enthusiastic. I guess speeding up with excitement when you talk *is* sort of a little-kid thing, but I miss that about him.

"Let him eat, Lily," Lucy says with a yawn. She and Hilary and I all came straight from AP bio, and we're still recovering from getting too much information hammered into us too quickly.

"Fine." Lily dismisses him with a wave. "But get me a slice of pie, will you?"

"What kind?" he asks, standing up.

"Just pie," she says. "Pie is intrinsically good."

"Is that going to be your whole lunch?"

"Best lunch possible," she says. "Since it's *pie*."

"Anyone else in need of some pie?" Finn asks, glancing around the table. "Or anything else?" His eyes move quickly past me. He's wearing a plain white T-shirt and jeans. He used to wear polo shirts that were too small and shorts that were too big, but now his jeans and tee fit him well, slim enough to be flattering but not so skinny that he looks like he escaped from 2010.

We all pass on the offer. Finn leaves the table, and Hilary says to her sister, "You can't eat only pie for lunch."

"Just watch me." Lily plucks her ukulele out of the tote bag at her feet and strums it, singing, "Pie is fine. It's very nice/ Especially with lots of spice/ Like cinnamon and ginger too/ My sis would like it, but she's a poo."

"Oh, well, that's brilliant," Hilary says. "Taylor Swift must be looking over her shoulder."

"She should—I'm breathing down her neck." Lily strums a few more chords, humming along with them, then says, "So who here is already madly in love with Finn Westbrook?" She raises her own hand.

Hilary lifts her hand with an uncertain waver. "I wouldn't say I'm madly in love with him, but there's potential for that."

"Did you see his eyelashes?" Lucy asks. "They're longer than my thumb."

"They're thick too," Hilary says. "And he's *nice*." She takes a sip from her can of Diet Coke. "Mostly, though, he's fresh blood. I am so sick of all the guys here." She munches a carrot stick thoughtfully. "Also? He has a good body."

"He's not muscular enough," Lucy says. "I like guys who are built."

"I don't," Hilary says. "They look stupid in clothes. Finn looks good in his clothes."

"You're totally in love with him," her sister says.

Hil shrugs. "Yeah, okay, fine."

"Too bad, he's mine."

"She branded him last night," Lucy says. "A big *L D* on his rump."

"How would *you* know what he has on his rump?" Lily asks.

Lucy laughs. "Don't worry—I'm not interested in this competition."

Finn comes back to the table with a full tray, ending the conversation. There's an empty space next to me and one next to Lily. He takes the one next to her—to be fair, that's where he sat before—and looks around. Four pairs of female eyes are watching him. "Why am I the only guy sitting here?"

"You feeling lonely for some fellow testosterone?" asks Hilary. She must have flat-ironed her hair that morning, because it's straight and silky. She's wearing a floaty bohemian dress and Grecian sandals. She's as classic a beauty today as Lily is a quirky one. "We could burp a lot if that would make you more comfortable."

"Tempting as that offer is . . ." Finn offers Lily a plate from his tray. "I got you a slice of pizza."

"I said I wanted pie."

"Pizza *means* pie. And you refused to be specific."

She pouts. "It wasn't nice of you to be clever about this. Not when I'm desperate for a sugar rush."

He puts down the plate and picks up another, which he puts in front of her. "Relax—I also got you a slice of cherry pie."

"Hooray!" Lily says. She strums a tune on the uke and loudly sings, "Pie, pie, pie, pie, pie" in an ascending scale.

"Oh, for god's sake." Her sister puts out a hand and covers the strings. "Everyone's looking."

"Let them look," Lily says, shoving Hilary's hand

away. "When are you going to realize that I'm not like you—I don't care what other people think?"

Finn points a finger at her. "I like you," he says seriously. "Now give me back the pizza. I'll eat it if you don't want it."

She smiles, puts down the ukulele, and picks up the slice of pizza in both hands. "Changed my mind," she says. "Pizza first. *Then* pie."

"Glad I got myself a sandwich too, then."

Hilary asks Finn whether Sterling Woods—our school—has changed much since he was here in ninth grade.

He thinks about that, chewing quietly. Another change—the old Finn was a messy eater, too enthusiastic about sharing information and stories to wait until his food was swallowed to talk. He's learned table manners somewhere in the last couple years.

When he's done with that bite, he says, "This place looks the same. But it feels different to me. For one thing the freshmen look like little kids. Not that I'm one to judge: I was one of the smallest kids in my class."

"Oh, right." Lily gestures at me. "Anna said you were really short."

Great. Thanks for bringing that up, Lil. I mumble something about how I never said that exactly, but Finn just shrugs. "She's right, I was."

"Who did you hang out with?" Lily asks him. "Do

you still have friends here?"

"Josh Starr was probably the guy I was closest to, but he doesn't go here anymore."

"He went to boarding school, right?" Lucy says.

"Yeah, his family's got this Exeter tradition. But I was wondering about Otis Chan, who was another good friend. I hadn't heard from him for a while, so I tried to track him down when I knew I was moving back, but his old phone number didn't work. And I haven't seen him. You guys know what the story is?"

"He dropped out of school last year," Lucy says. "I mean, not permanently, but he's in rehab and won't graduate with the class."

Finn flops back in his chair, staring at her. "You're kidding me."

"She's not," Hilary says. "He was a total stoner."

"You could smell it on him," Lily says. "Even at, like, eight in the morning."

"That's crazy," Finn says. "He and I spent a ton of time together. He was one of the most anti-drug people I've ever met."

"He got over that," Lucy says drily. "And he wasn't a social smoker—he was one of those alone-in-your-room kind of burnouts."

"That's so weird. When I knew him, all he wanted to do was play Dungeons and Dragons."

"Yeah, well, it's not *such* a huge leap from that to

being a stoner," Hilary points out.

"I guess." Finn shakes his head. "Man, I hope he gets his act together. That's really sad." He sighs and slumps his shoulders. "So I guess I don't have any good friends left here."

"Don't worry." Lily pats his arm. "We'll be your new friends. You'll like us even better, I promise."

"Will you play League of Legends with me and then go to the Apple Store?" he asks. "I'm a total nerd."

"Sure," she says. "If you'll go to thrift stores and used-vinyl-record stores with *me*. I'm a total hipster."

Hilary rolls her eyes and groans at this, but Finn just nods and assures Lily that it's a deal. They'll be there for each other.

I stay pretty quiet during lunch. It's all too weird for me. There's Finn sitting at our table, and half the time I'm thinking, He's completely different—I don't even know this guy, and the rest of the time I'm thinking, Oh my god, it's him, and he hasn't changed at all. It's the small things—the head movements and the way his grin spreads across his face and the large, soft brown eyes and the quick shifting in his seat with sudden enthusiasm—that haven't changed.

But he doesn't look at me the way he used to.

Actually he doesn't look at me at all.

There's a polite flicker of attention in my direction

when someone says something to me and I respond, but he turns back to the others as soon as possible.

Meanwhile, there are my friends, all laughing with him and listening to him and flirting with him—and don't think the irony escapes me, that this is the exact same guy who three years ago no one looked at twice.

Except for me. I looked at him more than twice back then.

And then I looked away.

And now he's the one looking away. Not in a rude way—no, he's been extremely polite to me. Far more polite than he is to the others. Like we're strangers who've been thrown together through mutual acquaintances. Like he knows the other girls much better than he knows me. Like *I'm* the newcomer.

I stay quiet during lunch because I'm afraid I might cry, right there in front of everyone. Or throw up. Or fall on the floor, kicking and screaming. I can't talk much because I'm focusing on not doing any of those things.

I wonder if I should grab him and pull him aside at some point and let him know how bad I feel about what happened in ninth grade. Just put it out there. Maybe an apology would make things less weird between us. Maybe he'd even forgive me. Maybe that's all he's waiting for.

I can't do it now—not with Hilary and Lily fighting

for his attention. But later that day I see him walking alone between classes, so I call out to him and he turns. For a second I swear he looks happy to see me—and then his face goes blank so quickly, I wonder if I imagined that. But he waits politely enough for me to catch up.

"Hi," I say.

"Hi," he says. Warily.

"Do you have a sec?"

"Not really. Class starts in two minutes."

"This will take less than that." I move to the lockers on the side, so we're out of the way of the kids streaming by. "I just wanted to say that I'm glad you're back."

"It's good to be here," he says evenly.

"And also—" God, this is hard. I take a deep breath. "Also, I know things got a little weird between us back in ninth grade, and I'm sorry for whatever part of that was my fault." There. That's enough, right? It's obvious what I'm referring to—and that I'm apologizing. I raise my eyes to his face, hoping to see it soften.

"Thank you," he says, without meeting my gaze. He shifts his binder from one hand to the other. "I'd better get to class." And he walks away again.

So much for an apology making everything okay again. Maybe I should have said more.

Or maybe I should have said less. Like nothing at all.

I actually touch my cheeks, because my face feels so hot from the inside that I figure they must be radiating heat, but they feel normal. I walk to class quickly and stare at the teacher with burning eyes and hold myself together until school's over and I'm alone in my room at home. Then I let it in—I let in the self-loathing and regret that come from knowing I threw away and kicked to the curb something I wish I still had and can't ever get back.

I let it all wash over me, and hope that there's something cathartic in feeling this awful.

As the week goes by and it becomes clear that Finn Westbrook is going to be a permanent addition to our table and that my attempt to apologize didn't change anything, I force myself to get used to having him there. What choice do I have? It still hurts to see him sitting there and feel no connection at all, but the hurt burrows down deep, farther away from the surface. After a while I don't have to worry that I'll burst into tears. I'm able to join in the conversation. I laugh even. I watch him get more and more comfortable with my friends, watch him tease them casually and easily.

He doesn't tease me. Not ever.

He says hello to me and also good-bye, and between the greeting and farewell is a world of indifference. He basically treats me the way I treat my great-aunts: he's polite and not the slightest bit interested in me.

Or at least that's how it looks and feels.

But deep down I think he's mad at me.

Deep down I think he might actually hate me.

I guess I'll just have to get used to that too.

three

A couple of weeks into school, Phoebe invites a bunch of people to watch the Video Music Awards on the enormous flat-screen TV at her house this coming Thursday night. Hilary can't go to the party, because the twins' dad is a music producer, and she's actually *going* to the VMAs. She and Lily take turns going as his date.

"I'd rather be with you guys," she says the Saturday before the party. The five of us are at In-N-Out Burger—Phoebe, the twins, Lucy, and me.

Lucy looks up from the hamburger she's dismembering—she never eats anything without taking out some of it and rearranging the rest, partially because she's a picky eater and partially because she's a control freak—and says, "Fine, you go to Phoebe's, and I'll take your place. Shall I tell Beyoncé you say hi?"

"It's not like I get to really talk to her or anyone else

who's famous," Hilary says. "At best we, like, shake hands."

"If you complain one more time about going . . ." Lucy says.

"Yeah, stop complaining," Lily says cheerfully. "You got to buy a new dress."

"It's just not fair. I *wanted* to go last year and you got to, and I don't want to go this year and I have to."

"All right, that's it," Lucy says. "Should we tell your father I'm his date for the evening, or should I just surprise him?" She pulls out a piece of tomato, inspects it, scrapes something off it, then sticks it back on the hamburger.

"He won't notice," Hilary says. "He can't even tell me and Lily apart, and look at us. Just *look at us*."

"My dad never calls me by the right name," I say. "Only by my older sisters'. Sometimes he'll call me 'honey' really awkwardly. He's not the honey type, but it gets him out of having to remember my name."

Phoebe says, "All parents have trouble with names. I'm an only child, and my dad sometimes stops and says, 'Uh, you.'"

I nod, but our family situations are totally different. She once told me that her parents cried so hard at her middle school commencement that her mother burst a blood vessel in her eye and had this weird red spot in all of the photos they took that day. And that was just middle school. I can't wait to see what happens at our high school graduation—maybe she'll explode.

"Oh, hey, Anna?" Phoebe says. "Speaking of your father . . . I keep meaning to ask—is it true he does alumni interviewing for Stanford?"

"And self-interest rears its ugly head," Lily says. She's drinking a chocolate milk shake for her lunch, said that was all she wanted, although she keeps sneaking fries from the rest of us.

Phoebe flushes. "Shoot me for caring where I go to college."

I say, "He's not interviewing this year—he's not supposed to when he has a kid applying to colleges."

"He got your oldest sister in, right?"

"Molly would have gotten in anyway. She's totally brilliant."

Phoebe raises her eyebrows skeptically. "Maybe. But I bet it didn't hurt that your dad is a major alum. Can you just tell him it's totally my first choice and ask him if he has any advice?"

"Sure," I say. "But I honestly don't know if it will help."

"Ask for me too, while you're at it," says Hilary. Lucy echoes her.

"It can't be everyone's first choice," Phoebe says, annoyed.

"It would be, if I thought I could get in," Hilary

says. "Anyway, it's not Lily's. She wants to go to Bard or Vassar. Right, Lil?"

Lily doesn't respond, because she's already rising to her feet and calling out to the guys behind the registers, "This music sucks! Can't you play something good?"

"No," one of them calls back, laughing. He's young and cute. "We don't get to choose it."

She draws closer. "If you could, what would you play?"

"I don't know. The Shins, maybe?"

They talk about music for a while, and somehow it all ends in his slipping Lily a free order of fries when his boss is looking the other way.

On Tuesday I'm working alone in the art room after school when the assistant art teacher comes in. She's never actually taught me—I've only had classes and independent studies with the main art teacher, Mr. Oresco, who's round and balding and whose praise means everything to me—but Ginny Clay arrived this year to teach a new class called Digital Art and to sub for Mr. O when he's sick. I doubt she'd have gotten hired if she hadn't been a Sterling Woods alum: she graduated from here the year before Molly, which means she's barely out of college and doesn't look much older than most of the students. She doesn't *act* much older either—she's a giggler, and she's blond and very pretty, but from what

I've heard about the class she teaches, she's not actually that good at either computer science *or* art. A lot of the students are way ahead of her in both, and they all say she just sends them over to the computers and sits at the front of the room reading magazines while they use various programs. If someone has a question, she usually asks another kid to help him out.

She was captain of the volleyball team her senior year here, when Lizzie was on the team. The two of them were friends, so I've known her for years. Because I'm her friend's little sister and she's now in a position of authority at school, she seems to think it's her obligation to criticize and advise me.

I do not enjoy when she does either.

"Hey, Anna!" Ginny spots me and pounces with delight. She's wearing tiny volleyball shorts and a shrunken tee and has her blond hair pulled up and back in a neat ponytail. She's also the assistant volleyball coach for the girls' team, but it's not like the uniform is required for the coaches—she must just like how she looks in it. The senior volleyball coach wears a tracksuit and a whistle.

I'm drawing at a table. I don't use an easel unless a teacher makes me. When I was a kid, I always drew standing up at our dining room table, and I guess the habit of working that way stuck. Mr. Oresco says I'm going to destroy my back if I don't switch over to easels and I know he's right, but I get so lost when I'm drawing and painting that I don't even notice if my back starts to ache.

I toss a "hello" back in her direction and kind of hunch over my artwork, but of course that's not going to stop Ginny, who's the sort who'll peer over your shoulder even if you don't invite her to.

"Oh, Anna," she says plaintively as she peers over my shoulder. "Aren't we *ever* going to get you to take some chances with your artwork?"

I stiffen. Everything about this statement annoys me, from the assumption that she's been mentoring me to the implication that I'm artistically stunted. I say, "This isn't done yet," because it's not, and because I'm hoping that will stop her from analyzing it.

"Oh, Anna," she says again—and now just those two words are enough to make me want to drive a sharpened colored pencil through her eye. "It's not a question of done or not done. Nothing artistic is ever really *done*, is it? The important thing is whether you're extending yourself. Are you stretching creatively? This feels so similar to what I've seen from you before."

I don't want to defend myself to her. I shouldn't have to. But it's hard not to respond when someone's standing two inches from you criticizing something you've made. "This is for my application portfolio."

"Art schools are going to want to see your range,"

says Ginny, who—just to be clear—never studied at an art school. She went to USC, where she majored in Human Performance. "I'm sure you have plenty of samples of *this* kind of thing." She flicks, almost contemptuously, at my drawing. "You need to show them you can do something like a vase of flowers. Or a plate of fish!" Maybe she notices my expression, because she quickly adds, "Or anything that's colorful and close-up—the point is to let them see there's more than one side of you."

"I really have to finish this." I bend over my work.

"You should be using an easel, you know."

"I like to work this way."

"Your poor back." She starts rubbing it with the palm of her hand, which just makes me stiffen it more. "Oh, and when you see her, will you tell Lizzie that I can't wait until Saturday night?"

"Okay. You guys doing something?"

"Yes—with you! I'm joining your family dinner to say good-bye to her before she leaves. I am going to miss her *so* much. And I bet you will too." Ginny throws her arms around me, and I'm enveloped in a cloud of musky perfume. "We'll just have to spend more time together." She gives me one last big squeeze before releasing me. "It's crazy how late her school starts, isn't it? It's that silly quarter schedule. But at least it means she's not gone yet, and we're going to have so much fun at dinner!

But now I have to run to practice." She turns to go. Then looks back. "And try to branch out a little artistically will you, Anna? You have so much potential. You just need the maturity and courage to make it blossom into something *real*. Love you! Bye!"

With a swish of her barely clad butt, she's gone.

I bend back over my work, but my focus—my lovely, wonderful, stress-relieving, happy-making focus—is shot, thanks to her visit. I put aside the black, thin pen I was using and drop into a chair. I study the picture.

Ginny's right about one thing: you can definitely tell that the same artist is responsible for all the work I've produced over the last couple of years. Somehow I started doing these weird landscapes—vast wastelands, most of them, often burned red and black, although sometimes they're wet with huge lakes or unevenly covered with tiny stones—lands that don't look like they should belong on Earth, and maybe they don't. I'm not even sure in my own mind whether they do or not. I usually do that part in a mixture of watercolor and pastel, to get some texture into it, but I've experimented with almost every kind of paint and surface—I just like the watercolor/pastel combination the best so far. Anyway, then I go in with ink pens—I use the sharpest I can find—and sketch in something small and weird. Something that doesn't belong in the landscape at all. Sometimes it's humans—two middle-aged women having tea, maybe, against a menacingly red Martian-looking landscape. Sometimes it's something mechanical: a robot trying to dig its way out from behind a rock. Sometimes it's animals, like a couple of tiny rabbits chasing each other on the edge of a world that's covered in ice.

I stopped questioning why I made the kind of art I did a long time ago. It's just what I do. I go into a kind of trance, and it makes me happy and it feels right. I don't paint vases or still lifes or portraits. (Sorry, Ginny.) I do *this*.

My art started turning into this at some point in my tenth-grade year. Sometimes I'd lie in bed after working on one of these pieces and I'd still be thinking about it and working on it in my head, and then suddenly I'd picture myself in the backseat of Lizzie's car, and Finn—the ninth-grade Finn who was long gone by that point—would pull out his phone and say, "Let me show you this incredible photo I just found," and I'd say, "And let me show you this."

And I'd hold up my picture. And he would like it.

And then I'd tell him how his photo inspired it.

And he would like that too.

I'm heading out the door for Phoebe's VMA party on Thursday night when I stop on our threshold and scan the empty street.

My car is nowhere in sight.

I go back in the house and shout for Lizzie. She's not there—which explains the absence of the car. She must have driven off while I was in the shower. Nice of her to check to see if I needed it. Which I'm pretty sure I already told her I did. Which probably explains why she left without checking.

Dad's not home either, so no chance of borrowing *his* car.

Phoebe's house is pretty close, but not close enough to walk. So I text Lucy:

I need a ride. Get me?

Already at Phbs—she says she'll tell Lily to grab you.

The doorbell rings about ten minutes later, but when I open the front door, it's not Lily.

It's Finn.

"Hi," he says. "Someone here call for a cab?"

He's wearing khakis and a green button-down shirt that looks soft, not stiff. He's rolled the sleeves up to just below his elbows. It's the first time this fall that I've seen him wearing glasses. They're black and small and rectangular and a lot cooler than the oversize ones he used to wear, but even so they make him look more like the old Finn.

"Why are you here?" I say, a little stunned by his sudden appearance on my doorstep.

"Phoebe asked me if I could grab you."

"She said Lily was going to."

His lips compress briefly. "Sorry," he says. "You're stuck with me. But it's a short ride."

Oh, god—I just offended him. "I didn't mean it like that! I was just confused."

"Shall we go?" is his response. He's already turning around and heading toward the car.

I follow him, and we get into the car.

"1044 Burlingham, right?" he asks as he pulls away from the curb.

"Yeah. It's about two minutes away—I carpooled with Phoebe and her sister for two years."

He doesn't say anything to that, and I wish I hadn't brought up carpools.

I look down and smooth my skirt over my lap. I feel self-conscious. I'm wearing a long, gauzy skirt with a tight green sweater on top and short black boots. The last glance in the mirror back home had been reassuring, but suddenly I'm filled with self-doubt. The skirt is too boho, the sweater too preppy—Lily could pull off the clash of styles, but I look silly, like I'm in some kind of costume. I tug on my hair, which I straightened with a flat iron but which is already softening into its usual waves, and desperately try to think of something to say so we don't just keep sitting there in silence. I come up with a brilliant "Is it nice being back in LA?"

"Yes," he says. "It feels like home. More or less."

"Cool."

"Yeah."

Could this conversation get any more hollow?

He doesn't look at me at all, just drives, one hand on the steering wheel, the other resting on the gear drive like it's a stick shift, which it isn't—the car's an automatic. I bet he was driving a manual car back wherever he's been for the last few years and hasn't gotten out of the habit of keeping his hand on the shift. It's a glimpse into the mystery of his life away from LA.

I say abruptly, "We had fun during carpool, didn't we?" As soon as the words are out of my mouth, I realize how pathetic they are. What am I hoping for?

A connection. That's what. Some tiny shred of friendship that might have survived the last two years.

I don't get one.

Finn says tonelessly, "Yeah. Good times."

I know when I'm hitting my head against a brick wall. Sometimes I even know enough to stop pounding. So the only other thing I say on the drive is, "There's Phoebe's house. The one with the red door."

"Thanks." He parks, and we start walking toward the house together. Eric Manolo pulls up, and Finn calls out to him. Eric gets out of his car and comes bounding up to us with his round cheeks and big, friendly smile, and Finn asks him about his car, which I guess is some kind of new hybrid or something, and the two of them talk about that until we reach the house.

I drift back behind them and try to get my mind off that miserable car ride. I stare at Eric's back and wonder why he's here. I like him a lot: he brings a mellow, good-natured vibe wherever he goes, which I'm always grateful for, given how type A Lucy, Hilary, and Phoebe can all get, especially when they're together. But Phoebe hadn't said anything about inviting him, and even though we're all friends with him, we almost never see him outside school.

Eric and Finn join the others, who are in the family room eating guacamole and watching people being interviewed on the red carpet, but Phoebe isn't there, so I go looking for her. I find her in the kitchen unwrapping plastic cups. "Oh, good," she says. "Stay here a sec—I need help carrying stuff into the other room." She's wearing jeans and a fitted T-shirt, with her light brown hair pulled back in a ponytail, and I feel overdressed in my skirt and sweater. Phoebe has a fresh-scrubbed, athletic kind of look—she's thin and strong. Makeup looks wrong on her face since she has big features, but when she keeps her clothing, face, and hair simple, she looks like the kind of girl who'd start off in the movie as the hero's best friend and then he'd realize he's in love with her. Speaking of which . . .

"I didn't know Eric was coming," I say.

"Yeah, we were talking at school today about something else, so I said he should come." She sounds a little too casual about the whole thing. Like she's trying hard to make it no big deal.

"Cool. I like Eric."

"Grab the soda for me, will you?"

I put my hands on the Coke bottles and then freeze, listening. "Wait—what is that sound?"

"*That* is the sound of a crazy dog whining in my parents' bedroom."

"You don't have a dog."

She sighs. "We do now. My mother was walking by a dog adoption fair in some parking lot and said he looked right at her and asked her to take him home."

"In so many words?"

"My mother is cray-cray, in case you haven't noticed."

Phoebe's mother *is* a little nuts. I've only met her a few times, but she's the kind of woman who takes your hand when she meets you and peers intently into your eyes and says things like, *Thank you for being such a special friend to my daughter.* Squirm-inducing. "Is he cute?"

"Not even a little bit," Phoebe says with disgust. "I've been asking for a pug for years, and Mom goes and picks up this weird pit-bull-mix thing with tiny, mean eyes. It loves *her*—follows her around and sleeps with her. But it growls at me and my dad, and he got so annoyed that he told Mom she was going to have to choose between him and the dog."

"The dog's still here," I point out. "Should I be concerned?"

"Dad hasn't left yet. But he is pretty pissed."

"Is it a boy or a girl?"

"It's a girl but looks like a boy." Phoebe plucks at a stubborn bit of plastic wrap clinging to a cup. "Which is why I call it *it*."

"Does she always make that noise?" It's an unpleasant cross between a howl and a moan.

"It's mad because I locked it up. Dad said I had to because it snapped at him this morning. He's worried someone might get bitten tonight, and we'd get sued."

"Shouldn't you just return her to the adoption place if she's that dangerous?"

"You try telling my mother that. She literally said, 'You don't give a child back because it misbehaves; you teach it not to.'" Phoebe picks up the plastic cups and a stack of paper plates. "Help me bring everything in, will you?"

I pick up the soda bottles and say, "Uh, Phoebe? I just wanted to ask you—why'd you have Finn pick me up? Lucy said you were going to ask Lily to."

She looks over her shoulder from the threshold. "He called for my address right after you texted, so I asked him instead. Why? Was there a problem?"

"No," I say. "I was just surprised."

* * *

80

Sometimes crazy things happen at the VMAs—like the year Kanye West interrupted Taylor Swift when she was accepting her award and said it should have gone to Beyoncé—but this year's show is pretty dull, and we end up talking more than watching. Unfortunately I get stuck for a long time on the sofa between Phoebe and Lucy, who decide a party is a good time to discuss the upcoming SATs and proceed to dissect every question they struggled with the last time we all took them.

I'm worried about the SATs too—my first scores were lower than I'd hoped, and I've been taking a class on Saturday mornings to try to get them up—but I don't get why they want to talk about that stuff tonight when the point is to relax.

Since I can hear them laughing a lot, I assume the other guests—Lily, Finn, Eric, and Oscar Green—are having a much more fun conversation on their side of the room, but after that car ride, I feel like Finn would prefer me to keep my distance. Too bad: Oscar's one of my favorite people these days. He's funny and self-deprecating and adorable, and normally I'd go sit with him . . . but not right now.

Lily and Finn are squeezed together in a big, puffy armchair. It all looks very cozy.

At least Lily's made me feel less overdressed. She's wearing a party dress—a *real* party dress—the kind a little girl would wear to a big formal event. It's a light blue satin, with poufy sleeves and a floaty tutulike skirt so big, it covers Finn's lap too. It probably *is* a little girl's dress: Lily's so small and slender, she sometimes shops in the kids' department. She's also wearing knee socks and platform heels and has on some kind of headband encircling her head above spit curls. She looks crazy. Adorably crazy. But crazy.

She's brought her ukulele, and when Taylor Swift performs, she pulls it out and sings along. We all applaud, and she gets up and curtseys, grinning and bobbing.

"You're better than she is," says Finn, and Eric chimes in with his agreement.

When Lily thanks them, she only looks at Finn.

The evening grinds on. Lucy and Phoebe stop talking about the SATs and start talking about grades and college applications. I alternate between sort of listening to them and sort of watching the TV. The others keep laughing.

I get up to pour myself some more Diet Coke, but the bottle is empty. I call over to Phoebe, who says to get another bottle from the kitchen.

I find the Diet Coke in the refrigerator, and I'm turning around with the bottle in my hand when I stop, because there's a dog in the doorway.

Her eyes are narrowed, and her head is lowered. She's pretty big. She's growling at me, lips pulled back from the sides of her mouth, showing her teeth.

And, Granny, what big teeth you have.

I like dogs. My parents refused to get us one—or any pet—because they didn't want to be "even more burdened than we already are," but a lot of my relatives and friends have them and I'll pet and cuddle and throw balls with pretty much any sweet dog I come across.

But I don't like *this* dog. Mostly because she already seems to have decided that she doesn't like me.

"Good doggy?" I suggest hopefully.

Good Doggy's upper lip twitches to show a fraction more tooth.

"Just let me get by you, okay?" I say. She growls deep in her throat.

I can't remember if you're supposed to look an angry dog in the eyes or *not* look it in the eyes. I try looking right at this dog, and she instantly narrows her eyes so malevolently that I quickly look away again. I take a step toward the door, thinking maybe she'll move aside—maybe she's just fooling around—but instead she lowers her shoulders into what looks like some kind of pre-lunge position, and I step back.

I want to yell for Phoebe, but I'm seriously scared that shouting will make this dog attack me. So I say, "Uh, Phoebe?" very quietly into the empty air. Maybe she'll hear me. "Your dog is kind of blocking my way. She's kind of terrifying me. Like I think she might kill me."

I can hear the sound of applause and music coming

from the family room. The TV's on really loud. No one's going to hear me talking that quietly.

"Okay," I say to the dog. "It's just you and me. And I really want to get out of here. So you're going to let me. Right, doggy? Nice doggy?" Trying to keep my voice soft and gentle, I take a careful step toward the door. The dog holds her ground but doesn't do anything else. "That's right. Good dog." I take another step. And another. I'm almost there—

And that's when she starts barking—so sharply and furiously that I instantly cringe back. "Stop it!" I say. "Just stop it!" And since I'm shouting, anyway, I scream for Phoebe. Possibly a little hysterically.

The dog crouches, ready to spring at me—at least I think she is—so I back up, my arms going up to shield my face, but before she can move, she's suddenly pulled back. She turns her head, snapping furiously at whoever's got her—which is Finn. He's *there*, in the doorway, dragging the dog back, and while he's wrestling her, he manages to get out a panted and urgent, "Are you okay?" and I say, "I'm fine." He yells over his shoulder for Phoebe to help him control the dog, and she appears, shoving past the other kids who are piling up in the hallway to see what's going on. She says, "Stop it, Rowley! Stop it now!" and the dog seems to respond at least a little bit to her name, because she stops snapping and just glares at everyone and especially at Finn, who's desperately trying to keep hold of her without getting bitten. "Little help here, Phoebe?" he gasps. She reaches down, and he transfers the collar to her with an audible sigh of relief, backing quickly away.

He says to me again, "Are you okay?" and again I tell him I am.

"Someone must have let it out," Phoebe says. The dog ducks her head and pulls, straining against the collar, and Phoebe says, "Stop it, Rowley!" I have a feeling she says that a lot to this dog. "Who went into my parents' room?"

We all shake our heads.

"She must have gotten out by herself," Lucy says.

"How? She can't turn a knob. No opposable thumb."

"Maybe she bribed a guard," Oscar says.

"Come on," Phoebe says to the dog. "You're going back in. Stay away from my parents' room, guys." She drags the dog by her collar down the hallway.

"You okay?" Lucy says to me.

"Fine." Now that I'm safe, I'm also embarrassed. "I'm sorry I screamed. It's just—it kept blocking my way. And growling at me."

"That is one scary-ass dog," says Eric sympathetically.

"You should have seen Finn when you screamed," Lily says. "He was out of the room before the rest of us even realized it wasn't coming from the TV set. Total hero." She takes his arm. "Come on, hero. I'll buy you a drink." He laughs and willingly follows her back down the hallway. The rest of us follow. I'm still clutching the Diet Coke bottle to my chest. In the family room, I pour myself a cup with shaking hands.

A little while later, Lucy says she has to go home to work on an English paper, and I hitch a ride back to my house with her. Some nights you just want to have end.

I try to get out of eating dinner at the Swan on Saturday night with my father, Lizzie, and Ginny Clay.

I know. Poor me. Having to eat at one of the newest, fanciest restaurants in all of LA. But honestly I would rather eat at a fast-food place. The food at these gourmet places is never worth the pretension and the endless discussion about it.

Dad says I have to come. "It's Lizzie's last night at home."

Lucy had told me I could use her as an excuse—that I could say she was having some sort of emotional crisis. ("Which I am, you know," she said. "I'm freaking out about the SATs." And, yes, even dealing with *that* sounded more pleasurable to me than this dinner.) So I try that, but Dad says, "Your friend will survive for four hours without you" and refuses to hear any more arguments. It's fine when *he* wants to withdraw and ignore the demands of family, but when he decides we should be together, I don't get a say.

86

Dinner turns out to be just as delightful as I'd anticipated.

The waitress has committed the horrible crime of not being super thin, and every time she stops by the table and leaves again, Lizzie murmurs something like, "She's heading back to the kitchen. They'd better hide the bread." Ginny Clay opens her big green eyes wide at every comment and covers her mouth with her hand, laughing and protesting.

"You're terrible!" she says with delight. "Stop making me laugh! I feel awful laughing!" Then she laughs some more.

The couple sitting next to us—whose only sin was picking this restaurant for a romantic dinner—are also considered fair targets for Lizzie's delicate wit.

"Should we tell her her boyfriend's gay?" Lizzie asks, jerking her head toward their table.

"Oh, I don't know," my father says with a wink. "Ignorance is bliss. Maybe the situation works for them." Dad's looking handsome tonight in a jacket and tie. He likes to dress up for dinner out. I'm wearing dark jeans and a leather jacket over a silk top, Lizzie is wearing black pants and a tight sweater, and Ginny Clay is wearing a narrow skirt and a brightly colored, flowing top with a wide neck that shows the lacy camisole underneath.

"Now you two stop that!" she protests with a giggle.

"They're just having a nice date!"

"Ginny, Ginny." Lizzie shakes her head fondly. "You are so innocent. You probably still believe in the tooth fairy."

"Oh, is that who that guy is?" says my father with a nod toward the next table. "The tooth fairy? That explains everything." And the three of them laugh while I check my texts under the table so no one will notice.

Dad calls the waitress over and tells her that Ginny needs a refill on the white wine that she and Lizzie both ordered. (Lizzie's still six months shy of her twenty-first birthday, but the waitress didn't ask for ID.) He orders himself another scotch while he's at it.

Lizzie says, "I like your pants," to our waitress, who thanks her for the compliment. After she's walked away, Lizzie whispers, "That's because they make me think of sausages and I love sausages!"

Ginny slaps her wrist. "You're awful! So terrible!" Then she turns to Dad. "Thank you for ordering for me. I love being taken care of." Dad smiles magnanimously as she goes on with a pretty little flutter of her hand. "Although I really shouldn't have any more wine. I'll get tipsy. And in front of one of my students!"

"I'm not actually one of your students," I say.

She brings a slender-fingered hand to her chest. "Maybe not officially, but I feel like I'm mentoring you." She turns to the others. "Anna has so much talent." She touches my father lightly on the wrist. "But you already know that—there is no way she could have gotten this far without a supportive parent."

"I try," he says. Which is debatable.

"I've just been urging her to push herself a little more." Ginny taps her chin thoughtfully. Her blond hair is piled on top of her head, and tonight she's wearing the kind of small black glasses that pretty young women wear to make themselves look like pretty young *intellectual* women. "She needs to spread her wings artistically, but I think she's scared of stepping out of her comfort range."

My father peers at me. "Anna, I hope you're not going to be one of those people who go through life crippled by the fear of taking risks."

I roll my eyes. "Really? But that sounds like such a *good* plan."

"If I could wish one thing for my girls," Dad tells Ginny, "it's that they have the courage to take chances in life. That's how you succeed."

"You are so right," she says eagerly. "That's what made the great artists great—Van Gogh, Picasso, Gauguin . . . they all took risks." What a genius: she can distill all the greats down to one single shared quality that I lack.

"Are *you* a risk taker?" my father asks Ginny.

She tilts her head sideways and slowly fans her long,

mascaraed eyelashes at him. "Just try me."

Dad lifts his chin ever so slightly and smiles.

"I think Ginny was flirting with Dad," I say to Lizzie later that night. We're in her room, where she's desperately trying to finish all her packing. The taxi to the airport's coming early in the morning. Dad didn't want to give up his training session at the gym to drive her. "Not after that huge meal," he said cheerfully, when he told her to call the cab company.

"Flirting? Don't be ridiculous." Lizzie holds up a pair of shorts. "Are these too long? Do they look like mom shorts to you? I mean, not our mom—she couldn't squeeze into these if her life depended on it. But you know what I mean."

"They're fine. You can always roll the bottoms up. But didn't you see how Ginny kept touching his arm? And she kept telling him how brilliant he was. . . . You really didn't see that?"

"She was just being friendly. That's how she is." She smirks. "You should try it sometime."

I ignore that. "I just thought it was weird."

"Plus she's only a couple of years older than me. Dad's not a cradle robber."

"He's dated younger women before."

"Not *that* young. And even if he did, Ginny's not his type. I know Dad better than you." That's a frequent refrain from her: how close she and Dad are. How similar they are. How Molly and I are more like Mom, which she pretends isn't an insult but we all know is one. "What about these pants?" She holds up jeans with a floral print. "I thought they were kind of cool at the store, but now I'm thinking they're stupid. You want them?"

"Not after you called them stupid."

"They'd probably be too tight on you, anyway. They barely fit *me*."

I give up and leave the room, telling her I have to do homework. We forget to say good-bye that night, and she's gone by the time I get up the next morning.

four

A few days later, Lucy and I are studying together at the Starbucks near school when Jackson Levy walks in with a guy I don't know. Lucy bounces up from her chair and calls out to Jackson, who waves before placing his order with the barista.

Lucy gazes at him as she sits back down. "He's so perfect," she says. "Have you ever seen anything so perfect?"

He *is* handsome in a beefy all-American sort of way, with a killer body. Even from fifteen feet away, I can see his biceps bulge where his T-shirt sleeves end.

"I hear he's gotten three offers from colleges already," Lucy says dreamily. "They all want him for their lacrosse teams. He told me that Yale is his number one choice. Which is yet another reason we belong together—it's mine too."

"Yeah, but the odds of both of you ending up there—"

"I can dream, can't I?" She sneaks another look at him. "I love that he's so built. I could never date anyone short or skinny."

"You have a serious daddy complex," I say.

"No, I don't. I just like the way it feels to get crushed against a big, strong chest."

"Yeah, that's not how a little girl feels with her dad *at all*."

"Shut up."

Once Jackson and his friend get their enormous iced triple venti drinks, they come over to our table. "Hey," Jackson says.

"Hey," Lucy says, beaming.

Jackson introduces the guy he's with, whose name is Wade Porter. He has gray-blue eyes and wavy black hair and is wearing a crimson Harvard T-shirt. He's a lot more slender than Jackson, and since I don't have Lucy's daddy's-girl issues, I prefer that. He is, in fact, totally attractive.

"Anna and Lucy go to school with me," Jackson tells him.

"Wait a second," Wade says. "You go to Sterling Woods?" We both say yes. He looks at me intently. "And your name is Anna? You're not Anna Eliot, are you?"

"Yeah. Why? Am I famous?"

"This is going to sound weird, but you and I are related."

"Seriously?" I've never heard of him before. "Is this some kind of new pickup line?"

"Nope." He grabs a chair from another table and sits on it. Jackson does the same thing, but he has to go farther to find a free chair, so Wade starts talking before he's settled. "We're cousins—not close ones, obviously—third or fourth and probably a bunch of removeds. I think my grandmother was first cousins with your grandmother? They were both Latimers before they got married."

I stare at him, surprised. I thought he was joking at first. "Whoa—that's totally right. But how'd you know I was her granddaughter?"

"I applied to Sterling Woods for ninth grade, and we were looking at the roster of kids, and my mother pointed to your name and said, 'Oh, look—Anna Eliot—she's your cousin.' Some relative had done a big family-tree thing a few years before that he sent around with everyone's name on it and where they lived, and she had thought about getting in touch with your father because you lived so close and then chickened out. My mom's like that," he adds. "She's kind of shy. But she did Google your dad."

"Googling," I say. "The next best thing to a family reunion."

"I'm jealous," Lucy says. "I want to discover a long lost relative."

"Which one of us is the long lost one?" I ask Wade.

"I've always known where I was," he says with a smile.

We compare relatives. There are a couple of great-aunts and uncles we've both heard of, but other than that there's not a lot of overlap.

Lucy and Jackson break off into a separate conversation. I can hear her talking about the SATs. Seems like a bad choice of topics—sort of the opposite of fun and sexy—but at least she's not being phony.

I know I should be worrying about the AP biology notes in front of me—we have a huge test in two days—but I'm kind of liking both the idea and the reality of connecting with this distant cousin of mine, so I keep the conversation going. I nod toward the T-shirt he's wearing. "So what's the story with that? You get recruited at Harvard?"

"Recruited? For what?"

"Aren't you a lacrosse player?" I'd assumed that was how he knew Jackson.

"Nope. I play on my school's tennis team, but—" He glances around like he doesn't want anyone else to hear, then leans forward and whispers, "I'm not actually very good. I'm just hoping no one notices." He leans back. "You play anything recruitable-ish?"

I shake my head. "Not even close. Do you know where you want to go?"

"Where I *want* to go? Sure. An Ivy would be nice, but Stanford's my top choice. Now ask me where I think I can get in—sadly that's probably a different list. What about you?"

I tell him a little about my hopes for getting into an art school, then ask him how he knows Jackson (it turns out they met in preschool), and then Jackson glances over and says, "We should get going, dude," and Wade nods and they both stand up.

"It was cool meeting you, cuz," he says to me.

"Sure was, cuz," I reply.

And he has me send him a text so we'll have each other's phone numbers.

After they leave, Lucy says, "Your long lost cousin is pretty cute."

"Too bad it could never work out between us. Our kids would have three heads."

She rolls her eyes. "That's only when you're like siblings. You guys are so distantly related, you're probably as genetically similar to him as you are to me."

"Then why won't *you* sleep with me?"

"I do," she says. "Practically every weekend."

"Oh, right." I open my bio book. "That wasn't exactly the kind of sleeping together I meant, you know."

"Well, it's all you're getting," she says with mock primness. Then she stops goofing around and gets serious about biology, because Lucy hates getting anything less than an A on a test.

"Homecoming after-party is always the best party of the year," says Lily at lunch the following week. The plate in front of her is half filled with French fries, half with beets from the salad bar. She said those were the only two foods that looked good to her. She's been alternating eating them, dipping first one then the other into mayonnaise. On the one hand: disgusting. On the other: somehow she's managed to make it look delicious, and I sort of want to sneak a taste.

"What are you talking about?" Hilary says. "Remember last year? They oversold tickets, and we got turned away at the door. And the year before that when the shuttle bus we were on broke down and it took two hours before they got us another one? And by the time we got there, everyone was drunk and it was too crowded? You said you'd never go again."

"Third time's the charm," Lily says cheerfully.

"The triumph of hope over experience," I say. "That's Samuel Johnson, in case anyone was wondering."

"No one was," Lily says.

I stick out my tongue at her. She wiggles her fingers at me. They're stained with beet juice.

"So are we going to try to go this year or not?" asks Lucy.

"To the after-party?" Hilary says. "We have to. We're seniors."

"It is our moral obligation," I agree.

"But no shuttle buses," Lily says. "We'll find some-place nearby to park."

Hilary says, "We're not supposed to do that." Lily just gives her a look and she sighs. "Yeah, I hate the shuttle buses too."

"So who's driving?" Lily points a pink-tinged finger at Finn. "You have the most ecologically responsible car, so you should."

"Okay, but we can't all fit in my car."

"Lucy can drive too."

"Hold on," Lucy protests. "If I drive, I can't drink."

"See? That's why you should drive," says Lily. "You're actually responsible about this stuff."

"Yeah," Lucy says glumly. "I am." She turns to me. "You have to promise me not to get drunk either. It's not fair if I'm the only one who's sober."

"Finn has to drive too," I point out. "So he'll be sober."

"But he won't be in my car. I want another ratio-nal person in my car with me. You don't have to be stone-cold sober, just not wasted. Okay?"

"Yeah, fine." So now I'm committed to being in Lucy's car.

Which . . . you know . . . means I can't be in Finn's.

He's clearly devastated by that same realization. You can tell by the way he's laughing at something Lily says so hard that his head has fallen back and his mouth is partially open. Total devastation.

If you've never been to an after-party, then you haven't missed much. We all go because we all go. *Not* because anyone really enjoys it.

"We're lemmings," I say to Lucy, when we're in her mother's minivan. I'm up front with her. Phoebe and some friend of hers named Ronna, who goes to a different high school, are sitting together in the middle row, and Eric and Oscar are in the way back. "We do what everyone else does, even if it's a mistake."

"Is it a left or a right on Garden?" is her reply.

We should have taken a shuttle bus. At least then we'd have been let off right in front of the club. But instead we have to search and search for a parking space and discover that the public lots charge a twenty-dollar flat rate on weekend nights, which we're not willing to pay. We end up driving all the way up the hill to find a neighborhood that isn't permit parking only. We have to walk what must be a quarter of a mile back down to

Sunset Boulevard, which is rough on all the girls, since the whole point of after-parties is to wear your shortest skirts and your highest heels. Lucy and I are both sober, but the others were drinking in the car, so they're laughing and stumbling behind us as we lead the way.

"Whose idea was it to skip the shuttle?" Lucy says irritably as we wait at the light to cross to the club. "Oh, well, at least I can go inside and get drunk and forget all about this—oh, wait, no, I *can't*, because I have to drive us home again. Isn't this just fun for me?"

"It's not all bad," I say. "Jackson's here—I just saw him go inside."

"Really?" She turns to face me, reaching up to tighten her ponytail. "Do I look okay?"

"Seriously amazing." The theme for the after-party is always something sexist and borderline offensive for the girls—like "zombie whores" or "nympho schoolgirls"—but the boys get easy costume assignments like "cowboys" or "heroes." This year the theme is "trashy cheerleaders and jocks" which is why all of us girls are wearing our shortest miniskirts with tight tank tops and the guys are all wearing whatever team uniforms they already had lying around.

"Now do me," I say.

She fixes my locket, pushing the clasp back behind my neck where it belongs, winds my ponytail around her finger to curl it, and pronounces me perfect.

"Was Jackson with anyone?" she asks me as the light changes and we cross, the rest of our gang right behind us.

"Just that guy we met at Starbucks."

"Your long lost cousin?"

I nod and smile. I'm kind of looking forward to another family reunion tonight.

I find Wade by the guacamole—or what used to be the guacamole. There's not much left: just some green mush and a few chip crumbs around the bowl.

"Hey, cuz!" I have to shout—the music's loud.

He looks up, registers it's me, and says a welcoming "Hey!" He leans in to say, "I like that we barely know each other and yet we already have nicknames. Also? You look really great." He's got on a baseball jersey in lazy deference to the party theme.

"Looks like I'm too late for the guacamole," I say.

"Don't blame me. I swear it was like that when I got here."

"After-parties aren't known for the plentifulness of their food," I say. Then: "Is *plentifulness* a word?"

"I'm kind of doubtingful."

I laugh. "So . . . if there's no guacamole and we're standing at the guacamole table . . . what does that make us?"

"Hungry," he says. "And ready to give up on the idea

of food to go dance." He tilts his head back and peers at me. "Yes?"

Most definitely yes.

He gestures toward the dance floor behind me. I turn too quickly and collide with Lily. "We were coming to say hi," she says in that half yell you have to use at a party. "When did you guys get here?"

The "we" is her, Finn, and Hilary. Hilary's dressed like the rest of us in a little flippy skirt over some kind of biker shorts and a cropped spandex tank; her hair's in the requisite ponytail. But Lily—who has no problem wearing short skirts and tight-fitting tank tops on any normal school day—has deliberately ignored the dress code for tonight and gone grunge for the evening, with loose jeans, her red Doc Martens, and a flannel shirt.

"How exactly are you a cheerleader?" I ask.

"Let's just say I root for the *softball* team," she shouts back with a grin.

I greet Finn with a polite nod, and he nods back at me. That's what we do these days: bob our heads like two friggin' birds drinking water. He's dressed normally, in jeans and a dark green polo shirt, and is wearing his contacts.

I introduce Wade to them, and the girls start pelting him with questions, like what school he goes to and how he figured out we were cousins and whether he's friends with various people they know at his school, and so on.

Wade is friendly and answers all their questions, but after a while he turns to me and says, "Still up for that dance?" and I nod eagerly.

Lily says to Finn, "Let's dance too," but he shakes his head. "I don't do that. Sorry."

"You don't dance?" she says. "At all?"

"I had a bad experience at a dance once." His gaze flickers across my face. No one else notices, but my stomach clenches with shame. "I don't usually even go to them. I'm only here tonight for a sociological experiment."

"Yeah? What are you studying?" asks Hilary.

"The effects of a multitude of very short skirts on the developing male brain." Everyone but me laughs. I force a weak smile.

"It's not the brains that are reacting," Lily says with a leer. She shrugs. "If you're not going to dance, then we'll have to go without you, right, Hil?"

"I don't think people are doing that," Hilary says, studying the dancers. "It's, like, mostly couples."

"Oh, who cares?" Lily says. "If we want to dance, we should dance, with or without someone who happens to have a penis."

"Hear, hear!" says Finn. "And to show my support, I'll come watch."

"I bet you will," says Lily with a toss of her head. Finn leans against a wall while the rest of us join the crowd on the dance floor. It's a relief to leave him and my discomfort behind. The music is loud; the room is hot; the floor is packed—perfect dancing conditions. I intend to enjoy this.

We start out in a group, the four of us all dancing together, but pretty soon Hilary shouts, "I'm done," and goes back to where Finn's alone at the side of the room. Lily keeps glancing over at them, and after a while she leaves the dance floor and joins them.

Wade and I keep dancing, but the heat that started off feeling welcoming and inviting turns overwhelming and sickening after a while, and there's one drunk kid who keeps bumping into me—at first I think it's by accident, but after his hand lands on my butt more than once, I start to wonder—so after a song ends, I shout, "Let's take a break and get something to drink."

We make our way to where a bunch of sodas and juice are set out on a counter. Wade asks me what I want, but I say I'll take care of my own drink. I'm kind of paranoid about that actually: we had these people come talk to the school about drugs and alcohol when I was in eighth grade, and one of the things they said was that open bottles and cans can be spiked with all sorts of crap, and the only way to be sure what you're drinking is safe is to open a new bottle or can and pour it yourself. So I find an unopened Diet Coke can and pour myself a cup while Wade gets himself a Sprite.

"Do you want something stronger?" he asks me. "I know a couple of guys who were going to smuggle some stuff in."

I tell him about my promise to Lucy to stay sober, and I realize I should probably check on her. We search the crowded room, greeting people we know and talking to each other as much as we can, given how noisy it is. Wade doesn't seem to be in any hurry to leave my side, and I'm not in any hurry to leave his: I'm liking his company, and I'm also liking the way girls from my school are eyeing him approvingly. Everyone will be asking me about him on Monday. I'm thinking that maybe when they do, I won't mention that we're distantly related, because even though it's not creepy, it sounds like maybe it *could* be creepy.

"Is it a coincidence that I don't see Jackson anywhere either?" Wade asks after we've completed a lap around the room.

"Good question. There's an outside, right?" We find the open doors that lead to some sort of courtyard area, which turns out to be Hookup Central—couples are on every piece of furniture, mouths plastered together, hands exploring. And there are Lucy and Jackson. He's leaning against a tree, and she's leaning against him.

Well, good for her. She's been wanting this for a while.

It's kind of awkward standing in the middle of all

these kissing couples. Wade and I may be having fun together, but we're nowhere near *this* yet. Maybe if I were drunk. Maybe if he started something. . . . But he doesn't, and I'm not, so we have a few uncomfortable moments of standing there trying not to look at any of the couples or at each other, and then I excuse myself to go use the restroom.

Back inside I spot Phoebe and Eric off talking in a corner. That's all they're doing—talking—but somehow they've created their own space bubble, and I don't want to go over and interrupt. Maybe it's the way she's looking down as they talk and he's leaning in close that makes me reluctant to break in on them. I squint at them and consider. Phoebe and Eric? Not a couple I would have put together. But that makes it kind of interesting.

After I've used and left the bathroom (long wait, of course—dozens of girls in line along with a few sheepish guys), someone grabs my arm.

"Hey!" I say. It's Oscar. He's wearing board shorts and a sleeveless muscle tee, because (he told us earlier) going surfing is the closest thing he's ever come to feeling like a jock. He usually slicks down his wavy light brown hair, but tonight he's left it naturally unruly, which makes him look about three years younger. "You having a good time?"

"Not really," he says. "I am so tired of this, Anna."

"Of after-parties?"

"No. Of being the only out guy in our grade, not just at Sterling Woods but at every major private school in the LA area."

"That can't be true."

"Maybe it's an exaggeration. But look around you." He flings his hand out. "See any other gay guys? And you know what really pisses me off?"

I link my arm in his. "What really pisses you off, Oskie?" We start to walk toward the area of the room that has the drinks.

"What really pisses me off," Oscar says, putting his mouth closer to my ear so he doesn't have to shout, "is that half the guys here are going to come out of the closet one day. But it's not going to do me any good. I'm going to finish up my senior year without a single date, and then I'm going to come to the tenth reunion and all these guys—and I could name some of them right now—are going to come over to me and tell me how they wanted to come out but didn't have the guts and how *now* they're all rah-rah-we're-here-and-we're-queer and everything and I'm going to want to kill them for all the time lost and the fun we could have had." He shakes my arm. "And I should be *allowed* to kill them. I really should."

I squeeze his elbow. "You're just much cooler and braver than anyone else. I think my sister's pretty cool and brave, but even she didn't have the guts to come out in high school." Oscar and I had a long, intense conversation about Molly a couple of weeks ago, so he knows the whole story.

"You know what being cool and brave gets me?" he asks. "Nothing. Because there's no one to be cool and brave *with*. My nights are lonely, Anna."

"My nights are lonely too," I say, but at that moment I spot Wade, who greets me with a welcoming smile, and I can't really blame Oscar for his skeptical silence.

I sleep over at Lucy's house, and when we wake up the next morning—or actually the same morning, since we went to bed at 2:00 a.m.—or actually the same afternoon, because it's now 1:00 p.m.—I have a voice mail on my phone from my dad. "I need you to come home before six," he says. Which surprises me, because when both of my sisters are out of town, Dad and I tend to lead pretty separate lives. His complete indifference to my whereabouts when I want to be completely independent makes up for his complete indifference to my whereabouts when I don't.

Lucy drops me off at home mid-afternoon, and I go straight to Dad's office. I knock and wait for his "Come in" before opening the door—all of his daughters were trained to do that at an early age.

He looks up from his computer screen. "Thank god you're here," he says, which is most definitely not the way he normally greets me. I'm lucky if I get a distracted "How's life? Good? Good" as he passes me in the hallway.

"What's going on?" I ask. "Is everything okay?"

"Yes, fine." He absently runs his fingers through his hair, then realizes what he's done and smooths it carefully back into place. "I just felt it was important that you join us this evening."

"Us?" I repeat.

"Yes, me and, um, your friend Ginny Clay. Your teacher. Ms. Clay. Ginny." He's avoiding my gaze, so he misses my horrified double take. "There's a, um . . . a exhibit. *An* exhibit. At the MOCA. It's an artist she admires. She, uh, mentioned this exhibit to me in an email and said she thought it would be very inspiring for you and your work—"

"For me and my work?"

"To inspire you and your work, yes."

I'm staring at him with my very stoniest of stares, but he's fiddling with the glass paperweight on his desk and doesn't get the full effect, or any effect at all, really.

Gently rocking the paperweight from side to side, he says, "We'll all go together, see the artwork, and have dinner downtown. Oh, you'll be excited about this—I made a reservation for us at Jersey."

"Why would I be excited? I've never even heard of it."

"Your sister's been saying we should go for months."

"Because she cares about that kind of thing. I don't."

"It's the hottest new restaurant in LA," he says, looking up with what seems to be genuine surprise at my lack of interest. "My assistant had to work very hard to get this reservation. We had to track down a client of mine who invested in it and—"

"I can't go, anyway. I have to work on a paper."

"You can work on the paper now. But you're going tonight." He sits up straight and lowers his voice. Suddenly he's an imposing figure—even a little scary. "We planned this evening for you. I will graciously assume that your lack of gratitude is a teenage reflex, and now that it's over we can move ahead with our plans. Be ready to go at six o'clock."

"I need to get an A on this paper," I say, but already my voice is losing its confidence. Maybe it's the way his eyes are narrowing—it still scares the hell out of me, even though I'm not a little kid anymore.

"You will be ready at six o'clock," he growls. "Or lose the use of the car for the next two months."

"You don't think that's a little harsh?"

He puts on his reading glasses. "Be ready to go at six," he says.

I can't even pick up the phone to complain to my friends—it's all way too embarrassing. The idea that

Ginny Clay thinks she has something to teach me about art. The idea that she and my dad send each other emails (!). The idea that I've been *ordered* to go to dinner with them.

I assume I'll tell Lucy about it eventually, but for now I just curl up into a fetal position and try to reread the James Joyce story I have to write the paper about. The words don't make sense. Life has become senseless.

Ginny drives up to our house at 6:02.

"Answer the door!" my father shouts from his room, after she rings the bell.

"Why can't you?" I yell back.

"Just answer it, Anna!"

I walk slowly down the stairs. Ginny keeps ringing and knocking, but I don't increase my pace. I reach the door in my own sweet time and open it.

"Hi, Anna!" she sings out, and throws her arms around me before I can dodge them. When I can slip out of her grasp, I see that she's dressed exactly the way someone in a movie would dress to go to an art exhibit, in a smart little black linen dress with her hair pinned up in a French knot to show off sculptural silver earrings and a matching silver necklace. She's wearing black spike heels, and I sincerely hope they'll pinch her feet when we walk through the gallery.

"Is that what you're wearing?" she asks me.

I look down at my jeans and T-shirt: I'm in

comfortable weekend mode. "I guess."

"We're going to a museum and a nice dinner," she says with a smile. "Don't you think you should change?"

"I'll put on a sweater." I was going to, anyway—museums are always cold. So are fancy restaurants. I have no idea why they keep the air-conditioning up so high at both. They just do.

"And maybe some nice shoes?" she suggests. "Just to dress it up a little?"

"Whatever." I move toward the stairs.

"You might want to brush your hair too," she calls after me.

On my way up, I pass my father, who's coming down. "Where are you going?" he says sharply.

"To get a sweater."

"Well, hurry up," he says. "You were supposed to be ready to go."

"You made me answer the door!"

I keep trudging up. Behind me, he and Ginny greet each other, her voice high and chirpy, his low and precise. I glance over my shoulder. She's thrown her arms around him, just like she did with me.

And he looks about as comfortable with it as I was.

In the garage he opens the front passenger door and gestures to Ginny to get in.

She pauses. "Doesn't Anna want to sit here?"

"She's fine in the back."

"Yeah," I say. "I have to work, anyway." I brought the James Joyce book with me. Mostly so I'd have an excuse to ignore them.

My father whispers, "I expect you to participate in the conversation," as he passes me on his way around the car.

"You can expect whatever you want," I mutter, low enough so he doesn't actually hear me.

Once we're on our way, Ginny chatters away enough for all three of us. She tells us she's "just incredibly excited" to see this exhibit and that she thought of me immediately when she heard about it. "One of the reviews I read called the artist 'fearless,' and I instantly thought, *That's* what Anna needs: to expose herself to fearlessness. She needs to touch, feel, see, taste, and experience utter fearlessness."

"So we'll be licking the canvases?" I say, and then flash a huge fake smile at her when she glances back at me.

"Your daughter has a very strange sense of humor, Mr. Eliot," she says to my father.

"Please," he says. "Call me Richard. Mr. Eliot makes me feel like an old man."

"That's ridiculous!" she cries out. "You must have had your kids incredibly young, because you don't look any older than most of the guys I date." She giggles, hand to her mouth. "Oh, wait! That sounded wrong, didn't it?"

I pull out my phone—anything to withdraw from the conversation. But Ginny glances back and catches me. "Oh, Anna," she says reprovingly. "I hope you won't be staring at your phone all night long. You'll miss out on so much. Right, Richard?" She turns back to him.

"Huh?" says my father, who had been taking advantage of a red light to check his texts.

We hit traffic and by the time Dad parks in the museum lot, he tells us we have ten minutes to see the entire exhibit. "They won't save our dinner reservation, so we can't be late."

"Look at the brave colors!" Ginny cries out to me as we gallop past a wall of canvases. "Look at the textures! This is what courage looks like!"

"It's also what vomit looks like if you mix food dye into it."

She raps me on the arm. "This is exactly what I'm talking about, Anna. You're close-minded."

"I am not," I say. "I just don't like these." The paintings are lumpy. And the colors are dreary.

"He's challenging our ideas of what's beautiful and what isn't. He's daring you to expand your definition of fine art."

"But they're ugly."

"Art isn't just about what looks *pretty*," she says. "Wallpaper is pretty. Art is provocative. Right, Richard?"

My father looks up from his phone, which his eyes haven't left since we entered the gallery. "You're the expert on all of this, Ginny. Anna and I are here to learn from you. But it's getting late—I think we'd better head out."

"Lead the way," Ginny says. "I'm starving!"

She couldn't have said anything to delight him more. He says, "Wonderful! Let's order everything on the menu and try it all!"

Once we're seated at the restaurant, Ginny tries to discuss the artwork, but I'm done with the subject, and even though Dad feigns an interest in what she's saying, it's obvious he's much more invested in studying the menu. "Yes, yes, brilliant work . . . I wonder if we should get four entrées or focus more on the appetizers. . . . The artist was definitely—I can't remember if I like bacon lardons or not—Anna, do you remember? No, you wouldn't, but Lizzie would know—you could tell the gallery wanted—definitely four entrées and five or six appetizers. Just to try everything. We can bring the leftovers home. Mail them to Lizzie, maybe, eh, Anna?" He looks up. "Can you picture her opening that care package? A pile of old pasta and bacon?" He chuckles delightedly and plunges back into the menu.

Ginny laughs. It's possible she's forcing it, but I can't tell for sure.

I pluck a breadstick out of the basket and settle back in my chair. The restaurant has an industrial look to it—an uneven brick floor and the ceiling opened up so you can see the pipes running along it—but the tables are covered with thick white tablecloths and the utensils are heavy silver. It's luxurious—but ashamed of itself. And, having seen the menu prices, I kind of agree it *should* be.

Dad orders for the table. "You don't mind, do you?" he says to Ginny, who gives a slightly anxious nod. I see why later, when our first few appetizers arrive and he asks her why she's not eating anything. She confesses that she's a vegetarian.

My father groans. "Please tell me you're not a vegan."

"Oh, no," she says. "I mean, I try to be when I can, but it's too hard all the time."

"I don't understand why people feel they need to take these stands," my father says. "We evolved to be omnivores. I would never allow my daughters to be vegetarians."

That would be news to Molly—she's been a vegetarian since eighth grade. Dad just never noticed. She doesn't make a big deal out of it.

Ginny murmurs something about the environment and the healthfulness of whole grains and plants.

My father waves all that away. "The restaurants I frequent all use high-quality meats—grass-fed beef and free-range chicken. And don't tell me that a vegetarian diet is healthy. The fattest people I know are vegetarians. All that pasta and bread."

"I hope you're not including me on that list!"

"Of course not." My father smiles at her reassuringly and takes a sip from his cocktail—a house specialty, with cucumber, basil, and some other garbage floating around in it.

My father offers to order Ginny whatever she'd like, but she insists there'll be plenty for her to eat. There really isn't, though—even the vegetables he's ordered are laced with prosciutto. Ginny eats bread from the bread basket and smiles valiantly as she watches us stuff ourselves. I have to admit that the food is good.

"I'll have to do a double workout tomorrow," Dad says as we walk out of the restaurant with several take-out boxes. Ginny laughs like he's made a joke, but he means it. Working out is his trade-off for eating like this.

Back home she gets into her own car and leaves, and Dad and I walk into the kitchen together. "Nice girl," he says vaguely. "Too bad she feels she has to do that ridiculous vegetarian thing. But so many do these days. I'm sure she'll outgrow it." He glances sideways, and I follow his gaze. He's looking at his reflection in the window. He straightens up a bit, shoulders back, stomach in. "I'm not an old man yet," he says. "When I tell people I have two daughters in college, they think I'm joking."

"You look good for your age," I say, which is true and seems to satisfy him.

He gives our reflections a brisk nod and heads down the hallway. "Go write your paper," he says before disappearing.

Up in my room, I text Lizzie a photo of Ginny and Dad sitting next to each other at the restaurant.

Pretty soon I get a text back.

What was Ginny doing at Jersey with Dad?

He took us both there.

What? I can't believe he went to Jersey without me. He knows how much I want to try it.

That's the part that bothers her?

Five

On Tuesday, Lily and I walk out of our last class and down the hallway to the courtyard behind the school. Lucy and Hilary are supposed to meet us here, but they have Mr. Flood for history during this period and he always keeps his students late. Whereas our math teacher, Mrs. Doninger, is of the *It's a beautiful day—go enjoy it!* school of teaching.

"Another sunny day," Lily says with a sigh as we drop our books and bags on the grass near our favorite tree.

"What have you got against the sunshine?" I ask, plopping down on the ground and leaning back against the rough tree bark.

"Just that it's always the same here, and it's boring. I'd kill for a thunderstorm. Or a tornado. I've never seen a tornado." Lily stretches out next to me. She's wearing thigh-high boots over a pair of leggings today and a purple-and-yellow-striped tunic. She looks like one of those French dolls with the porcelain heads and stuffed bodies, and she's heightened the effect by making her skin look extra pale, except on her cheekbones, where she's wearing a lot of blush. She rests her head on my thigh. "You mind?"

"No." I absently brush my fingers through her hair. It's blown straight today, very simple. "I like your hair like this."

"I'm thinking of shaving this part." She raises her hand and lifts the hair at her temple. "You wouldn't notice it when I wore it down, but if I wanted to pin it back, you'd see the shaved part."

"How would your parents feel about that?"

"Dad wouldn't notice; Mom would hate it; Hilary would hate it even more."

"And that's why you want to do it."

"No, it's not! I'm not like that."

"Come on, Lil. You like shocking people."

"I just want to do my own thing, that's all." She rolls onto her back, her head still resting on my thigh. "Anna?"

"Mmm?"

"Do you think Finn likes me?"

I hope she can't feel the muscles in my leg tense up. I force myself to be honest. "Yes," I say. "I do."

"Me too." She swings herself up to a sitting position

120

and, with some effort, pushes off her boots, then crosses her legs like a little kid. "So why doesn't he do anything about it?"

"You mean like ask you out?"

"Yeah, or try to get me alone or tell me he likes me or *anything*."

"Maybe he just hasn't had a chance. We're always in a group—"

"Oh, please." She waves her hand. "I've given him opportunities. Believe me. Do you think it's because of Hilary?"

"What do you mean?"

She plucks a blade of grass and twirls it between her fingers. "She obviously likes him too. It makes it awkward. For all of us."

"But he likes you better?"

"Are you asking or saying?"

"I don't know. But—" I stop.

"What?" She turns to look at me, her eyes eager.

I'm struggling to figure out what to say. I want to tell her not to rush anything, but not because I think it's good advice. Because I don't want Finn to be going out with anyone who isn't me. And that's not fair. So I don't say that. Instead, even though it's painful, I finally say, "I think he does like you better. I mean, maybe he doesn't want to hurt Hilary's feelings, and it's probably weird that you're sisters. But it's not like you two are interchangeable. He's got a right to choose you over her, and you have a right to choose him back."

Lily slides over so she's next to me. She rubs her cheek against mine. "How are you so wise?"

"I'm not."

"Could have fooled me." She glances over her shoulder. "Oh, there they are." She jumps to her feet and waves her arms in wide sweeps.

Hilary and Finn and Oscar descend on us. Oscar takes the spot next to me, and Finn sits across from us, leaning back on his elbows, with a twin on either side of him. Hilary's hair is braided down her back and she's wearing jeans and a very tight short-sleeved sweater and looks really pretty. Today she kind of blows Lily out of the water: Lily's too cutesy with her pink cheeks and garish tunic.

I wonder if Finn thinks so too.

He happens to glance up while I'm staring at him, and I drop my gaze, embarrassed. "Where's Lucy?" I ask, as if that's all I've been thinking about—why Lucy isn't here right now.

"She wanted to ask Flood about our big research paper," says Hilary. "You know the way she is about this stuff."

I do. Lucy's so neurotic about papers and tests that she'll grab teachers whenever and wherever she can—right after class, before review sessions, if she sees them in the hallways—just to make sure she's studying or writing the right things. Most of the teachers are thrilled she's such a dedicated student, but I swear I once saw a history teacher make a sudden U-turn in the corridor when he saw her coming.

"Hilary and I have something we want to talk to everyone about," Lily announces, shifting to her knees. "But we'll wait until Lucy's here."

"Are we in trouble?" Oscar says. "Because if we are, it's all Anna's fault."

"Don't throw me under the bus," I say with mock indignation.

"What exactly did you two do?" Hilary asks.

"I didn't do anything," Oscar says. "That's my point."

"We're not going to yell at you," Lily says. "This is a good kind of conversation. It involves an invitation."

"Cool," says Oscar. "And, now that I know we're not being yelled at, I can admit that Anna is totally blameless. Mostly totally blameless."

"Remind me never to murder anyone with you," I tell him.

Lucy emerges a few minutes later, her forehead puckered with concern because, she tells us, "Mr. Flood didn't seem all that enthusiastic about my topic."

She slumps down forlornly next to Hilary, who says,

"I was there when you first described it to him, and he said it was great."

"I know, but today he was all 'I just want to make sure you're not trying to do too much.'" You can tell when Lucy's especially on edge, because she starts twirling her hair around her index finger. Right now she's twirling a strand from her ponytail like crazy.

"I may be going out on a limb here," Finn says, "but is it possible he just wants to make sure you're not trying to do too much?"

She shakes her head. "It's obviously code for 'I hate this topic now that I've had time to think about it.'"

"Yes, I'm sure that's it," Lily says. "Now shut up about school, Lucy, because Hilary and I have this unbelievable invitation for you all, and we've already waited for you for forever—"

"More like three minutes," Hilary puts in. "Lily's not good at waiting."

"No, although while we were sitting here I found a four-leaf clover." She holds it up for us all to see.

"That's not really four leaves," Finn says, leaning over to peer at it. "It's three, but one of them has a little extra piece on it." His voice speeds up a little. "Do you know that there are approximately ten thousand three-leaf clovers to every four-leaf one? In nature, I mean. People have actually figured out how to breed for them." For a moment I hear the old Finn in his voice, the one who got excited about gene research and alternative fuels. He gestures at the clover. "But this isn't one of them."

Lily pushes him away. "Just for that, you don't get to share my good luck."

"No one in this group is capable of being quiet for more than two seconds," Hilary says, crossing her arms over her chest.

"That's so unfair," I say. "I've been waiting patiently to hear the news."

"Look at Miss Goody Two-Shoes," Oscar says. "Little Miss Innocent. Miss I-Would-Never-Get-Oscar-in-Trouble-Oh-Wait-Yes-I-Would-and-Do-All-the-Time."

"Will you all please shut the frack up?" Finn says.

"Frack?" Oscar repeats. "Is that how we're swearing now?"

"It's from *Battlestar Galactica*," I say. "Finn loves that show." And then I realize I only know that because he told me so back in ninth grade.

"I do," he says quietly.

"Oh, forget it," Hilary says, throwing her hands up in the air and letting them fall down. "You guys are too annoying to invite anywhere."

"I'm not annoying," Lucy says. "Invite me."

The rest of us beg her to forgive us, and Hilary relents. "Okay, fine. So you guys know Coachella, right?"

"A-doy," Oscar says. "I've only gone for the last two years."

Coachella's the best music festival on the West Coast: three days of nonstop outdoor concerts in the California desert, incredible bands, and a lot of weed. So I've heard. I've never been. It's super-expensive and you have to buy tickets almost a year ahead of time, and I've never saved up enough money or planned ahead enough to make it happen.

Hilary goes on: "So that's huge, but it's in the spring, and Dad thinks there's room for something similar in the fall. His company's lined up all these bands—some really good ones—"

"—and a few bad ones," Lily says. Hilary shoots her a look, and she shrugs. "Just keeping it real."

"Mostly good ones. Anyway, it's only two days, and it won't be as huge as Coachella—at least not this year—but it won't be as hot either, and the really really amazing thing is that because it's being run by Dad's company, he said he could get us and some friends VIP passes, and we can have a van take us there—it's in the Santa Ynez Valley, a couple of hours away—and he can set us up with hotel rooms and everything."

"So what exactly is the question?" Oscar says. "Do we want to go? Because the answer's sort of obvious."

"Wait," Lucy says. "When is it?"

"November tenth and eleventh."

"But that's the weekend before early applications are due."

"Bring your laptop."

"Right," Lily says. "I'm sure there'll be lots of time to work . . . when we're not watching the bands play . . . or partying . . . or eating junk food . . . or doing ten million other incredibly fun things that have nothing to do with college applications." She leans forward and grabs Lucy by the shoulders. "Come on, Luce! Don't be such a dud. It's our last year of high school. Are you really going to spend the whole time worrying about college? Can't we have fun for one weekend?"

"We can invite Jackson if you want," Hilary adds slyly. "Ah, look—that brought a smile to her face."

"It did not," Lucy protests, smiling.

Hilary glances at me. "We can invite that friend of his too, if you want, Anna—the guy who was draped all over you at the after-party."

"He wasn't draped over me!" I protest, and the others laugh. Except Finn, who's apparently too busy watching a tiny bug crawl across his hand to be interested in whether or not Wade Porter was draped over me at the after-party. "He wasn't," I say again, frustrated. "We're just friends. *Cousins.*"

Hilary shrugs. "Whatever."

"There is nothing bad about this offer," Oscar says. "Which is why I'm sure my parents will find something to object to about it."

"You can promise them we'll be good little boys

and girls," Lily says. She holds up two spread fingers. "Scout's honor."

"That's a peace sign," Lucy says.

"Fine. Peaceful Scout's honor."

"We won't really be good little boys and girls, will we?" Oscar asks hopefully.

Lily grins at him. "Good? No. But we'll be great."

I glance over at Finn. He's carefully lowering his hand to the grass and staring down at it. He's letting the little bug crawl to safety.

six

'm happy I'm retaking the SATs at my own school. Usually I forget to register ahead of time, and by the time I finally *do* remember, there's no room left at Sterling Woods and I have to get up super early to drive a long way to some school I've never even heard of and wait in line with a thousand strangers and take the test in a room that's totally alien and unwelcoming (because any school that's not yours feels wrong)—so I'm relieved I remembered this time.

(Okay, the truth is I didn't actually *remember* to sign up early online: Lucy did. When I happened to be over at her house. So we both signed up.) And now I'm very glad I did, because it feels like home when I arrive at Sterling Woods at 7:45 that Saturday morning. A home where you have to wait in line with a couple of hundred other people to go inside to take a four-hour test. So . . . not a great home. But a home.

Lucy and I had agreed to meet at the courtyard fountain so we could wait in line together. When I join her there, she's already talking to Finn, who greets me coolly. He's wearing his glasses and red-plaid pajama pants and a T-shirt. Lucy's wearing capri leggings and a Yale hoodie ("To inspire me," she says defensively, when I raise my eyebrow at it) and has her hair pulled back in a ponytail so severe that no errant lock can possibly swing in front of her eyes, causing her to fill in the wrong circle, thereby lowering her score. (I know how her mind works.) I'm wearing the most comfortable sweatpants I own and a tank top under a zip-front sweatshirt.

"You guys both look like you just rolled out of bed," Lucy says.

"I *did*," Finn and I say at the same time, and we grin at each other before remembering that we don't make eye contact anymore. He drops his eyes first.

"Did you at least have some coffee or Coke or something?" Lucy asks as we all head together toward the line that winds from the front entrance almost to the gate. "I made myself drink a cup of coffee even though I don't like it, because I read a study that said caffeine really does help you do better on tests."

"It also makes you have to go to the bathroom," I say. "Risky trade-off."

"Yeah, well, I always have to pee a million times before a test, anyway," Lucy says, and, sure enough, as soon as we're in line, she excuses herself and runs off. Leaving me and Finn alone.

"Guess no one else is taking the test here this morning," I say, to head off any potentially awkward silence.

He glances at the long line in front of us. "No one?"

"Of our friends, I mean."

"The twins are taking it at University High," he says. "And Oscar's not retaking it. I don't know about the others."

"Why isn't he retaking it?"

Finn shrugs. "I assume he's either happy with his scores or just doesn't think he can get them up any more."

"Either way, I'm jealous."

A pause. "You remember your number-two pencils?" he says, after a moment.

"And my calculator, yes." Another pause. "I feel like we should be quizzing each other or something. Cramming."

"It's kind of too late for that."

"Then distract me. I'm getting nervous."

"This seems like a good time to remember that many of the greatest minds of our era never even graduated from college," he says. "Like Steve Jobs. Bill Gates. Mark Zuckerberg."

"That guy who pushes a shopping cart on the Promenade . . ."

He shakes his head. "Wrong attitude, Anna." It's nice to hear him say my name teasingly. First time in a very long while.

Lucy returns to the line a moment later. "Oh my god, it was so gross—some girl was literally throwing up in there."

"You really have to stop doing that before tests," I say.

"Very funny." She twists around to look at the line behind us and then stands on tiptoe to see how far it goes. "They have to let us in soon, or we'll start the test late."

"It doesn't matter," Finn says. "They time each segment separately."

"Still . . ." She tugs at her blond ponytail, shifts from side to side, scratches at her elbow. "I hate this waiting. It's worse than taking the test."

"You think that," I say, "but wait until you hit a question you can't answer. And then you'll be all, 'I want to be back in line with Anna and Finn.'"

"No, I'll be more like, 'I want to die.'" She fidgets some more. "I'm going to the bathroom again. I can't tell if I really need to or if I'm just thinking myself into it, but either way—"

"Use a different bathroom," I call after her. "A less vomit-y one." She nods and switches direction.

"Odds are good someone's throwing up in all of

them," Finn says. "It's crazy to me that people get so nervous."

"That's because you're a super-genius with a photographic memory. I'm surprised you're even retaking this."

"I'm not," he says. "It's my first time."

"Really? You didn't take it last spring?"

"I was too lazy."

"No," I say accusingly. "You knew you wouldn't have to take it more than once—you knew you'd do great."

"I did okay on the PSATs," he admits, and I know him well enough to know that "okay" means he probably got perfect scores. "I figured it would be similar."

"Plus you were too busy inventing apps and making a fortune."

He leans against the wall. "You've heard that rumor, have you?"

"You never talk about it. But everyone else does."

"I *helped* invent an app," he says. "With this older guy I know—my astronomy teacher back up in Seattle. It was sort of my idea, but I couldn't have done it without him. And I didn't make a fortune off of it. I made a little spending money. That's all."

"So the rumors that you're going to buy the island of Manhattan—"

"Grossly exaggerated," he says with a smile. "But

I'm looking into Queens." The line starts to move. He stands up and we do that walking-in-line thing—a tiny step, then waiting, then another step, then waiting . . . "They're checking IDs," he says, craning his neck to see what's holding us up.

I pull mine out of my pocket, and he tilts his head to see the picture on it. "You look different."

"It's two years old." I start to lower my arm, and he puts his hand on mine to stop me.

"That's how you used to wear your hair," he says, still examining it, holding my wrist to keep it where he can see it. "The bangs . . . I always liked the bangs. I was surprised you didn't have them anymore."

I flush. "I grew them out a couple of summers ago."

He releases my arm. "Did you get a good essay out of it? 'What I Did Last Summer'?"

"I'm saving it for my college essay. 'How Growing Out My Bangs Taught Me Compassion.'"

"Work a third-world country in there somehow," he says. "Colleges like to see some global awareness."

The line takes us through the front door.

"Progress," Finn says.

"Look." I point to a kid who's clutching some beads and murmuring to himself. "Is he actually praying right now?"

"There are no atheists in the SAT line."

"Remind me to ask him in a few weeks if it helped."

134

"I'm guessing the success of his prayers will correspond to the number of hours he spent studying. Okay, now look at this." We're stopped again, and Finn's right in front of a painting. It's a parched landscape: cracked red clay bordered by small, withered trees. It looks like maybe it was once a water hole, but a drought has dried it up. Kneeling down next to the empty hole are two minute scratchy figures: a small girl and her dog. She's petting him, but he's looking away from her, at something in the distance. If you follow his gaze, you can just make out a tiny creature peeking out from between a couple of the dead trees across the dried-up pond from them. It's so small, you have to squint to see that it has too many limbs and a malevolent gaze. "Now that's actually good," Finn says. "I mean, you look at it quickly, and it's just this interesting landscape. But if you keep staring at it, you notice that there's something else going on, and it's more tense than tranquil. Almost scary."

I'm starting to respond when Lucy slips through the door and rejoins us, fingers anxiously twisting in her ponytail. "The bathroom scene was intense. All these girls freaking out together—it was like a support group for people who are terrified of taking tests, except they were only making each other crazier." She glances at the wall over Finn's head. "Oh, Anna—your picture! I totally forgot that was right here. I always come in the other way. I love this one. It's so weird."

"Wait, you did this?" Finn says to me. Then, his eyes narrowing: "You might have said something. Or signed it at least."

I smile sheepishly. "I did. On the back."

"Anna thinks signatures on the front of pictures are distracting," Lucy explains to him.

"Plus how can you make someone look stupid for not knowing you painted it if you sign it where they can see?" Finn says irritably.

"I didn't make you look stupid." We're almost at the front of the line where they're checking everyone in. "You said exactly the right thing about it. And it meant more to me because you weren't just being polite."

"You should have told me."

"I was about to, but Lucy interrupted."

He just shrugs and stares off into the distance, his arms crossed over his chest. He's clearly pissed off, which isn't fair. He was the one who started talking about the painting—I didn't trick him into it or anything. And I really *was* about to tell him.

It's especially frustrating, because for the first time since Finn has come back to LA, he was talking to me like I was a normal person and not someone he has to be wary of.

On the plus side . . . he really liked my painting. Not knowing it was mine, he liked it. And that thought must be making me at least a little bit happy, because when I give my name and ID to the proctor, he says, "That's the first smile I've seen this morning."

The three of us are sent to different rooms. As we part, we wish one another luck—Finn even tosses good wishes my way, so he can't be *too* mad.

I'm glad I end up in my ninth-grade English room, because I loved my teacher that year, and the way she has the room decorated still feels cozy and welcoming to me. And I'm also kind of glad the three of us were split up. I really don't need to sit near Lucy, who'll be chewing her lip and twirling her hair and groaning out loud when she doesn't know an answer. She wraps herself in anxiety during exams. And I think it would be hard for me not to glance over at Finn if we were in the same room. And I really need to focus on the test: I don't want to have to take it again in December.

seven

I get a text that afternoon from Lily, inviting me over to their house to celebrate being done with the SATs. I'm superstitious enough to wince a little at the "being done" part, but I text back that I'll be there at eight.

Their housekeeper lets me in—Lorena lives with them, and I've seen her way more often than I've ever seen either of the twins' parents, so I give her a big hug and she tells me to go on back.

As I walk through the curved archway that leads to the great room in the back of the house, something rains down on me. A bunch of somethings. I instinctively throw my arms up to protect my head, and Lily laughs. She was waiting for me with a handful of M&M's— "Minis," she points out, "so they wouldn't really hurt. It's like getting married," she adds. "Finally being done with the SATs. It's a rite of passage."

"Stop saying stuff about being all done with them."

I stoop down to pick up some M&M's to throw back at her. "You're going to jinx us all."

"I said the exact same thing," says Lucy, who's perched on their enormous coffee table next to Hilary. She looks a thousand times better than she did this morning: her blond hair is all blown out and down on her shoulders, and she's even wearing a little makeup. Mostly she looks a lot less like she's ready to jump out of a window. She and Hilary are both wearing jeans and sweatshirts, like me, but Lily's got on a short black skater dress that has a white outline of a skeleton on it that lines up with the bones of her real body.

"How'd it go?" I ask Lucy. We didn't see each other after the test.

"I don't know," she says. "I don't know I don't know I don't know I don't know."

"You guys?" I glance back and forth between the twins.

"It was great!" Lily says. "This one girl came running in ten minutes late and got into a huge fight with the proctor because he wouldn't let her start, and she actually tried to grab a test and start filling it out, and he had to wrestle it away from her and call security to escort her out of the building. It was amazing."

"Were you there?" I ask Hilary, who shakes her head.

"I was in a different room. Thank god. It was hard enough being in a strange school with no one I knew."

"And now we're done talking about the SATs," Lily says. "Oh—that's the doorbell! It'll be Finn or Oscar. Someone help me throw M&M's." She takes a new handful out of the bowl and positions herself at the door.

Lucy whispers to me and Hilary. "Wait—just quickly—did you guys get that reading-section question about dictators? Was the answer 'malevolent' or 'culpable'?"

Hilary and I both shake our heads quickly. You can't let Lucy start with this stuff. It won't end. She'll be asking for reassurance about questions all night long.

The guys walk in together. I didn't see Finn right after the SATs, but since then he's put in his contacts and showered and combed his hair and changed into jeans and a sweater. He looks older and less familiar. Oscar just looks like himself: very handsome and neat, with an Oxford shirt tucked in behind a canvas belt.

Lily pelts them both with M&M's and is reaching for more when Finn grabs her arm. "No more," he says with mock sternness.

She nods meekly, but as soon as he lets go, she whips another handful at him.

"I warned you," he says, and gets a fistful of his own, which he throws rapidly, one by one, right at her face. They're so light, they can't hurt much, but she shrieks and puts up her hands and promises not to throw any more. He stops, and she instantly grabs some more and tosses them right at him. He calls her a "liar and a traitor" and reaches for a handful, which he pelts her with, and then she grabs the entire bowl and dumps them over his head.

She crouches down, still clutching the bowl and helpless with laughter, as he shakes his head, sputtering a little. "You got a bunch down my shirt," he says, and pulls his sweater and tee away from his body to release them.

"Bet you missed a few," she says with a waggle of her eyebrows. "You'd better strip down."

"*You'd* better clean these up," he says.

"Lorena will do it later." Finn picks them up.

Eric and Phoebe arrive together while Hilary's calling in a pizza order. The way they walk in side by side turns my suspicions about them into a certainty. Which is great for Eric, who's one of the nicest guys in the world but hasn't had a lot of luck with girls. He's grown out of the worst of his baby fat, but he still has a round face and he's not exactly ripped, and the fact that Phoebe— who's only dated alpha-type jocks up until now—is willing to see past all that makes me proud of her.

But it also makes me nervous. If they go out and then break up, it'll ruin our group.

Then I remember: we graduate in seven months. So maybe it doesn't matter all that much. Besides, Lily and

Finn are probably going to start going out soon too. (Not a welcome thought. But true.) Maybe this kind of thing is inevitable in a coed group of friends.

Lucy nudges my leg with hers and bobs her head questioningly in Phoebe's direction, and I nod my agreement: *something is definitely going on with them.* We'll get it out of Phoebe before the end of the evening.

"What do people want to drink?" Hilary asks. We're in the kitchen now, which the family room connects to with another enormous arched opening—their ceilings must be like fifteen feet high—and she's pulling out snacks to hold us until the pizza gets here. "We have Coke, Diet Coke, sparkling water, juice . . ."

"Anything stronger?" Eric asks hopefully. "We all had a tough day."

"Not Oscar," Lucy says. "He didn't have to take the SATs again."

"We can't all be natural geniuses," Eric says.

"True, true," Oscar says loftily. "But don't you ordinary folk worry about a thing. We superior beings will fix the world for you, so you can go about your daily lives without a care in the world, like the lower-order animals you are."

"Whatever," Eric says. "No one's answered my question."

"We can have wine," Hilary says. "Our parents are cool with that."

"What about beer?"

"Our parents are cool with wine," she repeats. "Take it or leave it, Manolo."

He looks at Phoebe like he needs to check with her—another sign that something's going on with them. She flicks her light brown hair behind her shoulders and says, "Wine sounds good to me. Do you have rosé?"

"I doubt it, but I'll check." Hilary opens a door in the back corner of the kitchen. It's filled with intersecting diagonal shelves; a bottle nestles in every diamond-shaped hole. There are dozens of holes, dozens of bottles.

Hil picks out two bottles and brings them back to the counter. "No rosé, sorry, Phee. Just red and white. Who wants what?" She hands Finn a bottle opener, and he sets to work uncorking the bottles.

"Hold on!" Lily says. "I have an idea." She grabs a glass from one of the cabinets. "Phoebe, this is for you." She fills it partway with red and then adds some white and holds out the glass. "Look! Instant rosé!"

"I don't think you're supposed to do that," Oscar says.

She makes a face at him. "They made fun of Thomas Edison too."

"Actually I don't think they did," Finn says. "As far as I know, he was well-respected in his own lifetime."

"But they *would* have laughed at him if he'd mixed

red and white wine," I say.

"Phoebe? Back me up here," says Lily. "Tell them it's delicious."

"I'm not drinking it," Phoebe says, backing away.

"Fine. *I'll* drink it." Lily takes a big sip. "Delicious. You guys are cowards. Take a chance on something new."

"What the hell," Finn says. "I'll take a Lily-rosé."

She grins at him. "You're not a coward."

"Maybe not," I say. "But he did just give in to peer pressure."

Oscar laughs. "Anna's right. *You* may be a maverick, Lil, but Finn's just following your lead."

"I don't have a problem with that," he says. "You follow Lily, you're going to end up somewhere interesting." They clink glasses and toast each other.

That wasn't the point I was trying to make.

Later, after we've all agreed that wine and pizza make the best combination ever, Lily declares that she wants to make brownies. When she can't find a brownie mix in the pantry, she pouts for a while and then brightens up. "I'll make some from scratch! What goes into a brownie? Flour? Sugar? Eggs?"

"Look up a recipe," Hilary says.

"That takes all the fun out of it." Lily disappears

into the pantry. "Just you wait," she calls out. "These are going to be fantastic."

"Can we watch a movie?" Oscar asks Hilary, who says, "Absolutely."

Finn stays with Lily in the kitchen while the rest of us head back to the sofas in the family-room area. Eric and Phoebe are already sitting close together. They move apart when we enter. Then shift back again. I cock my head at Phoebe, who shrugs at me with an uneasy smile. I give her a surreptitious thumbs-up, and she looks relieved.

Oscar and I squeeze into a big armchair together. He's nice and warm, and I'm cozy and a little sleepy from the wine and exhausted from taking the SATs that morning and at risk of falling asleep until Eric talks Hilary into live streaming *Arachnophobia*, which is an old movie about enormous spiders and not at all the kind of thing that puts you to sleep. I am, in fact, wide awake (and clutching Oscar's arm so hard, he has to ask me to stop) when Lily comes in with her pan of brownies. She sets it down on the coffee table and orders Hilary to pause the movie.

When she tries to cut the brownies, they turn to mush under the knife. They're very runny and slimy.

"They look not unlike turds," Oscar whispers to me as Lily scoops out pieces and passes them around on napkins. People take their first tentative bites. We instantly recoil, one by one.

"Ugh!" says Hilary, wiping her tongue with a napkin. "Lily, these are disgusting. They're, like, raw. And they taste weird."

"Yeah," Lily says cheerfully, spitting her bite back onto the napkin. "My brownies suck."

"They really do," Finn agrees.

"Toss them here," Lily says, holding out the pan. "I'll throw them out."

"And next time use a recipe," Hilary says as we hand back our brownies.

"Never!" As Lily stands up, a napkin-wrapped brownie falls out of the pan onto the floor. She kicks it toward the kitchen. Bits of goo fly out of it.

"What are you doing?" her sister says. "Pick it up!"

"Score!" Lily says as she kicks it again with a giggle.

"You're making a mess!"

Oscar puts his mouth to my ear. "Here's the thing," he whispers. "I love John Green as much as the next gay teen. But the whole manic-pixie-dream-girl thing? It gets a little annoying in real life."

I kind of agree with him and can't help glancing over at Finn, to see what he thinks. Except I can't see his face, because he's on his feet, bending down, carefully using a napkin to pick up the brownie crumbs off the floor. When he stands up, his back is still to me, but I hear Lily say to him, "A noble experiment, right?"

Finn's back shrugs. He says something I can't hear. All I know is that Lily looks—for just a second—uncharacteristically uncertain. Maybe even embarrassed. Then she turns around and goes on into the kitchen.

And Finn follows her.

eight

Wade Porter and I have been texting. Nothing too major—we just check in with each other every now and then. We keep agreeing that we should hang out together sometime, but with the SATs hanging over us for the last couple of weeks, that just wasn't going to happen.

But now they're over, and I get this:

Could I drop by your house just to say hi on Tues evening? I have a physics test that morning and need something to look forward to.

I didn't think we were at the dropping-by-each-other's-houses stage of things yet, but why not? I text back a *Sure* and my address.

Dad's home and in his office when I hear the doorbell. I race down the stairs to get to the door before Wade rings again—Dad will ignore a first ring on the assumption I'll get it, but a second one risks bringing him out, and I don't really want to launch into the whole introduction thing.

I fling open the door.

Only it's not Wade—it's Ginny Clay.

"Hi, Anna!" she sings out. "Surprise!"

"What are you doing here?" I ask. That sounds too rude. I fix it. "I mean, hi, what are you doing here?"

She squeezes by me. She's wearing cigarette jeans and a cropped cardigan over a long, narrow top. Her blond hair is sleek on her shoulders. She's carrying a brown paper bag with a fragrant baguette sticking out of the top.

"I just found the most amazing new gourmet food store in Santa Monica," she says. "I wanted to buy everything there, but I couldn't just buy it for myself, and then I remembered how you're all such foodies in your family, and so I figured I'd satisfy my greed by buying everything I wanted to for you guys."

"Really?" I say. "You bought us food? For no reason?"

"Mmm-hmm." She's still smiling. "Is your dad home?"

"I'll get him." I'm halfway down the back hallway before I realize she's followed me.

I knock on Dad's office door and get permission to open it.

"Surprise!" Ginny sings out as she pushes by me and enters.

Dad looks slightly stunned by her sudden appearance. He's not used to being interrupted when he's working, and he's definitely not used to people barging into his office. But his social skills are strong. "Ginny," he says. "How nice to see you." He snatches his reading glasses off of his face and puts them on his desk, then runs his hand through his hair, settling it all in place. He rises to his feet. "To what do we owe the honor?"

Ginny repeats the explanation she gave me. "You've taken me out to such nice meals," she says at the end. "I wanted to give something back. Can I show you what I got?"

"Not here," my dad says hastily. Food is not allowed in his office. "In the kitchen. In the kitchen."

In the kitchen Ginny unloads her purchases. The crusty baguette. Some kind of fig jam. A soft cheese I've never seen before. Dark Belgian chocolate. Pickled miniature vegetables. A bottle of red wine. And a small carton of quail eggs.

"How cute are these?" she says, showing us the tiny speckled shells in their little carton.

Dad says, "This is all just terrific, but I'm afraid I ate a late lunch today."

"And I had an enormous sub a couple of hours ago," I say.

"Oh, that's fine," Ginny says, a little too brightly. It's seven thirty, and I'm sure she thought she'd be getting to us right around our dinnertime, but the truth is, we don't actually bother with sit-down meals in our house: Dad and I just eat when we're hungry. And I'm usually starving right after school. And then again later, but that's just for stuff like ice cream and brownies. And popcorn. And chips. She says, "This will keep. I didn't mean for us to eat it tonight necessarily. It's really more of a house gift." She gives a little stilted laugh.

"Well, thank you," says my father. He clears his throat. "Can you stay for a glass of wine?"

She says eagerly, "Only if you're not busy. I don't want to interrupt anything."

"A pleasant interruption is far more enjoyable than the work I was doing," Dad says gallantly. He stands up a little straighter. "Anna, get the wineglasses."

I get out three. He pours two and puts down the bottle. I pick it up and pour a little bit into the third glass. "Cheers," I say, and drink it.

Dad shoots me a look, but he lets it go.

"Shall I put out the bread and cheese too?" asks Ginny, who's probably starving.

"Sure," Dad says amiably. "We'll have a little party. Anna, get out a cheese board."

I hand Ginny a cheese board from the drawer, then pour myself a little more wine.

"Enough," Dad says, just as the doorbell rings. "Who could *that* be?" he asks.

"A friend of mine." I put down my wineglass and speed out of there.

This time it really *is* Wade. He's waiting there on our front step, looking slim and handsome in a polo shirt and khakis. And a belt. And loafers. He seems kind of dressed up, actually. Like for a date. Only we're not going on a date—he's just dropping by to hang out, right?

Which is why *I'm* wearing sweatpants and a hoodie and a ponytail.

"Hey," I say.

"Hey." He leans forward and pecks at my cheek.

Well, this is awkward.

I say, "Come on in."

"Who's here?" he asks as he steps over the threshold and hears Dad's and Ginny's voices coming from the kitchen.

"My dad and a friend."

"His girlfriend?"

"No! God, no."

"Oh, sorry. Who is she?"

"Just this friend of my sister's. She teaches at my school now."

"So your sister's here too?" I shake my head, and he says, "She's your sister's friend, but she's here even though your sister isn't?"

"Yeah, but I have no idea why. Let's just go to the family room so we don't have to deal with them."

"I don't mind," he says. "I like meeting people."

I shake my head—I can imagine the little knowing smile Ginny will give me when she sees Wade and assumes it's romantic. Which it may or may not be. I'm honestly not sure yet. But Wade's already heading toward the sound of their voices, so I follow him into the kitchen.

Ginny looks up from the bread she's smearing with fig spread and spots Wade. "Well, hello there," she says. "You must be the reason Anna went running for the door so quickly." She gives me a sly wink.

I reluctantly introduce everyone.

My father strides forward to shake Wade's hand. "Good to meet you."

"Great to meet you too, sir," says Wade, pumping away enthusiastically. *Sir?* Boys in California don't say "sir." Do they? "Has Anna told you how we're related?"

My dad shakes his head, so Wade explains that we're cousins. Dad asks what his mother's maiden name was, and Wade tells him, and Dad says, "Oh, yes, I know exactly who she is. I met her mother—your grandmother—a few times when I was a lot younger. Please send them both my regards."

"I will," Wade says.

"Are you two kids hungry?" Ginny asks, like she's our hostess. Like this is *her* kitchen. "We have tons of food. Cheese, bread . . . quail eggs . . ."

"Oops, too bad—I had quail eggs for lunch today," Wade says, and Dad and Ginny laugh appreciatively.

"How about some bread and cheese?" Ginny says.

"Sure," Wade says with a quick glance at me.

I shrug, and we join them on the stools around the kitchen island. It wasn't exactly how I wanted the visit to go, but the bread and cheese are good, and I'm hungrier than I realized.

Somehow—I'm not sure how or why—we get onto the subject of colleges. I guess it's inevitable. It's all anyone asks us seniors about, and it's all we think about, so conversations these days always seem to end up there.

Ginny asks Wade if he's applying early anywhere, and he says, "Yeah. I mean, I know it's probably ridiculous, because it's such a long shot . . . but it is the best school out there, and I figure I have no chance of getting in if I don't even try, right?"

"That's the spirit," says Ginny.

My dad nods absently, because he's reading something on his phone.

Wade raises his voice slightly. "You went to Stanford, didn't you, Mr. Eliot?"

Dad looks up. "I did. Best four years of my life. Seven years, if you count law school."

"Law school definitely counts," Ginny says.

Wade says, "Any advice for someone desperate to get in?"

"Yes," Dad says. "Get good grades and do well on the SATs."

"I'm working on it," Wade says.

"I've done quite a bit of alumni interviewing for Stanford," Dad says. "We're always looking for the exceptional."

"The exceptional. Got it. Will you be interviewing this year, sir?"

Sir again.

"Not this year, no. When you have a child applying, they make you take the year off."

"But she's not actually applying to Stanford, right?" Wade looks at me for corroboration, and I nod.

"I'm hoping Anna will change her mind," Dad says, which is probably true, since he's said that to me several times. If we spent more time together, it would probably stress me out, but he can only put pressure on me when he's actually with me, so it hasn't been too big an issue.

"I wouldn't get in, anyway," I say.

"Oh, Anna," says Ginny, who clearly enjoys saying "Oh, Anna" to me. "That sounds like fear talking. Wade's got the right idea—you have to take the shot if you want a chance to make the goal."

"I don't know why you think I'm so afraid of

155

everything," I say irritably, tearing a bread crust into small pieces. "I'm not."

"I worry that you're holding yourself back out of a fear of looking stupid."

"How nice for you that you don't have that problem," I say sweetly.

"Funny," she says icily. She glances at Dad, but he's looking at his phone again.

"You done yet?" I ask Wade, who obligingly slides off his stool, even though he still has a chunk of bread and cheese in front of him.

I was thinking we'd go to the family room and hang out there for a little while—maybe watch some TV and talk—but in the hallway he says he should probably get back to his homework and college applications. At the door we say good-bye, and then he bends down to kiss me. He kisses my cheek, straightens up, hesitates, and then leans back down and kisses me again, on the lips this time. It's light and brief, but it's definitely on my lips. Then he smiles at me and leaves.

I call Lucy to ask her what she thinks that meant.

"He likes you," she says without any hesitation.

"It was a very quick kiss."

"Well, did you respond? Pull him back in?"

"Not really. Did I mention it was very quick? I mean, his lips landed and then were gone. Stealth kiss."

"How'd you feel about it?"

"Fine. I felt fine about it."

"Calm down," she says sarcastically. "You're fogging up my phone."

"I don't not like him. I'm just not sure I like him yet. I was hoping I'd have a better sense after he came over tonight, but we spent the whole time with my dad and Ginny."

"Who's Ginny?"

"Ginny Clay."

That only confuses her more. "Why was Ginny Clay at your house if Lizzie wasn't there?"

It takes a while to explain the whole Ginny Clay story, so we never get back to our discussion of Wade, which is maybe just as well. What insight could Lucy have into the viability of this relationship when she doesn't know anything more than I can tell her?

And when you toss around phrases like "viability of this relationship," doesn't that sort of mean you're not in love?

But why *aren't* I in love? Wade is perfect.

I'll have to work harder at falling in love with him. That's all. I need a boyfriend so I can stop lying in bed at night wondering whether Finn and Lily have finally decided to stop worrying about Hilary's feelings and let themselves become a couple.

nine

At lunch every day, we plan our weekend at the music festival. The twins' father is arranging a van for our group, which so far seems to be Phoebe, Hil and Lily (obvs), Lucy, me, Oscar, Eric, Jackson, and Finn.

"Don't you dare break up with Eric before then," Hilary says to Phoebe, as Lucy and I follow them out of school at the end of the day. "That would complicate everything. Wait until after the trip to break his heart."

"What makes you think I want to break his heart?" asks Phoebe.

"History," says Hilary, who has a point—none of Phoebe's boyfriends have lasted longer than a month or two.

But so far she and Eric seem to be doing just fine as a couple. Eric is so happy she's his girlfriend that his round face radiates joy whenever he sees her. He jumps up to hold her chair for her, goes to her volleyball games and cheers wildly when she scores a point, opens doors for her, carries her books, pays for her meals, and rubs her shoulders.

And Phoebe . . . uh . . . lets him do all those things for her.

It works for them, I guess.

We reach our hangout near the tree and sit down on the grass to talk some more about plans for the festival—most importantly what clothing we're all bringing—and then my phone dings and I glance down at it.

"Crap," I say, jumping back up to my feet. "I totally forgot I was supposed to meet Mr. Oresco in the art room. We're supposed to go over my portfolio, see what I still need to add to it."

"I should head off too," Lucy says, scrambling up after me. "I've got to start that English paper."

"It's not due for another week," Hilary points out.

"I know, but I have so much else coming up. . . ."

As I walk back into school, I wonder if Lucy will be different in college. So much of her anxiety is about getting in—I hope she'll be able to relax once she's there. Maybe she'll stop caring about her grades or whether teachers like her and start partying like a beast.

Or maybe she'll just pick a new goal—graduate school or a fellowship or a cum laude degree—and obsess over *that*.

Yeah, it'll be that second one. Anxiety is her

caffeine—it keeps her going. Keeps her focused. Keeps her busy. I can't imagine a Lucy without stress—it wouldn't be Lucy.

I reach the art room, where Mr. Oresco and I spend the next half hour sorting through the pile of art I've produced since ninth grade, weeding out the bad pieces ("Don't call them *bad*," he chides me. "Art is a process, and sometimes that process takes you down paths that you decide not to pursue—but it's all valuable." Yeah, whatever—I'm still planning to burn the work that embarrasses me) and seeing what's left once we're down to the pieces that don't make me cringe.

"I love the direction you've been going in," Mr. O says, after we've finished making our piles. "I think the tension in your pieces is phenomenal. And there's something to be said for having a distinct and memorable point of view, so if you want to submit a portfolio that's all in this one very strong voice, I'm fine with that. But—"

I brace myself.

His voice is gentle as he goes on. "You might want to try your hand at something like a portrait or still life—something with a lot of detail, just to show some range. You don't have to include it unless you're happy with it, so there's no risk in trying, right?"

He's being reasonable, supportive, and intelligent—everything Ginny Clay wasn't when she told me I was a coward—so I tell him I agree.

I thank Mr. O, put my work on the shelf where I keep most of it, and head out to the mostly deserted hallway, where I spot Finn and Lily standing near the back door. Their heads are close together as he shows her something on his phone.

I stop where I am. It hurts to see them like that and I don't want to have to start smiling and pretending it doesn't, so I think about slipping away quickly, but just then Lily lifts her head, sees me, and calls out a greeting. She's wearing a pair of bright red jeans tucked into purple boots and a dark blue tank top. Crazy colors, but they work together. She says with a laugh, "Save me, Anna! Finn's showing me the most disgusting photos of dust mites and bacteria and stuff like that."

"Cool," I say, and force myself to move toward them.

"Cool?" she repeats. "I would have gone with 'revolting.'"

"And they're all around us." Finn pockets his phone. "Not to mention on top of us."

"Thanks for the nightmares." Lily swats his arm. "Is Hilary already out back, Anna?"

"Yeah. I was just going there."

We all head toward the courtyard. My steps are dragging. I let myself fall a little bit behind them.

I knew this was coming. We all did. But it was so slow. . . . I think maybe I had convinced myself that Lily

161

liked Finn much more than he liked her. That conversation she and I had under the tree had at least told me that Finn hadn't singled her out yet. But now . . .

Let me show you something. Another guy might mean something crude by that. But Finn . . . Finn just likes to share things that interest him with people he cares about. I remember what that felt like, the enthusiasm that burned in him lighting a spark in me until we were both blazing with curiosity and interest.

And now he's sharing all that with someone else.

Hilary jumps to her feet the second she sees us. "Where were you?" she says to Lily. "I said I wanted to go home right after school. What didn't you understand about that?"

"Cool your buns," says Lily. "I was talking to Finn."

Hilary glances at me. I quickly make sure I have an amused eyebrow-raised kind of expression on my face. The kind of expression that says, *Yeah, I found them alone together, and we all know what* that *means.* The kind that adds, *Not that I care one way or the other.*

It's a lot to communicate with a twist of the lips and a lift of the forehead, but I think I may have succeeded. Hilary swallows visibly and then says in a low, harsh voice, "Let's just go. The essay tutor's going to be at our house in like three minutes."

"Oops—totally forgot." Lily turns to Finn. "So . . . text me?"

He nods and tilts his body toward her so their shoulders brush against each other. As PDAs go, it's pretty tame, but Hilary and I exchange another look. She heads off with a brusque "Bye, guys," as she grabs Lily by the elbow. Their heads are close together as they walk toward the parking lot—they're talking. And I can guess what about.

Poor Hilary. She's got to be disappointed. But she's also got to have seen this coming. Finn's always made it clear he likes the way Lily does whatever she wants. It's like he decided at some point that the one thing that mattered to him most in a girl was that she not care what other people think.

Yeah, I wonder what made him feel that way.

Finn and I are still standing there. It's kind of pathetic—even when it's awkward and we have nothing to say to each other, I like being with him, so before he can just say good-bye, I quickly say, "Mites and bacteria, huh?"

He shrugs sheepishly. "I should probably stop trying to get other people to find that kind of thing cool." His voice picks up speed. "I mean these things are all around us—even inside us—and we've got the technology now to really see them. But no one likes to think about it. It grosses people out to think about sharing our buildings and bodies with all these other creatures. But that's the way it's always been. It's how we evolved.

It's healthy, in its own way. We're our own ecosystems."

"It's the creepy-crawly thing," I say. "No one likes bugs. And everything that's infinitesimal looks like a bug when it's magnified."

"Not everything," he says with a laugh.

"Everything," I insist.

"Most things do. I'll give you that." He shifts his book bag on his shoulder. "What's so bad about creepy-crawly things, anyway?"

"Spiders," I say. "And earwigs. And scorpions. And centipedes."

"They're all beautiful if you get down on their level and really look at them."

"I will never find an earwig beautiful."

"I bet I could find a photo to change your mind," he says. And his hand slips into his pocket like he's going to grab his phone. But then he pulls it out empty and takes a step backward. Away from me. "I better go. It's getting late."

I want to beg him to show me a photo of a beautiful earwig, but I don't. I just nod and say an indifferent "See you."

As he walks away, he does pull out his phone, but from the way he's thumbing it, I can tell he's sending a text.

Well, Lily told him to text her. I guess he didn't want to waste any more time before he did.

ten

The next morning I run into Dad in the kitchen and remember to tell him I'm going away right after school on Friday and won't be back until Sunday night.

He absorbs that as he inserts a coffee pod into the Keurig. "Away? Could you be more specific?"

"I'm going to a music festival. My friends' father will be there."

A slight furrow on his brow. "Do I need to call him?"

"No. It's all fine. Everything's arranged."

"Okay, great," he says, relieved. "Have fun. The Keurig needs more water." He walks out of the room, mug in his hand, his parenting done.

I refill the water tank, both grateful and sad I'm free to come and go as I please.

That afternoon I sit on the floor in the family room with the shades pulled all the way up to let in lots of light and contemplate the pad of art paper on my knees. I've laid out a circle of photos around me: family, friends, and even some magazine ads I've clipped out over the years.

I pick up a photo of Lucy from about two years ago. We were really into *America's Next Top Model* back then, so we'd take turns photographing each other. Most of the shots just stayed on the computer once we downloaded them, but I liked this one enough to print it out: Lucy had been leaning toward the camera with what was supposed to be a seductive pout, except she started giggling.

It's a side of Lucy I get to see, but most people don't— she can be goofy when we're alone, even though she's terrified of making a fool of herself out in the world. I want to capture that. So I set to work drawing. I draw and I draw and I draw. I erase a lot and toss the paper aside to start again four or five times. I keep working at it, though—I'm not going to give up; I'm going to keep fighting until I stop feeling frustrated at the gap between what I want my drawing to look like and what's on paper. I try different styles: loose and abstract, detailed and sharp, cartoonish, rough, polished . . .

I hate them all. By the time the light coming through the window has faded enough that I either have to turn on some more lights or give up, it's an obvious choice: I crumple up every piece of paper I've used and toss them all in the wastebasket.

I feel so frustrated, I could scream. Why couldn't I capture what I love about the photo—what I love about Lucy—on paper?

Maybe the mistake was picking Lucy as a subject. She has a funny little nose that's cute in real life but looks weird when I try to draw it.

I try to convince myself Lucy's nose was the problem and that I should try again with a different subject. But deep down I'm afraid that I really just can't do a decent portrait.

I hear Dad moving around out in the hallway and call out to him—it's getting late and I'm hungry and sometimes if I catch him at the right time, we can order in some dinner together.

Footsteps come closer in response to my shout, but the figure in the doorway isn't Dad.

"Molly?" I say, and jump up. "Molly!"

We hug each other tightly.

"What are you doing here?" I ask, stepping back, and then, before she can even answer that, "Wait—what's wrong?"

Now that I get a good look at her face, I can tell she's feeling miserable. And it occurs to me at that moment that she shouldn't be home now. She should be at school.

"Nothing," she says. Then she bursts into tears. "Everything." She shakes her head, struggles to regain her calm. "Nothing."

"Oh, for god's sake," I say, and for the first time in our entire sibling relationship, I feel like the older sister. I take her by the arm and lead her over to the sofa. "Just tell me what happened. Start with why you're home."

"It's no big deal, really," she says, her voice still unsteady as we settle side by side. "I was halfway home, so I figured I'd come the rest of the way and see you."

"Why were you halfway home?"

That's when the story comes out. Her girlfriend, Wally, lives in San Luis Obispo, and she and Molly decided to drive down together from Stanford for the weekend, so Molly could meet Wally's family and they could have some home-cooked meals and escape from the pressure of school for a couple of days.

"So I said to her before we left, your family's cool with me coming, right? And Wally said they'd be fine with it. It wasn't until we were almost there that she admitted to me they have kind of a 'don't ask, don't tell' policy—she's never come out formally to her parents, but she said they know—they just like to be able to ignore it. So fine, right? I mean, I was sort of like that with you guys—"

"Except none of us knew or even guessed," I point out.

"It's not my fault you're oblivious. But at least when you guys found out, you were fine with it. And I wasn't scared about telling you. I just had to get over my feeling that it was kind of private." Molly pauses, plucking at the fabric on the sofa arm. She's cut her hair since I last saw her. It's chin-length now, with choppy, uneven ends. It suits her long, narrow face. She's wearing a Stanford tee and running shorts and flip-flops. She manages a humorless smile. "The fact that Dad and Mom don't care about our personal lives—it's not all bad, you know?" I nod, because I do know what she means. They may not be involved parents, but they're not interfering parents either. "And at least they're always polite in front of other people."

"I'm guessing Wally's family wasn't so mellow?"

"It was awful, Anna." She lets her head fall back on the sofa cushions and stares at the ceiling. "Not at first. At first they were really nice. They have this little house in an area that's zoned for horses. Her mother and sister are these crazy horse people. It's really beautiful there, and we walked around a lot yesterday, and the meals were great, and her little sister—she's around twelve—is cute and sweet and wanted to hang with us. So it was all good. And then last night, after everyone had gone to bed, Wally said we should use the hot tub, so we went in, and one thing led to another—" She stops and looks at me uncertainly.

"You made out in the hot tub," I say. "I get it."

"We weren't out of control or anything—just enjoying each other's company. Totally PG." A reluctant smile breaks through her misery. "Well, maybe PG-13. Anyway, then we go to bed—her mother had put an extra mattress in Wally's room, but we were really sharing her bed. Which I kind of thought they knew. Anyway . . ." She hugs a pillow to her chest. "Turns out her sister had been spying on us in the hot tub. She told their parents everything she saw, and by the time we got up this morning, everything had changed. They couldn't look at us, wouldn't talk to me . . . Wally started freaking out—I mean, seriously freaking out. I'd never seen her like that. I was like, 'I thought you said they were okay with it,' but she was like, 'You don't understand.' And she was mad at *me*—I mean, she didn't say it out loud, but I could tell. Like it was all my fault—if I hadn't come to her house, if I hadn't gotten in the hot tub with her, then everything would still be okay, and she could still pretend to be whatever her parents wanted to pretend she was." Molly tugs hard on the pillow fringe. "So then her parents finally call her into their room to talk to her. When she comes out, she's sobbing, and she tells me I have to go. No one says a word to me, and when Wally's little sister comes into the hallway when I'm there, her mother grabs her and pulls her away like I'm going to *contaminate* her or something—like I'm going to leak lesbian all over her. So I just pack up my stuff and get in my car. But instead of driving back to school, I drove here." She touches my arm. "I wanted to see you, Anna. I needed to see someone who'd be on my side."

I throw my arms around her. "I hate them," I say. "They're idiots. They're jerks. They're assholes."

"They're not that different from tons of people. I might as well get used to it. I've been living in this bubble at school—pretty much everyone at Stanford's open-minded. But that's just not true everywhere."

"What about Wally? Have you guys talked since you left?"

Molly shook her head. "She texted me. Said she's sorry, but there was nothing she could do and she'll see me back at school. I didn't answer. I'm pissed at her. Really pissed. Like done-with-her pissed. If she couldn't stick up for me when it mattered, then she's not some-one I want to be with."

"I hate her family."

"They were so nice to me at first. That's the most upsetting part. When they thought I was just her friend, they liked everything about me . . . and then wham! I kiss her on the lips in front of the kid, and suddenly I'm the devil."

"Idiots."

"Yeah." She tosses the pillow across the room. "Screw them. Screw her."

Footsteps approach, and my father leans into the room. "I heard voices. Molly? Is that you! What a nice surprise!"

She gets up so they can hug.

"What brings you home?" he asks.

She hesitates, then says casually, "I was visiting a friend who lives just a couple of hours away and thought I'd come home for the night."

"Are you hungry? Can I take you girls out for a nice dinner?"

"I wouldn't mind Katsuya," she says.

"Sounds good to me. Just give me half an hour to wrap up some work and we'll go. Can one of you make the reservation? Thanks." He leaves.

I tilt my head at Molly. "Katsuya? How very Lizzie of you."

"Our sister may be superficial and shallow," Molly says, "but she has excellent taste in restaurants."

"Meh," I say. "Aren't you going to tell Dad what happened?"

She shakes her head. "No. I thought about it in the car. If I tell him and he gets angry, he'll want to ream them out and that would just be embarrassing. And if I tell him and he doesn't get angry, I'll feel hurt. Either way, it does more harm than it helps, you know?" I nod, and she adds, "It helped just talking to you. That's all I needed."

She goes upstairs to change, and I go into the kitchen to make the reservation. That's when Dad comes out of his office and says with studied offhandedness, "Hey, I just had an idea."

"He wants to invite Ginny Clay to come to dinner with us," I tell Molly, who's upstairs in her room, changing into jeans.

"Who's that?"

"Lizzie's friend. The assistant volleyball coach? Remember? She came to Lizzie's graduation party. She's tall and blond. Very blond. Ridiculously blond."

"Oh, her." Molly makes a face, which proves to me that she does indeed remember Ginny accurately. "That's weird—why does Dad want to invite Lizzie's friend to come to dinner with us?"

"Honestly? I think they're interested in each other. Like in a going-out kind of way."

She looks horrified. "Are you serious? Isn't she basically my age?"

"Basically. A year older, I think."

She makes a retching sound. Then she covers her mouth with her hand like she's shutting herself up. She drops her hand and says, "I shouldn't be like this. I mean, if I expect other people to be open-minded about *me*, I need to be open-minded about other people. Two consenting adults and all that."

"Don't judge yourself too harshly just yet. Let's talk again after you've spent an evening with her."

"Ginny Clay is a ridiculous human being," Molly tells me, after she's spent an evening with her. We didn't go to Katsuya, because Ginny doesn't eat fish. We go to some high-end vegetarian restaurant Ginny likes, where one section of the menu is devoted entirely to "raw foods" and another to "vegan foods." I'm amazed my father agreed to go there. He said to Ginny at the beginning of the meal, "I'm giving you this one chance to convince me this kind of food can be appealing," and at the end of the meal, he said, "I am not convinced."

"Next week, a steak house!" Ginny said gamely, and he smiled at her with genuine delight, although that may have just been at the prospect of eating steak. No matter what, it sounds like they're planning to see each other again. I just hope they don't drag me along. I'm beginning to feel like some kind of weird beard.

"I just don't get it," Molly says now. We're in her room, sitting on her bed. She's curled up against the headboard, hugging her knees to her chest; I'm sideways, my back against the wall, my legs extended out in front of me, my feet hanging off the side of the bed. "Why her? She's not particularly bright or interesting or sophisticated. . . ."

"She's pretty," I say. "Dad likes pretty things. And

it's not like he's ever had good taste in women."

"Mom, for example."

"For example."

Molly releases her knees and stretches, yawning. "Anna, I'm sorry, but I have to kick you out. I've got to get up brutally early tomorrow if I'm going to make my one o'clock class. I'll probably be gone before you even get up."

"Okay." I scooch off the bed and onto my feet. "I'm glad you came home, Molly. I mean, I'm sorry it was for the reason it was, but it's good to see you."

"Yeah, ditto." She reaches out her hand and squeezes mine. "Thanks for being here when I needed you."

"I'm very good at being home," I say. "It's my finest quality."

"Be careful," she says, "or you may make us lose our Most Dysfunctional Family award."

"Nah," I say. "We've still got that one covered."

eleven

"Four days and counting until we leave for the music festival," Hilary announces at lunch on Monday. "Is everyone excited?"

"Ms. Malik just told us we're having a quiz in AP bio next Tuesday," Lucy says. "I'd say I'm more conflicted than excited. And more nervous than conflicted."

"Thank you, Ms. Buzzkill," says Hilary. "So sorry this once-in-a-lifetime opportunity to see some of the best bands in the country perform may cut into your study time for a test you're going to ace, anyway."

"I believe she's being sarcastic," I say to Lucy.

"How shocking," Lucy says. "I've never been exposed to sarcasm before."

"I believe *she's* being sarcastic," Finn says to Lily.

"I'm pissed," Lily says, ending the joke.

"And why are you pissed?" asks Finn.

"Well, first of all, someone put raisins into the

chocolate chip cookies." She waves the offending cookie in the air.

"That's because it's an oatmeal raisin cookie," Finn says.

"What?" She flings it across the table onto Hilary's tray. "Poseur! Why do people even make these things when no one likes them?"

"Just because *you* don't doesn't mean other people don't," Hilary says. "Not everyone has the exact same opinions as you. Thank god."

"Well, they should. Because I'm always right."

"You'd hate it if everyone thought like you. Then you couldn't go around saying, 'Look at me, I'm so special and unique and different!'"

"A, I don't talk like that," Lily says. "And two, 'special and unique' feels repetitive."

"So what else are you pissed about this lovely school day?" Finn asks her.

"I'm pissed at how boring my life is."

"She suffers," I say. "Lord, how she suffers."

She glares at me. "I don't mind that I have a perfect life—"

"She's a stoic," Lucy says.

"—not usually. But our stupid college-essay tutor told us to come up with five different ideas. He said we should draw on pivotal moments in our lives—something that's changed us." She turns to Finn. "And do you know how many pivotal moments my life has had? None. Nothing important has ever happened to me. Nothing ever will."

"You're a twin," Lucy says. "That could be a cool topic."

Lily rolls her eyes. "Look at Hilary. Just look at her. Could anything be more boring to write about than *her*?"

"Screw you," her sister says.

"What are *you* writing about?" I ask Hilary.

"I was alone with my grandmother when she died," she says. "My mother's mother. We were at the hospital, but my mom had taken Lily to use the bathroom and I was just sitting there by myself, and she was taking all these long, slow breaths, but then she just *stopped* and some alarm went off, and the nurse came in and said she had died."

Lucy rubs Hilary's arm. "I'm so sorry. That sounds scary and sad."

"It was *weird*," Hilary says. "I barely knew her. We never visited—she and my dad didn't get along, and Mom said she was kind of evil. But we went because she was dying and then—"

"And then she died," Lily says. "And cute little eight-year-old Hilary instantly thought, Now I know what I'm writing my college essay about. Good thing Lily has a small bladder or she might have stolen it from me."

"Right," Hilary says. "That's exactly what I thought as I gazed at Grandma's lifeless body. You're a mind reader." She looks around the table. "What's everyone else doing for their essays?"

Oscar says, "I'm playing the gay card—talking about the summer I came out to my family."

No one says anything right away, and I bet the others are thinking what I am: that colleges must receive a million essays from gay kids about how they came out or didn't come out or how hard it's been or how accepting people have been and so on. Oscar must know that it doesn't sound like the most original idea in the world, because he quickly adds, "It's a funny essay, not a serious one. When I came out to my grandmother, she started telling me that she had always suspected that her sister liked other girls, but 'in those days no one knew what that meant.' So I told her I was pretty sure that even back in those days people understood homosexuality, they just didn't talk about it. And she said, 'Well, all I know is that if I'd had a choice between a husband and a wife, I'd have taken the wife. We do all the hard work.' And then she told me to take that into consideration before I committed myself to a man."

"I love that," I say sincerely, and everyone else agrees it sounds great.

"What's yours?" Oscar asks me.

Since I'm applying mostly to art schools, my essay

(which is a work in progress) is about how I started drawing. After my mother left us, the school told my father I should see a therapist. The therapist told me to draw a picture every week; she would use it to start a discussion. I discovered I liked the drawing part more than the talking part, and it became my favorite thing to do—especially when I realized I could draw horses.

Everyone's quiet when I finish talking. Finn breaks the silence. He says slowly, "I wonder if that has something to do with the kind of art you make. The way there's always something hidden—"

I cut him off, excited. "It's so weird that you said that! One of the first things I drew was our house. I made it really big, and the sun was shining and there was grass in front—the whole classic kid thing. And the therapist looked at it and told me it was beautiful. And she put it down. And then like ten minutes later, we were talking and her eyes fell on it again and she suddenly gasped and said, 'What is that in the window? I didn't notice it before.' I had drawn this weird distorted face staring out. . . . I still have the picture, and it is genuinely creepy. I'm lucky she didn't have me committed."

"What was it supposed to be?" Finn asks.

"My mom," I said sheepishly. "The therapist seemed kind of disturbed by that."

"Because it's *disturbing*," Hilary says.

"You don't know my mother." I shake my head. "No,

I'm sorry, that was mean. She's not evil. I just drew her that way."

"How'd you start doing the landscapes?" Finn asks. "I saw more of your stuff online—on deviantART—and it's cool how you paint all these different kinds of worlds."

He had looked up my artwork. I try not to let my pleasure show and say, "Yeah, I kind of got into that after ninth grade." I look down at my half-eaten sandwich (too much mayonnaise, not enough lettuce—bleh). I say, "There was this guy I knew who was always showing me cool photos of other planets and faraway places. I guess I kind of absorbed more of that than I realized."

"This guy?" Finn repeats. He catches my eye, and I smile.

"Who?" asks Lily, who's been poking at a piece of tomato with a chopstick. "What guy? Someone at school?"

"Him," I say, and point at Finn.

"Him?" She registers that with a tiny, little frown of uncertainty. Her forehead clears. "Oh, right—you guys knew each other! I always forget that. You feel like a new kid, Finn."

"I'm new and old."

"You and your photos," Lily says, and bounces her elbow against his. "The first time you told me you wanted to 'show me something,' I was sure it was going to be pornographic. You sounded so excited. . . . And then it was just this weird fish."

"A batfish," Finn says. "Wasn't it awesome?"

"All I know is it was the opposite of porn."

"Were you relieved or disappointed?" Oscar asks her.

"A little bit of both."

"I save the porn for special occasions," Finn says in that slow—and, yes, if I'm being honest, *sexy*—drawl he's acquired since ninth grade.

"My birthday's coming up . . ." Lily murmurs.

"No, it's not," Hilary says.

Lily sighs. "You are the most literal person in the world."

"The word you're looking for is *honest*. Get to know it."

"Why?" Lily says. "It has no relevance to my life."

"That's for sure."

"Doesn't anyone want to hear about *my* essay?" Lucy asks plaintively. "I've written three and don't know which one to use—you guys need to help me decide. Or maybe I should just scrap them all and come up with something new." We all turn our attention to her—just as the bell rings. "Oh, come on!" she says.

"Don't worry about it." I pick up my book bag and rise to my feet, along with everyone else. "We'll have lots of time to discuss your essays this weekend, on the bus ride to the desert."

"It doesn't matter," she says sadly. "They all suck."

"Hilary," I say. "Tell Lucy her essays don't suck. I've got to get to history."

"Your essays don't suck," Hilary tells her. And then we all go to class.

"Bad news?"

I look up from my phone. It's an hour later, and we're between classes. I'm standing at the bottom of a stairwell, using the space behind the doorway to hide the fact I'm looking at my phone from any teachers who might be in the hallway. Finn must have spotted me when he was coming down the stairs. I have no idea how long he's been watching me from the bottom step—long enough to figure out that I'm frowning down at a text.

"Not bad exactly," I say. "Just a little sad. A text from my sister—the good one. The one you don't know."

He comes down the last step, so we're at the same level. "Molly?"

Of course he remembers her name. He remembers everything. "Yeah, that one. She had this weird thing happen when she was visiting a friend—" I raise my chin. "Not just a friend, her girlfriend—and the parents freaked out because they kissed and kicked her out."

Here's the thing about Finn: he's the kind of guy who, when you throw something at him like, *My sister's girlfriend's parents threw her out of their house for being a lesbian*, doesn't react instantly, doesn't just say the obvious things. Instead he waits, absorbing the information, watching me with his dark brown eyes, his fingers twitching along the strap of his messenger bag. "When did this happen?" he asks.

"Last weekend," I say. "Now she and her girlfriend are back at college together, and her girlfriend just assumed everything would go back to normal. But Molly's too angry for that, so they had a huge fight."

"Does Molly really like her?"

"Totally in love. Or at least she *was*. But Wally didn't defend her."

"Families are always the hardest thing to deal with. Maybe she just needs more time to figure out how to manage hers."

I stick my phone in my pocket. "How do you 'manage' bigotry? I hate people like that. I don't want them to exist."

"Imagine how hard it would be to have parents like that."

"It would be awful."

"Which is an argument for cutting the girl some slack."

"Maybe." The bell rings for the start of the next

class—we're late. I move toward the doorway, and Finn follows me, reaching past me to hold the door open as I pass through. I nod my thanks. "But she just stood there and let them be mean to Molly. How can you trust someone who doesn't stick by you when it matters?"

"Yeah?" he says softly. "How?"

And it's right then, as I'm walking through the door he's holding and out of the dank little stairwell that smells like toes and pizza, that I realize I took the wrong side of this argument and pinned myself, wriggling like a beetle, to the wall. I open my mouth and have nothing to say, and we look at each other and I realize he's been aware during this entire conversation that I've been incriminating myself up and down and sideways. I feel my cheeks turn red and I tell him I'm late for class and I run away.

Later, when my shame has dimmed to a mild burn instead of a raging inferno and Ms. Malik is droning on at the front of the class about species differentiation, something else occurs to me, something that makes me sit up straight in my seat, eyes wide open like I'm actually paying attention to what Malik is saying (which, of course, I'm not).

And that's that Finn—who was clearly seeing a parallel between Molly's situation and what happened between us back in ninth grade—picked the wrong side of the argument.

And by "wrong," I mean he picked *my* side—the side arguing for forgiveness.

Okay, that's interesting.

I don't hear a word Malik says for the rest of the class. I'm too busy thinking about this, wondering why Finn would choose to argue that side when everything that's happened between us this year has convinced me he believes the opposite.

Maybe he's changed his mind?

twelve

The twins' dad has arranged for the van to the music festival to pick us all up at our houses on Friday afternoon. We have just enough time after school to run home and grab our stuff.

At Lucy's house her entire family—mother, father, and little brother—come outside with her and even stick their heads into the van to say hi to the rest of us. They help her stow her bag, and her father reminds her to work on her college applications and to study for her bio quiz, and then her mother whispers something in her ear that makes Lucy roll her eyes at us and say impatiently, "I *know*, Mom. You can trust me." Then her brother tells her she's incredibly friggin' lucky to get to go to a music festival and says, "Mom and Dad better let me go to music festivals when *I'm* in high school." "Twelfth grade," says Lucy's mother, who has a warm smile and is very pretty. Lucy's father, who looks like a tall, graying, short-haired version of Lucy, cuffs his son on the shoulder and they all finally leave the van.

To put this all in perspective . . . when the van picked me up twenty minutes earlier, I was taping a note for my father—*Gone to the music festival with my friends. Be back late Sunday. A*—onto the monitor of his desktop computer: I figured it was the one place where I could be sure he'd see it. That was it for my good-byes.

Oscar's the last pickup. Once he's carefully arranged his bag in the back and buckled himself into the empty space next to me, the van driver appears in the open sliding door and asks for our attention. He's a skinny oldish-to-old guy. "Okay, kids," he says warily, "we're all on the same side here. You want a quick, pleasant, easy ride to the desert, and so do I. I am well aware that every one of you is under the age of twenty-one. Do you know what that means?" We can guess, but we just stare at him silently. He seems happy to answer it himself. "That means absolutely no drinking in my van. There's no smoking either. You all speak English, I presume? Do you need to hear it in any other languages?"

"*En español, por favor?*" Eric says jokingly.

The guy turns a steely gaze on him. "You really need me to translate? Or are you just being funny?"

Eric waves his hand. "Nah, man, you're good."

The driver rubs his hands briskly and says in a completely different, suddenly cheerful tone, "All righty, then! I'm going to hop up front and start driving. You need to stop for a potty break or anything, you just call my name. I'm Bill. Otherwise I'll leave you alone, and you can pretend I'm not even here. With any luck and not too much traffic, we'll be at your hotel before six. Keep your seatbelts fastened, relax, and have a great time!" He steps back and slams the door shut.

"Bipolar much?" whispers Phoebe, who's in the front row with Eric, but before any of us can reply, Bill reappears at the driver's door and climbs into his seat. And away we go.

I've got my laptop and a DVD of *Mean Girls*—I've seen it a million times, but it just gets better with every viewing, and after Oscar admitted a few days ago that he'd never seen it, I figured this was a chance to educate him and help pass the time. But when I insert it into my laptop, Lucy—who's sitting on my other side—complains that it'll be too distracting for her. She's trying to read through notes for her bio quiz.

"Switch places with Oscar," I suggest.

She does, so now he's sitting in the middle, but after we start the movie, she complains that she can still hear the dialogue.

I get out earbuds, and Oscar and I share them.

Lucy leans over Oscar to complain some more to me. "Why did you have to pick one of my favorite movies? I keep watching it even though I don't want to. Can't you guys just do homework like me?"

"Oh, for god's sake," I say. "Go sit up front with Phoebe and Eric if you're unhappy here."

She grumbles that I'm not being very supportive as she slumps down and leafs through her notebook.

Oscar taps something on his phone and tilts it toward me.

What's up with her?

I take his phone and quickly type in:

Jackson was supposed to come but his coach wouldn't let him.

"Ah," says Oscar.

A burst of laughter behind us makes us turn around in our seats. Finn has his phone out and is showing something to Hilary and Lily that's got them laughing hysterically.

"What's so funny?" Oscar asks.

Finn holds up his phone so we can see the photo. "Lily thought this was a Chihuahua."

"I was joking," Lily says. "But I don't know what the hell it really is."

"An anteater?" suggests Oscar.

"I already guessed that," Hilary says.

Finn shakes his head. "Anna, you want to guess?"

"A capybara," I say.

He raises his eyebrows. "Give the girl a cigar."

"Better not," I say. "Our driver won't like it."

"How about an apple?" Lily says, and tosses one to me. She has a bunch of snacks in a bag at her feet.

"I've heard of capybaras," Oscar says. "They're big rodents. But I didn't know they looked like that. I assumed they looked like giant mice."

"How'd you know?" Finn asks me.

"You've showed me pictures of capybaras before," I say. There's a tiny hole in the fabric at the top of my seat. I stick the tip of my pinkie through it. "You said they were your favorite rodent."

"I thought *I* was your favorite rodent," Lily says to him.

"It's a tie," Finn says. But he's still looking at me. Like a teacher whose failing student just surprised him by getting something right.

I hand Oscar the laptop so he can keep watching the movie. I want to try sketching him while he's distracted; I'm still determined to prove I can do a decent portrait.

He has beautiful, long-lashed eyes and this great, long, straight nose and I get all that down on paper— look, there's the nose, there are the lashes, there's his jawline—but it still doesn't look like Oscar to me. It doesn't look like anything other than lines on a piece of paper.

I feel a tap on my shoulder and turn my head.

"Do me now," Hilary says.

"I'm not a Disney caricaturist," I hiss. "I don't 'do' people."

"Sorry!" She flops back. "Forgive me for liking your drawing."

I twist around to face her. "Sorry, Hil. I didn't mean to snap at you. I'm just frustrated. I'm supposed to add a portrait to my portfolio, but I suck at them."

"I think that's *good*," she says. "It totally looks like Oscar."

"Show us," says Lily.

I shake my head and quickly flip the paper over. "Trust me. It's not good."

"Why don't you try sketching all of us?" Finn suggests, looking up from his phone. "Just quickly, without stressing about it? And then if one of the sketches comes out better than the rest, you can polish and use it. If not, no harm done."

It's not a bad idea.

"That's not a bad idea," I say.

"It's a great idea," says Lily. "Do me first." She strikes a pose, hand on her hip, head tilted back, eyelashes fluttering. She's dyed the tips of her hair pink for this weekend and is wearing a leather vest that ties up the front like a corset. Today must be Punk Day in LilyLand.

"Okay. But don't pose. Just be natural."

"How's this?" She swivels sideways and snuggles into Finn's chest. He pushes her away from him.

"Please don't," he says. "Your hair's in my face, and I need to send this text."

She slumps against the back of her seat and pouts. "Gallantry is dead."

"Gallantry doesn't like a mouthful of hair," he says.

She sits back up, tilts her head so she can grab a hunk of her hair in one hand, and moves back over toward him, then brushes the ends of her hair all over his face, giggling. "How's this? And this? And this?"

"Ugh!" he says, twisting away and putting up his hands to hold her off. "Stop it, Lily. That's gross."

"Welcome to my world," Hilary says, from his other side. "The second you tell her you don't like something, she does it *more*."

Lily shrugs and sits back. "I just thought if you got a better taste of my hair, you'd appreciate how delicious it is."

The look Finn gives her is not a pleasant one.

"How about I sketch you first?" I say to Hilary.

"No! Me first!" Lily says. "You promised."

"No, she didn't," Finn says.

"She gave me a promise with her *eyes*."

No one laughs. I say, "If you want me to sketch you, Lily, you have to sit quietly for five minutes. Are you sure you can do that?"

"Shut up," she says. "Why is everyone being mean to me?"

"Because you do things like shove your hair in people's faces," Finn says.

"Have a sense of humor," she says. She arranges herself in a comfortable sitting position. "Anna, sketch me—I'll stay like this."

I nod and arrange myself sideways, my back pressed against the side of the van, the sketch pad propped up on my knees. My toes press against Oscar, and he looks up from the movie and asks me what I'm doing.

"Preparing for my career as a Disney caricaturist."

"I wonder how that pays," he says, and goes back to the movie.

I spend the rest of the trip sketching everyone around me. They forget I'm doing it and relax back into staring at their phones or talking, which helps.

I'm not happy with any of the drawings. I'm relieved that no one remembers to ask me about them when the van stops. I don't want to show them.

thirteen

A tactical error: the first thing we do at the hotel is troop up to see the suite that Hilary and Lily are going to be sharing with their father, who's already at the festival. Then the rest of us take the elevator back down to our standard rooms.

The hotel is a concrete rectangle built around a courtyard, but the people who work there wear black uniforms and speak in hushed voices, so it feels kind of fancy once you're inside. You'd think we'd be happy just to get to stay there for free, and we *would* have been, but after seeing the twins' enormous suite with its three bedrooms and two bathrooms and two coffeemakers and one dining room table, our normal hotel rooms (two double beds, a chest of drawers, and a single bathroom in each) are a letdown. The girls have room 351; the guys room 353.

"At least we're next door to them," Phoebe says when we walk in.

"I think we actually connect," I say, because there's a door on the side of the room that shares a wall with 353, and I can already hear someone pounding on it. Lucy unlocks it, and Eric comes barreling through.

"We have one big room!" he cries out happily. Phoebe squeals, and they throw their arms around each other like it's been days since they've seen each other and not about ten seconds.

"We're not sharing our bathroom with you guys," Lucy says. "Boys are pigs."

"I'm not," Oscar says, coming in behind Eric.

"Maybe not," she says. "But you're still not using our bathroom. Girls need their own bathrooms, and the sooner you all understand that, the better your lives will be."

"Okay, but what about the sleeping arrangements?" Eric asks hopefully. "We don't have to separate into boys and girls, do we?"

"Yeah, we do," says Phoebe. "I promised my mother we'd be sleeping in separate rooms."

"It's not like she'd know."

"I *promised* her," Phoebe says again.

Eric scowls, and the rest of us laugh.

"I only promised her we'd *sleep* in separate rooms," Phoebe adds, pressing against his side. "I didn't say anything about when we're awake."

His broad face splits into a grin.

"I liked you guys better before you got all lovey-dovey." Oscar sits down on the edge of one of the beds.

"You're just jealous," Phoebe says.

"Yeah." Oscar rolls his eyes. "Eric's totally my type."

"Hey," Eric protests. "That hurts my feelings. Why aren't I?"

"That's not what I meant," Phoebe says. "And you know it."

"No," Lucy says, sitting next to Oscar. "What you meant was that the two of you are in love, and the rest of us are losers."

"What's wrong with me?" Eric asks Oscar.

"First of all, I was talking to Oscar, not you," Phoebe says to Lucy. "And second of all, you know very well I didn't mean anything like that at all."

"I just don't want to spend this entire weekend with you and Eric constantly rubbing our noses in how in love you are," Lucy says.

"My feelings are hurt," Eric tells Oscar, who says, "Let it go, man."

Phoebe's staring at Lucy. "Are you serious?"

"You're already doing it," Lucy says.

"Will you guys excuse us for a moment?" I say. I grab Lucy's arm and drag her up onto her feet and into the bathroom. I close the door and face her. "I love you, but you're kind of acting like a crazy person."

"I was just looking forward to this so much," Lucy says, and slumps down on the edge of the bathtub. "I pictured me and Jackson lying out on the grass together listening to music, and it was going to be so romantic and magical. And now he's not here, and it won't be romantic at all. I'm compromising on my college applications and schoolwork just by being here, and for what? Just to hear some bands with the people I see every day? I don't even care that much about music." She plucks at the terrycloth bath mat lying on the edge of the tub next to her. "I wish I hadn't come."

"Well, you're here now, so what's the point of sulking? Let's go have fun tonight. If you hate everything about it, I bet your dad would come pick you up tomorrow."

"Yeah, probably."

"So what's the big deal? Either you'll have a great time and want to stay, or you'll go home tomorrow. The most you'll lose is a couple of hours, and who works on Friday night, anyway?" I put my hand on the bathroom knob. "So can you just try to have fun for the next few hours?"

She promises to try, and we leave the bathroom. The guys have disappeared, and the connecting door is closed.

"We're all getting changed," Phoebe explains. She's

standing over her suitcase, pulling stuff out. "I sent the twins a text, and they're going to come down and meet us here. They have wristbands and stuff for us."

We spend the next twenty minutes putting on our festival outfits. Since it's already dark out, our goal is to dress warmly and still look good. I put on a pair of satin pants—they're cut like jeans, but they're black and shiny and tight—and a fuzzy green sweater that has some swing to it. Phoebe pairs patterned jeans with a silk top and a mannish jacket that she wears with the sleeves partially rolled up. Lucy says she doesn't see the point of getting all dressed up and throws a cardigan on over her jeans and T-shirt. Despite her lack of enthusiasm, she still ends up looking neat and pretty—I don't think she's capable of looking sloppy.

Hilary and Lily show up while we're putting on makeup and fooling around with our hair. Lily is still wearing the leather corset, but she's changed from jeans into a short, flippy skirt and cowboy boots. Hilary's wearing a long, narrow gray sweater over a pair of leggings and low-heeled, soft leather boots that come up over her knees.

"Oh my god," Phoebe moans when she sees her. "Those boots. I would kill someone for those boots. Several people."

"I don't know about people, but she killed at least two cows for them," I say.

"I did not," Hilary says.

"Well, someone did."

"And it was well worth it!" Phoebe says.

"Not to the cows," I say.

"Did anyone bring condoms?" Lily asks.

There's a moment of silence.

"Well, there's a conversation stopper," Lucy says.

"You planning on needing them?" Hilary asks Lily.

"I just think we should all know where some are," Lily says. "Semper fidelis, right?"

"Always faithful?" Lucy says. "That doesn't make any sense."

"Be prepared."

"That's the Boy Scouts motto. Semper fidelis is the marines."

"Huh," Lily says. "You sure about that?"

"Pretty sure."

Phoebe taps Lily on the arm. "Come with me," she says coyly, and they disappear into the bathroom together.

"When you think about it," I say, "'always faithful' and 'be prepared' imply very different things when you're talking about contraception."

"That's very deep," Hilary says. "Maybe you should write about that for your college essay." She gives a glum nod toward the bathroom door. "So I guess this means she expects to have sex with Finn this weekend."

Hearing her say it so bluntly makes me breathe in sharply with sudden discomfort. I turn the sound into a cough. And croak out, "You really think they're there?"

"This will be the turning point," she says. "We'll be outside, in the dark, listening to music, people making out all over the place . . . A lot will be happening tonight."

"Just not to us," Lucy says, and Hilary and I both give equally miserable nods.

Phoebe and Lily come out of the bathroom smiling. The rest of us leave the room without saying another word.

Fourteen

The twins' father has sent a limo. Inside there are brackets set into the car walls that Oscar says would normally hold liquor bottles, but not when there are underage kids being picked up.

It's funny—it's never really sunk in before how much richer Hil and Lily are than the rest of us. My dad's a lawyer, and Lucy's parents are both psychiatrists, and I don't know what everyone else's parents do—oh, right, Finn's are scientists—but basically we're all *fine* (more than fine—lucky and privileged), but the Diamonds are on a whole different level. I already knew they had a huge house and, you know, *staff*, but today the limo and the van and the hotel rooms all make it clear they're rich beyond anything I realized before. I honestly don't think I'd feel jealous about that, except that right now Lily is snuggling next to Finn in the limo, and the thought occurs to me that she has *everything*. And that seems unfair.

Rows of small lights—colored dashes—outline the limo's windows and doorways, blinking and changing colors, pink to blue to violet to green. They're mesmerizing, and I'm gazing at them in a dazed trance for a while before I realize everyone else is watching me.

"They're *pretty*," I say defensively, and everyone laughs.

Hilary pulls out a schedule for the festival and starts to plan our evening.

"There are three stages," she begins. "North, South, and Galaxy."

"That's all?" says Oscar. "There are like seven stages at Coachella."

"I'm so sorry this isn't as big as Coachella," Hilary says icily. "Would you like the limo to drop you off right now, so you don't have to suffer any longer?"

"Whoa!" he says. "I've been stabbed by the sarcasm sword."

She scowls at him. "I just don't want to hear the word *Coachella* again this weekend, okay? This is its own thing and it's its first year and it has to build and sometimes things are better when they're smaller and everyone says Coachella isn't what it used to be, anyway, and this will probably be bigger and better than Coachella one day."

"You just said *Coachella* like three times," Lucy points out to her.

"You also aren't making sense," Lily adds. "I mean, you said it's better when festivals are smaller, but you also said this will be bigger than Coachella."

"You know, he's your father too," Hilary says hotly. "You act like this festival doesn't mean anything to you."

"Are you kidding?" Lily says. "I'm thrilled to be here. I'm beside myself with joy."

"She's so happy, her hair turned pink," Finn adds.

"It's Kool-Aid!" she tells him happily.

"Excellent," he says, playing with the strands. He seems to have gotten over his earlier annoyance about having that hair in his face. "If we start dying of thirst, we can dip your hair in water and drink it."

"If you have water to put the Kool-Aid in, why couldn't you just drink that?" Eric asks.

"Hold on," Hilary says, looking up. "How did you get it so bright if it's only Kool-Aid? That doesn't work on dark hair."

"I bleached the ends," Lily says.

"You told Mom it was temporary!"

"The color's temporary. Just not the bleaching."

"She's going to be pissed."

"When *isn't* Mom pissed?"

"Good point," says Hilary. "Now can we please focus on tonight?" She goes on to list the three bands that will be playing right around the time we get there, and we all agree that we want to see the one playing the North Stage. They have a hit single on the radio right now.

"Okay, then there's no one good for like an hour or so," Hilary says, peering at the schedule. "That's when we should get something to eat. Dad said the food at the stands is pretty bad, and we should come join him in the VIP section—he has a chef cooking just for him and his friends. After that we should see Consternation at the South Stage and then—"

"You know," Lily says, "we don't have to have every single minute of this weekend planned out in advance. We could try to be a tiny bit *spontaneous*. Or does that make you feel all funny inside?"

Hilary throws the schedule at her, but it falls short. Lucy picks it up and hands it to Hilary, who throws it at Lily again, but Finn blocks it with his forearm. Protecting her.

"Look," he says quickly, before anything else can get thrown. He points toward the window. "We're here."

We all press our faces to the glass as the limo drives us past the security lines at the entrance. They're pretty long, and I ask Hilary if the festival's sold out and she says not quite but close. "Next year it will be impossible to get a ticket," she says. "You'll see."

The limo circles around the edge of the festival grounds to the back, where it drives through a private

VIP entrance. A couple of security guards stop us, check the driver's ID, glance into the back to check our wristbands, then wave us through. The driver lets us out soon after that. The girls and boys have to separate into different lines, because we still have to go through a metal detector and have our bags checked and get frisked. The girls' line is staffed by female security guards, and the guys get males. It's much less crowded here than it was at the general entrance, and the guards are polite and unrushed.

One of them pulls a water bottle out of Phoebe's hippie-style bag. "If I take a sip of your water," the middle-aged guard asks jovially, "will I get a surprise?" Phoebe manages a feeble shake of her head but without a lot of conviction.

"Your call," says the guard, dangling the bottle from her fingertips. "I can take a sniff or just toss it." Phoebe's mouth opens and closes silently. "Let's toss it, shall we?" the guard says, and drops it in a wastebasket before waving Phoebe on.

"What was it?" I whisper to her, once we've gotten through the line.

"Twenty bucks' worth of vodka," she moans.

"You're lucky you didn't get thrown out."

Oscar retrieves his backpack from the table and joins us where we're waiting to regroup. "That was the most sex I've had in months," he says, nodding toward the businesslike guard who frisked him and who is now quickly and efficiently patting down Eric.

"You really need to get out more," I say. "And also? Me too."

Once everyone's safely through, we explore the VIP area for a little while. It's completely dark out now, but the space is well-lit. There are tents and tables scattered all over a wide grass field, with a line of food stands and open bars at one end. Hilary forbids us to buy any food, because she says we'll be eating soon enough, anyway, and that food will be free and much better. Lily tries to score a drink at one of the bars, but the hot, tattooed bartender shakes his head at her wristband and shrugs regretfully.

"The red bands mean we're underage," Lily says when she rejoins us. "And he says they'll be fired if any-one sees them slipping us booze. I'll just have to find someone with a blue band to buy me a drink."

"Please don't get us all in trouble," Hilary says.

Lily opens her eyes wide. "I would never . . . !"

"Lily *is* trouble," Finn says with a grin.

She winds her arm through his and pulls him close. "You are going to know the true meaning of that state-ment before this weekend is through, I promise you."

"I can't wait," he says.

That's funny. I can.

* * *

We emerge through another set of security gates onto the actual festival field, which is wide and uneven. Two stages mark the north and south ends of the field, with the larger Galaxy Stage about equidistant between them, on the eastern side. They're all outdoor stages with no tenting. I'm glad it isn't supposed to rain this weekend.

We head toward the North Stage, snaking our way through groups of other people, most of them around our age. When we reach the stage, we decide to sit on the grass way in the back—it's crowded up front, but the speakers are loud, and we can hear just fine from far away, and we're all in the mood to relax.

I lean against Oscar and close my eyes and let the music throb through me for a while. When I open my eyes again, the first thing I see is Lily up on her feet, dancing, swaying her bare arms up in the air in time to the music. A guy walking by—shirtless with sagging pants that reveal skinny hips—calls out, "Go, leather dancing girl!" and she gives him a thumbs-up and flashes a grin at all of us.

Phoebe and Eric curl up together and start kissing. They're not alone. A lot of the people who have chosen to sit this far from the stage are couples who are making out.

"I feel left out," says Lucy, who has crawled over to sit with me and Oscar. "Where's *my* hookup buddy?"

"I'm willing to service you both in any way that will help," Oscar says gallantly.

"Even though we don't have penises?" I say.

"I'll make do. I'm a good friend."

There's no encore—"That's because they need to stick to the schedule," Hilary informs us—so we all get up and make our way across the field, back to the VIP area, so we can eat with the twins' father.

Dinner's incredible. It's in a tent that's been decorated inside and out with slender branches of sparkling lights. Over the entrance the lights spell out Star Bar.

"This is the place," Hilary says, and leads us inside.

I've seen the twins' father before, at school functions and stuff like that, but all I've retained from those brief encounters was the impression of a baseball cap, a fit physique, jeans, and a T-shirt. Oh, and black glasses.

My memory's accurate. When we walk into the tent, which is lit unevenly by standing lamps in each corner that create strange shadows on all the faces, the figure that detaches itself to greet us is slim and wearing jeans, a T-shirt, a baseball cap, and glasses.

"There you are!" says Mr. Diamond. He gives his girls quick kisses on the cheeks. "What the hell are you wearing?" he asks Lily.

"Leather corset," she says calmly.

He shrugs. "Cool." He turns to the rest of us. "You

209

guys know me, right? Hil and Lil's dad. Hope you're having a great time." The light falls more directly on his face, and for a brief moment, you can see that the guy is solidly in his fifties; there are lines around his eyes that the glasses can't hide and gray glints in his face stubble. Then he shifts, and his face falls in shadow and he could be our age.

We all tell him how happy we are to be there and thank him for his generosity. He waves his hand dismissively. "All I ask is that you talk it up afterward. Tell your friends it was the best weekend of your lives and that they should buy tickets for next year as soon as they go on sale. Will you do that for me?" We all say that we will, and he says, "Help yourself to the food, guys. There's soda too." He turns back to his daughters. "I'll see you two in the suite tonight. I want you back no later than one. Which means in the limo by twelve forty-five. Understood?"

"Yes, Daddy," says Lily with an angelic blink of her beautiful dark eyes. He turns back to his adult guests.

The buffet is laid out on a long table that runs half the length of the tent. It is, according to a sign, both vegan and organic, but despite that, it's pretty good. I especially like the kale chips they've put out in bowls around the room. They're crunchy and salty, and I keep eating them. "These demand alcohol," says Lily, who's dipping into the bowl as much as I am.

"Why isn't your mother here?" I ask. I've seen their mother only once or twice, but I remember her as being incredibly hip, with a youthful body and a shaggy rocker haircut. She was born in Korea, and her father's a dentist, but she gives off a vibe that's pure Hollywood.

Lily shrugs. "She never goes to Dad's work parties. That's why Hil and I get to go to all the awards shows. Basically Mom and Dad don't do anything together unless they can't help it. I think they kind of hate each other."

"But they're still married," I point out. "So they can't hate each other as much as my parents do."

"You are so competitive," she says, and we laugh.

ꜰɪꜰᴛᴇᴇɴ

After dinner we decide to split up. Phoebe, Eric, Oscar, and Hilary want to see the band that's about to play on the Galaxy Stage, but the rest of us want to check out the two smaller bands on the other stages—one's from Ireland and has a loud, raucous rock thing going on, and the other's got a country vibe and a fiddler.

We all agree to meet up at the North Stage in an hour, so our group decides to start at the South Stage and then head up to catch the second half of the other band's act.

On our way Lily threads her arm through Finn's. "Let's push all the way to the front this time," she says to him. "I want to be close enough to smell them."

As they move ahead of us, Lucy grabs my sleeve. "Hey, look—isn't that Jackson's friend? The one who's your cousin?" She points, and I see Wade Porter standing in line for a water fountain next to another guy. He glances around just as I look over there, and I wave. He squints at me in the dark then waves back with sudden recognition. He nudges his friend and leads him toward us.

Lucy and I stop to wait for them. Finn and Lily don't notice and keep walking. We call after them, but it's too noisy and they don't seem to hear us. Doesn't matter—we've got our phones. We'll figure it out.

Wade gives me a hug and says hi to Lucy, whose name he remembers, and then introduces his friend. Connor has bright red hair and the pale skin and freckles that seem to go with that.

"I can't believe you're here!" Wade says. He decided to come at the last minute, he explains. He and Connor didn't have any plans for this weekend—except the usual college application and school stuff—and heard an ad on the radio just that afternoon saying that you could get discounted festival tickets through some ticket site. So they did. They arrived only about half an hour ago.

"We're headed over to the South Stage now," he adds. "I was just waiting to refill my water bottle."

"We're going there too," I say.

"Fantastic—wait for me." He turns away but then turns back with a grin. "This festival just got much better." He heads over to the fountain.

Connor rocks awkwardly on his heels, then tucks his hands under his armpits and nods at both of us. "So," he says. And then. Nothing.

Lucy takes pity on him. "You having fun?"

He glances around warily. "About to." He untucks his hands, reaches into his pocket, and pulls out a joint. "We were going to find some place quiet to smoke this before the next show. Want to join us?"

I'm neutral. Weed isn't my thing, but I'm happy to pass one around in a group and have a hit or two. I look at Lucy, trying to gauge her level of interest. She looks equally uncertain, and then Lily suddenly appears at my elbow—she and Finn must have done a U-turn when they noticed we were missing, and now she's back and instantly zoning in on the object in Connor's hand.

"Is that what I think it is?" she asks.

He closes his fingers quickly. "No."

"She's our friend," Lucy tells him.

"Oh, then yes," he says, opening his fist back up.

Wade returns, screwing on his water bottle cap. He shoves the bottle into his backpack. "Better hide that," he says to Connor. "There's a security guard about ten feet away. But I think I know where we can smoke it." He hesitates and looks at me. "I mean, if you guys want to."

Lily says, "Lead the way. I've been hoping someone would come up with some weed."

I glance at Finn. Back in ninth grade, he used to maintain that anyone who used drugs was an idiot. "Brain chemistry is so fragile," he once said to me. "Why would you ever screw with it?" But I guess he's become more open-minded, because he just stands there, apparently willing to go along with whatever Lily wants. Maybe that's love?

Lucy is now quizzing Connor about his source. He says, "I wouldn't trust anything I picked up here—I bought this from my regular guy back home. He's captain of the tennis team."

"All right, then I'm in," says Lucy. I raise my eyebrows at her, a little surprised. She shrugs. "We're here to have fun, right?"

"I guess. I just thought you'd—"

Lily interrupts me impatiently: "Come *on*."

Wade tells us all to follow him and takes my arm. I fall into step next to him.

I check him out as we're walking. He's wearing jeans and a blue V-neck sweater over a T-shirt. He catches me checking him out and grins at me. Confident I'll like what I see. And I do. I like what I see. What's not to like?

Lily can't stop giggling.

"Could she be more of a cliché?" Lucy whispers to me. She and I are relatively sober. We each took one hit of the joint, but it was super strong and we waved it away after that. I don't like feeling either paranoid or catatonic, and too-strong weed makes me both. And Lucy never takes more than a puff or two—enough to get a little relaxed without losing any real control.

Finn didn't have any, so I guess he's still into protecting the, uh, *fragility* of his own brain. But the other three have been passing the weed around for a while, and now Lily seems to find Connor's hair the funniest thing in the world.

"It's just . . . the whole redhead thing . . ." She gasps. "It's so weird. And why do they call you gingers? Have you ever seen ginger? It's *tan*. Blond people should be gingers! I don't get it."

It seems to take Connor a while to process what she's saying, to think about it, and to formulate an answer, but finally he manages to get out, "It's because we're so *spicy*," and he and Lily snort with laughter.

We're sitting in a small circle, all the way at the edge of the field, in a dark, unused corner to the west of the South Stage. We're all sitting very close together, creating a tight wall with our bodies so the burning tip won't give us away in the dark. Not that the security guards seem to be cracking down on any kind of smoking. As far as I can tell, from the clouds of fragrant smoke we've been walking through all evening, they're okay with anything that requires inhalation. It's only underage drinking they seem determined to prevent.

Still, we don't want to take any chances.

Lily shifts over toward Finn and rests her cheek against his shoulder. "You'd look good as a redhead," she says, gazing up at him dreamily. "You have a red-headed personality."

"I don't know what that means," he says with a smile.

"This," she says, and rises up a little so she can put her mouth right on his.

Okay, it doesn't make any sense, but as a move, it totally works. Given the fact they end up kissing. Right here, in front of all of us.

In front of me.

Lily's clearly driving this thing, but Finn's hands willingly slip around her, scooping her body against his. She may be stoned, but he isn't. He knows what he's doing. And even though she started it—I mean, she really did; he was keeping some space between them, and then she put herself right in his lap and pressed her mouth against his—he doesn't seem to mind.

And why would he? They've been moving in this direction for days. Weeks. Just because he seemed to pull back a couple of times recently when she was acting especially . . . you know . . . *Lilyish*, that doesn't mean he doesn't still like her. Maybe deep down I was hoping it did, that every time she did something that annoyed him, she pushed him away a little bit. But I guess that was me seeing what I wanted to see. What's that physics thing about momentum? How things are hard to stop once they've started moving in a certain direction? That's them. Moving in a direction. Hard to stop.

Even so, I kept hoping. . . .

I don't know what I kept hoping.

Well, I tell myself with a sort of gallows humor, at least I know that Lily's got a condom in her pocket.

The thought does not console or amuse me the way I might have hoped.

I reach forward and snatch the joint out of Connor's hand. He's so stoned, he barely reacts. I take a long hit and let it burn in my lungs. It might help. It might not.

I hand the joint to Wade, and our fingers touch. He looks at me while he takes a drag and then after he hands the joint back to Connor he moves a little toward me, so our shoulders are touching. I was sitting with my knees up, but now I tilt them in his direction and let them rest against his leg.

He cocks his head at me with a sort of amused, inquisitive expression.

What the hell, I think.

I mean, really—what the hell? I have no one I need to be loyal to, and my head is now spinning nicely in a way that makes nothing seem to matter all that much. Why not have some fun? So I lean in toward him. And we kiss. I start it, but he responds pretty quickly.

Wade turns out to be an excellent kisser, which is a relief. He doesn't smush my lips; he doesn't try to lick the inside of my mouth; he doesn't clank teeth—he doesn't commit any of the cardinal sins of bad kissing. And he doesn't push for anything more than mouth contact, thank god. I'm not in the mood for more.

Speaking of which, even though the lower half of my face is busy, my eyes drift over toward Finn and Lily. They're still kissing. Their bodies are intertwined, but otherwise they're keeping it pretty clean, which is a relief.

I'm not a prude. I just don't think I can bear to be present if these two get any more intimate.

After a few minutes of this, I hear Lucy give a loud, fake, extremely annoyed cough. I dodge Wade's searching mouth long enough to check on her—and just in time to see Connor lean forward toward Lucy with his own lips pursed.

"You have *got* to be kidding me," Lucy snarls as she shrinks back, away from him.

It takes Connor a full three seconds to absorb that, then he sits back with a thud and takes a last hit of the almost-gone joint. He drops it almost immediately and sticks his fingers in his mouth.

He got burned.

sixteen

Thanks to a flurry of texts and some good luck in the form of an extremely visible tall man with a shaved head who's standing next to Oscar, we're able to meet up with the others at the North Stage in time to see the band we wanted to watch together.

The set starts. Up near the front of the stage, the audience is packed so tightly, people can hardly move, but back where we are everyone is either standing and dancing or lying on the grass being mellow. I'm one of those: I recline against Wade, who wraps his arms around me and takes the weight of my head against his chest.

His nice, manly chest, I might add.

Lily's all curled up on Finn's lap—I guess it's her property now—and Phoebe's doing the same thing on Eric's. Those two feel like an old, established couple compared to the rest of us. Lucy's got her head on

Oscar's shoulder; he strokes her hair idly and stares at a guy a few feet away who's wearing tight plaid pants and a leather vest over his naked chest. I wonder where Connor went to, but I can't dig up much concern. That last big hit made me sleepy. Plus . . . it's hard to care about Connor.

Hilary's on her feet a few yards away from us, dancing to the music. I don't know if she's really that into it or just doesn't want to be sitting near all the couples. Not that Lucy and Oscar are *really* a couple, of course.

Or Wade and me either.

Wait—are we?

I tilt my head back so I can study his face. He's a good-looking guy. Good-looking enough that I would find him totally cute if I really liked him. Which I guess I don't, at least not yet, since I'm sitting here studying him with detached curiosity. I'm weirdly calm. Shouldn't I be kind of excited? I haven't kissed that many guys— usually that kind of thing makes my heart start rattling.

Maybe it's the weed that's making me feel deflated. Unenthusiastic. A little bored even. Just one hit can make me feel cut off from myself. Maybe that's why I'm not feeling at all aroused or on edge, despite all the kissing.

Except . . . I'm not actually completely cut off from my own emotions right now.

Because, if I were, would I be feeling a stab of misery every time I look over and see Lily looking so comfortable and welcome on Finn's lap?

It's past ten when the band finishes. We stagger to our feet and regroup. Hilary suggests we all go back to the VIP area so we can have some space to sit and discuss the rest of the evening's plans, but Oscar wants to hear more music. She hands him the schedule and he scans it, then says, "No, you're right—there's nothing else good until eleven. Who's ever even heard of these bands? Swordfish Barnacles, Monkey Brunch, the Molten Pops—"

Finn and I both cry out at the exact same moment. "The Molten Pops?"

"Have you guys heard of them?" Oscar asks, looking up again.

"I have their album," I say.

"Me too," says Finn. "It's awesome."

"I've never even heard of them." Lily's been clinging to Finn's arm and swaying back and forth, humming to herself, but now she says dreamily, "The Melting Pops?"

"Molten," I say. "And they're really good. Weird, but good."

"I'm getting tired," Lucy says.

"Me too," says Phoebe. "I need to sit down. And I don't mean on the grass. I mean on a chair. And I could use something to drink. I'm dying of thirst, and they took away my water bottle."

"Your 'water' bottle?" I say with raised eyebrows.

"I would have used it for water eventually," she says defensively. "That was the plan."

"I need to pee," Lily says.

"You definitely want to do that up in the VIP area," Hilary says. "The bathrooms out here are Porta-Potties, and they look disgusting. I'm sorry, Anna, but I think we'd all rather have a break than see that band."

"Okay," I say, but then Finn says, "Why can't we just split up for an hour? Anna and I can go see the Molten Pops by ourselves. The rest of you go VIP it up." He glances at me. "Right?"

"Sounds good to me."

"Okay," Hilary says. "Meet us at the Galaxy Stage for Rock Basic at midnight." Rock Basic is tonight's headliner band—they get the closing slot.

"We could watch from there, right?" Lucy points to the hilly part of the VIP area that overlooks the Galaxy Stage. A bunch of people are gathered there already, waiting for the next show. "It would be less crowded, and we could find each other more easily."

"That's a good idea," Hilary says. "Let's do that."

"Connor and I can't get in there," Wade says in a low voice to me. "We're not VIPs. But I'm supposed to meet up with him and some other friends in fifteen minutes, anyway. So I can just take off now. If that's okay with you?"

"Yeah, that's fine." I've had enough kissing for the night, and I don't really know what else to do with him at this point. "I'll probably see you later tonight—or we can meet up tomorrow."

"Great," he says. "I'll text you."

I don't know whether I should give him a good-bye kiss, and I don't think he's any clearer on the subject, because there's an awkward pause and then he leaves with a wave and a nod.

"How did he manage that?" Eric asks, nodding after Wade.

"What?"

"His wristband. It's blue."

"I hadn't even noticed." But now that I think about it, Wade's kisses had an alcohol tang to them.

"Fake ID," Oscar suggests. "Or he has a big brother or cousin who lent him their license. Half the people drinking here are underage."

"Just not us," says Phoebe with a sigh.

"It's my father's event." Hilary has a real edge to her voice. "Even if you *had* fake IDs, I wouldn't have let you use them. He could get in trouble for serving minors."

"But he *is* serving minors," Eric points out. "Or the bartenders are, anyway."

"I can't control everything," Hilary snaps.

"But she tries," Lucy murmurs to me. "Lord, how she tries." Then she shifts closer to me and says in an even lower voice, "Don't ever do that to me again."

I don't have to ask her what she's referring to.

"I'm sorry," I whisper back. "I kind of got lost in the moment. It's been a while since a guy has wanted to kiss me."

"I was just left sitting there with you guys deep-tonguing all around me. And then that red-haired guy thought he had a *chance* with me—"

"I know. I'm sorry. I promise." Meaning, *I promise never again to make out with a guy while another couple is also making out, leaving you stuck with a loser who thinks maybe that means he has a chance with you.*

She knows what I mean, accepts my apology, and drifts off with the others.

Finn and I are suddenly alone. I mean, we're surrounded by thousands of people, of course, but we're alone compared to being with our group.

"Come on," he says with a jerk of his head toward the South Stage. As we start walking, he says, "So tell me how you know about the Molten Pops. They're pretty esoteric—I only know about them because the cousin of the bass player went to my old school, and he talked about his cousin the rock star all the time."

"Because of their cover art. I was doing this image search for an art project, and up popped this unbelievable drawing." I still remember seeing it for the first time. The colors were jarring and loud and wrong, and I couldn't stop looking at it. I'd scroll away because I needed to keep working—and then I'd scroll back to look at it again. "I clicked on it and found out it was the cover art for their album, and I got curious about them."

"I know about the artwork!" Finn says, all excited. Like the ninth-grade Finn, the one whose voice would sometimes get too fast and high because he couldn't wait to tell me something. He's peeking out again from this older, distant, crush-worthy guy. From this guy who was making out with Lily just a few minutes ago. It makes me feel happy and bereft at the same time. "The artist is the girlfriend of one of the band members. She's a children's book illustrator—I'll show you some of the pictures from her books later—they're pretty different, except that she uses color in kind of a similar way—"

"She loves neon green."

"And that electric purple. Don't you think it's cool how her lines are wavy? She never uses a straight line."

"I know! It's like a handheld camera effect on a still picture."

We reach the stage, but we're early, which means we can weave our way through the waiting rows of people and get close to the action.

We still have another ten minutes before the set

starts. Workers are busily removing the previous band's equipment and bringing out the new amps and stands.

Once we've settled on a spot, Finn pulls out his phone from his pocket and does a search for the children's books by the same artist. He shows me a couple of her drawings, and I like them, but not as much as the work she's done for the band.

It's funny. Back in ninth grade, when Finn and I would look at photos on his phone together, I never even noticed his forearms, but I can't stop looking at them now. They're long and slender and something about the way his wrist joins them to his hand seems oddly beautiful to me. Either I just didn't notice the way guys were made back then, or he wasn't yet made that way.

"Hey," Finn says, putting his phone back in his pocket, thankfully breaking the spell. "I was wondering. What happened in the end with your sister and her girlfriend?"

"Good question. I haven't heard from her since then. I should find out." Molly and I don't talk much when she's at school.

"You still think what her friend did was unforgivable?" He says it almost too casually, and I get the feeling he's been thinking about this.

Okay, here's my chance to come down on the right side this time—on the side that actually helps me out. "No." I shake my head emphatically. "I've changed my mind. People make mistakes. So long as they feel bad about them, they should be forgiven."

He stares at the stage even though nothing too exciting is going on there yet. "But what if there's some fundamental character flaw that isn't going to change? So there might just be more mistakes? How do you trust it's just going to be the one time?"

I have to say the right thing. I just wish I knew what that was. I take a stab and say slowly, "I guess it's up to whoever feels betrayed. If that person cares enough, they'll want to try again. I'd hope."

He doesn't respond to that, just stares at the stage with an unmoving face.

Well, I've exposed the wound this much—might as well pull the whole Band-Aid off. Either it will hurt like hell, or maybe it will have healed . . . and either way we both know we're not really talking about Molly.

"You and Lily . . . you're a couple now?" I say. He nods without taking his eyes off the workers in front of us. "That's great." My voice sounds flat, and I'm sorry the buzz from the joint is wearing off. I could have used a little more disconnect right now. "She's one of my favorite people in the world."

"I've never met anyone like her."

"That's because she's unique," I say, but as soon as the words are out, I'm remembering what Oscar said, about how she tries to be your basic manic-pixie-dream-girl cliché.

Whatever.

"She doesn't care what anyone else thinks," Finn says. "She does what she wants, no matter who's watching or what other people might say. She's true to herself."

I glance up, and his eyes are on me, dark and intent, but they flicker away as soon as they meet mine. And I think, He's talking about Lily. But he's also talking about me. About what I'm not. What I wasn't. What he doesn't think I can ever be.

But he's wrong.

"Lily's more out there than the rest of us," I say. "And she's more fun. And a little crazier. But that doesn't mean we're not all true to ourselves too."

He makes a noise. It's a short noise, but it conveys a fair amount of skepticism.

I take a deep breath. "You think because I cared about what other people thought back in ninth grade, I'm not my own person. But that was ninth grade. We were all—" I struggle to find the right word. "Unformed. Barely cooked. But now we're older, and it's okay to be different. It's *cool* to be different. When you're in middle school—or even in ninth grade—it's harder. Everyone just wants to fit in."

"Not everyone," he says. "I didn't."

229

"You were unusual."

"And I bet Lily didn't."

"I didn't know her then. But I bet she cared more than she does now. Everyone does. It's hard to be different when you're still trying to figure out who you even are."

"Some people are brave enough not to care."

"So you think Lily's brave."

He just sort of bobs his head.

It's painful, but I say it: "And that I'm not."

"You were either a coward or a hypocrite," he says, and his sudden harshness tears at me. "I've spent a lot of time trying to figure out which one."

I won't let myself cry. That would just *prove* I'm a coward. So instead I force a smile. "Yeah? Any conclusions?"

"No conclusions," he says. "Other than to learn from my mistakes."

Now that the band's going to play any second, people are crowding in around us. I feel weirdly alone and also so completely surrounded that I can't breathe. The press of the crowd forces us to move closer together, but we're careful to keep what little distance we can between each other.

"I'm guessing you think your mistake was to trust me," I say.

We're near enough to the stage lights that I can see

the expression on his face. But I can't actually read it. It's blank. I guess the fact he's closed himself off to me is expressive in its own way.

There's a pause, and then he says in a voice so low, I have to lean in to hear it, "At first I hated myself—hated that I was such a loser that you couldn't even look at me in public, let alone talk to me or dance with me. So I thought, I'll change. I'll change, and then I'll come back and she'll want to be with me because I won't embarrass her anymore."

"I didn't want you to change," I say. "It wasn't that—"

He cuts me off. "Then I got angry. I stopped hating myself and started hating you. I still wanted to change and come back a lot cooler than I'd ever been, but only so I would be able to reject you like you rejected me."

"I didn't reject you. You never let me explain—"

He cuts me off again. "And then I stopped caring at all."

"If you had just given me another chance—"

"Strangely enough, once I've been publicly humiliated, I don't rush back for a repeat experience."

"I didn't mean to humiliate you," I say, even though it's getting harder for me to talk without bursting into tears. "I swear it. I know I hurt you, but I didn't mean to. It just sort of happened. And I've been so sorry ever since."

"I know," he says a little more gently. There's a pause. I'm working my throat—lots of swallows and chin jerking—trying to keep it from swelling so much that he'll hear the thickness in my voice. And then he says lightly, "I admit I probably shouldn't have worn that brown suit to the dance. I don't know what I was thinking."

That lets me choke out a laugh that's really a small sob, but at least I can *pretend* it's a laugh. Maybe I'm fooling him. Maybe not. "You did get cooler," I say in a voice that I try to make sound as casual as his. But it's shaky. "I mean—look at you. Every girl at school wants to go out with you."

"I don't know about that," he says. "But all of that stuff—it's in the past." He actually puts his arm around my shoulder and gives me a brief sideways squeeze, releasing me almost immediately. "I'm glad we've been able to become friends again, Anna. And I'm really glad we finally talked about all this. It was sort of lying there all this time. I know you tried to talk to me right at the beginning of the year, and I wasn't very receptive. I guess I wasn't over being angry yet. But I am now. The past is the past, and we're friends again."

"Yeah," I say faintly. "Totally."

The band is finally entering the stage. They're a funny-looking group. Two of the three guys have enormous waxed mustaches, and the third has crazily overgrown muttonchops. They're wearing frilly shirts, leather boots, and blue jeans. People applaud as they find their way to their instruments.

We're silent.

Then Finn says to me, "So that Wade guy . . . ?"

"What about him?"

"You seem to be—" He stops.

"'Seem to be' what?"

"You know . . . It looked like you were both—" Another halt, and then he tries again. "I mean, maybe that's why it's easier to talk. Now that you're . . . you know."

I decide I don't have to help him out. To my relief— and maybe his too—the band launches into its first song, making conversation impossible. Everyone in the audience pushes forward with excitement.

The guy who's in front of me is wearing a wife-beater shirt and shorts, despite the fact that the temperature's probably about fifty-five degrees now and dropping by the second. Fumes of alcohol and stale smoke waft off of him. He's swaying unevenly—he doesn't seem to have a firm grip on balance at the moment—and the way he keeps taking sudden, uncontrolled steps both backward and forward is making me nervous. I wish I had more space between him and me, but people are pressing up behind us, and I have no space to use as a buffer.

"You okay?" Finn asks, glancing over.

I force a smile. "Yeah—this is so cool." But I'm

miserable. I'm miserable because it's too crowded, and people keep bumping into me. And I'm miserable because I can't cling to the hope anymore that Finn never hated me. He did. For a long time. And even though maybe he's stopped hating me—*maybe*—I'm miserable because he has now so completely friend-zoned me that I couldn't claw my way out of there even if I showed up naked on his doorstep. And I'm miserable because he thinks Lily is braver and more creative and more original than I am. And I'm miserable because he might be right about that. And I'm miserable because the jerk-face in front of me keeps almost stepping on my toes, and I'm cold, and everyone except me is having fun.

I look over at Finn. He's watching the band, but the second I try to study his face, he turns to me. He nods toward the stage, smiling—*he* doesn't seem to be at all miserable.

"How amazing is this?" he shout-whispers. "I've listened to this song a hundred times—it's amazing to hear it live!"

I'm shouting back my agreement when the guy in front of me decides he should holler and wave his arm and takes a compensating step back at the same time. He doesn't even notice that he's crushed my foot or that I'm yelping in pain. But Finn sees the whole thing. He grabs the guy's shoulder, and Big Foot turns around.

"Watch it!" Finn yells. "You just stepped on my friend's toes."

"Sorry," the guy says with an indifferent shrug. He's taller than Finn and probably weighs fifty to sixty pounds more, so he's not intimidated. He shakes off Finn's arm. "Chill, dude," he says as he turns back to the stage.

Finn glares at the guy's back and then says, "Change places with me, Anna." He doesn't wait for me to respond, just moves around and nudges me over into his old spot.

Now I'm behind the guy's girlfriend. She's way too out of it to stomp on anyone's toes—she's so stoned, she's practically catatonic. Her eyes are closed, and if she weren't on her feet, I'd have said she was asleep.

I shout my thanks to Finn.

"Your toes okay?" he asks.

"Basically. I'm lucky he's only wearing sneakers."

"Yeah, Doc Martens would have crippled you." We both turn our attention back to the band.

They start one of my favorite songs. I close my eyes and try to think about the music and nothing else, but Finn suddenly jumps, bumping into me. I turn, thinking our drunken friend stepped on his toes, and see that Lily's snuck up on us and is jabbing her index finger between Finn's ribs. He writhes and pushes her hand away.

"Got you!" she sings out. She squeezes between us. "Hi!" she shouts to me, even though it's a quiet song at the moment. "Those guys were boring, so I came to find you. It wasn't easy—I didn't know you'd be so far up toward the front, and you didn't answer your texts."

Someone turns around and hushes her. She puts her finger to her lips in exaggerated obedience. She listens to the band for a minute or two but then gets restless and pulls Finn's arm around her, then grabs his hair and tugs his head down toward her so she can kiss him on the lips. He gives her a quick peck and then pulls away, nodding toward the stage in an *I want to see this* kind of way. Lily pouts and looks around, shifting from one foot to another.

I'm watching the band again when she nudges my arm. "See those guys?" she says, pointing at a group of frat-boy types a couple of rows in front of us. "They're passing around a joint. Think they'd share with two cute girls who ask nicely?"

I shake my head and put my mouth close to her ear so I can whisper. "I'm not about to take drugs from strangers." Isn't that like Safety 101?

"Oh, please," she says. "They're smoking it themselves—do you honestly think they'd put anything dangerous in their own joints?"

"We don't know where they got it from. They could be idiots who'd buy from anyone."

"Oh, they're definitely idiots," she says with a giggle. "They're wearing USC hoodies. Are you coming with me or not?"

I shake my head, and she tugs on Finn's arm, then goes on tiptoe to tell him what she's planning to do.

I can't hear what he's saying, but he shakes his head, so I can guess.

Lily shouts, "You two are both buzzkills. Stay here and stagnate. I'll be back in a sec."

Finn grabs her arm. "Stay here."

She shakes off his hand and pushes her way forward. The woman who shushed her earlier glares at her, but Lily doesn't even notice. Within seconds she's up by the college guys and talking to one of them. She smiles flirtatiously and bats her eyes, and pretty soon they're grinning back and in just a few seconds they're handing her the joint.

I glance over at Finn. "She does what she wants," he says flatly.

"So I've heard," I say.

seventeen

ily stays with the frat boys for several more songs, helping them finish off that first joint and sharing another one. Since she's in front, I can watch her easily, and toward the end of the set, when she finally seems to be detaching herself from them, one of the guys grabs her around the waist. I can't hear what he's saying, but he obviously doesn't want her to go—and seems to feel she doesn't have the right to just walk away at this point. She laughs in his face and extricates herself and slips through the rows of people back to us. She sidles up next to Finn and leans against him. The guy who put his arm around her turns to see where she went. He sees her with Finn and looks briefly annoyed, but then he shrugs and turns back to the music, probably too wasted to care.

The band finishes, we applaud, and I follow the two of them—their arms still entwined—back toward the

VIP area. Lily suddenly lets go of Finn and runs ahead, dancing and twirling and flinging out her legs. Then she trips and falls down and doesn't move. We both rush forward to make sure she's okay—but she's just lying there laughing.

"You should see your faces!" she says. "You have identical expressions right now." Her hair's spread out on the field, which has to be muddy and gross—thousands of shoes have been churning it up all day—but she doesn't seem to care. She smiles dreamily up at us. "I'm a twin, but I don't look as much like Hilary as you two look like each other right now. Are you guys twins?"

"She may be a tiny bit stoned," I say to Finn.

"You think?" He sighs and extends his hand down to her. "Get up, Lily."

She bats it away. "Don't make me get up. I won't be able to look at the stars. You guys should lie down with me here. It's so beautiful."

"This is where people walk," Finn says. He's crouching on one side of her, and I'm on the other—both of us trying to protect her from the hordes of people walking by. "And it's cold and late, and if you'll just get up then the three of us can go to the nice VIP area where our friends are waiting for us."

"I thought you liked stars," she says to him. "Aren't you the star-app guy? The billionaire star-app guy?"

"Sure," he says. "That's who I am. Now get up."

He reaches down to her, but she slithers away from him. "I don't want to. I want to make grass angels. Like snow angels, only in the grass."

I grab her arm and shake it hard. "*Get. Up. Now.* I mean it, Lily. Three-year-old behavior is only cute in three-year-olds."

She scowls at me. "You've forgotten how to have fun, Anna."

"I never knew," I say crossly. "Now get up."

Finn yanks on one arm, and I yank on the other, and we haul her to her feet. We each take an elbow and steer her through the crowd. "I can walk by myself," she says haughtily. "You can let go of me."

"No, we can't," Finn and I say at the exact same time.

We march her up to the VIP gate, where the security guards study our wristbands extra carefully and shine their flashlights in our faces for a few seconds. I guess we look suspicious, what with Lily's giggling and asking them if they've ever shot anyone and then giggling some more.

It's crowded on the sloping lawn above the Galaxy Stage, and it takes us a few minutes to find our group. I help Finn maneuver Lily into a spot next to Hilary, and then I shift over to where Oscar and Lucy are sitting together.

I'm happy to be reunited with them. Oscar and Lucy.

Lucy and Oscar. My good friends. My best friends. Those good good friends of mine.

"Hey!" I say, wanting them to know how happy I am to see them, how much I love them both. "I am so glad you guys—"

Lucy cuts me off. "There you are. Finally. You said this would be fun, Anna. But I'm bored and cold, and I could be doing work right now or sleeping or something—anything—other than just sitting here. I am *so* going home tomorrow, and I'm really pissed at you for making me come tonight."

I turn to Oscar, but he's in a bad mood too. "I just want to go back to the hotel," he says wearily. "Enough is enough. I'm tired and it's cold, and I don't even like Rock Basic, and now that I've said that out loud, someone's probably going to beat me up."

"So let's go back to the hotel," I say. It hasn't been the greatest night for me either. I feel wounded and sad and jealous. And I can't even talk to anyone about it. I mean, I *could* . . . but the idea of explaining it all even to Lucy or Oscar makes me just want to curl up and go to sleep. And while it might be nice to get some sympathy, I don't want someone looking over at me to make sure I'm "okay" every time Finn and Lily kiss or hold hands from now on.

Lucy agrees we should go, so we call over to Hilary, who frowns and comes closer. "We all have to leave at the same time. It's a limo, not a shuttle bus."

"Yes, but you know what *is* a shuttle bus?" Oscar says. "The shuttle bus. From the festival to our hotel. They had a thing about it in the lobby. There's one every half hour, right outside the gates."

The others hear what we're talking about and join the discussion. Phoebe says that she and Eric want to go back too. Apparently she speaks for both of them now.

Lily says, "Let's go back to the hotel and get into the hot tub." She pushes her face against Finn's chest. "Doesn't that sound nice?" she purrs. "A hot tub?"

"I could go back," Finn says with a shrug.

"Fine. I get it. Everyone wants to go back but me. So we'll go back." Hilary takes out her phone and punches a text to the limo driver.

"What's up with Lily?" Lucy whispers to me as we all stand up and head toward the exit. Lily's holding on to Finn with one arm and wiggling the fingers of her free hand in front of her face, staring at them like they're fascinating. "Is she still stoned?"

"Not still. *Again.* She got high with some college randos."

"She's not normally such a pothead."

"I know. She clearly thinks it's what you're supposed to do at a music festival." Doesn't that make her more of a follower than I've ever been? "I wonder if her dad will notice."

"I don't get the feeling he's the noticing type."

"Neither is mine."

"Mine notices everything," Lucy says with a sigh. "I wish he didn't."

"Really? I love your dad."

"Yeah," she says. "Me too."

It's past midnight when we get back, but the hotel lobby and courtyard are still buzzing with activity—people are everywhere, laughing and talking and drinking and swimming. Most of them are around our age, so I'm guessing they're also here for the festival.

Even though she spent the drive dozing on Finn's chest, once we're out of the car Lily says again that she wants to go to the hot tub. We're all up for it, except Lucy, who says she's going to stay in the room and do some work.

We change, and then Eric, Phoebe, Oscar, Finn, and I travel back down from our rooms to the lobby together. The guys wear board shorts and T-shirts. Phoebe and I wear the hotel bathrobes over our bikinis. Everyone's in flip-flops. When the elevator stops at the lobby, a gray-haired couple is waiting to get on. They eye us suspiciously as we all emerge. "You're going swimming *now*?" the wife says.

"Just a quick one," I say, feeling oddly guilty.

The man holds open the elevator door with one arm

and glances around at all of us. "So what's going on tonight? We've stayed here a dozen times before, and it's always been quiet—just a normal hotel. But tonight it's crazy."

I explain about the music festival, how it's on a fairground just a few miles away from the hotel. He shakes his head unhappily but thanks me for the information.

"They should have told us when we booked our room," his wife says as the elevator door closes behind them.

"Well, that was a downer," Eric says. "Our mere presence made them sad."

"Eh, they'll pop a bunch of sleeping pills and be fine," Oscar says. "That's what my parents would do, anyway."

We head through the big French doors in the back of the lobby, which lead onto a series of outdoor pathways, one of which leads to the pool and hot tub area. There are groups of people talking and laughing and calling out to one another, but once we get inside the pool gate, only two people are actually in the hot tub: a guy who's sitting down and a girl in a bikini who's straddling him. Their mouths are pressed together, and his hands are roaming around her back.

We hesitate, but then Phoebe shrugs. "It's a public

place," she says, and barges ahead. The rest of us follow her and start taking off our bathrobes and flip-flops around the edge of the tub.

The girl becomes aware of us and slips sideways off of the guy's lap. She whispers in his ear and he nods, and before we even get in, they climb out of the tub and walk away.

"What about Hil and Lily?" asks Phoebe as she and I dip our toes carefully in the water to see how hot it is. Not as hot as I'd like, but hot enough. "Where are they?"

"It takes them longer to go up and come down," Oscar points out. "All those extra flights."

"One of the downsides to having a penthouse suite," I say. "Extra elevator time."

"All that canned music," he says. "It's just miserable."

Eric wades right into the tub and makes a braying sound as the hot water hits his chest. "Nice. Can someone turn on the jets? I forgot."

"No, don't," Oscar says, following him down the steps and settling on the bench. "I find them overstimulating."

"Seriously?" I say. "You delicate hothouse flower, you."

"I can't help it if I have hypersensitive sensory-input issues," Oscar says. I don't think he's entirely joking.

"I like the jets," Finn says, stripping off his tee and joining the two guys in the water. "That's two for, one against."

Phoebe says, "I don't like them. It's nicer when it's quiet."

Finn looks at me. "Deciding vote," he says. "Looks like you have to have an opinion of your own for once, Anna."

I stare at him. "What's that supposed to mean?"

"Yeah," Phoebe says. "Anna's as opinionated as any of us."

"Well, not as opinionated as *you*," Oscar says to her. "But she's right in there with me and Eric."

"All right, then," Finn says, and crosses his arms over his chest. "Jets or no jets?"

I don't actually care, but I pick no jets because he voted for them, and he just implied—not for the first time, not even for the first time this *evening*—that I care too much about what other people think. Also? He's made me sad tonight. Even if our conversation was supposedly just clearing the air and all that . . . I feel a little bit broken at the moment.

So I say, "No jets."

Ha. Showed *him*.

Oscar pumps his fist in triumph. "She loves me the most." Not exactly the message I was going for, but I'm okay with it.

"Or me," Phoebe says. She steps down into the tub and immediately snuggles into a spot next to Eric.

"Keep your hands where we can see them," Oscar tells them.

"Does the sight of other people's affection make you uncomfortable?" Phoebe asks sweetly. "Maybe you should see a therapist about that."

"Trust me, I have."

I pause on the second step of the hot tub to let my legs adjust to the heat and realize Finn is watching me. It's too dark for me to see his expression. His eyes glitter a little in the dark, but he looks away the second I glance at him. I'm suddenly self-conscious about being in a bikini: I'm so much curvier than thin, athletic Phoebe, who's the only other girl out here now. I quickly sit down on the bench between Oscar and the steps, gasping as I sink into the hot water.

"Oh, good," Finn says, looking past the rest of us. "Here they are."

I turn. Hilary is striding toward us. She's wearing a bikini and a sari kind of thing that ties at her waist. Lily is following more slowly. She's still wearing her leather corset, but she's changed back into jeans. She's also barefoot.

"I couldn't get her to put on her bathing suit," Hilary says when she reaches the tub. "I tried, but she's being weird."

"She's really stoned," I say, but Hilary instantly shushes me.

"I can't hear that," she says. "Seriously. If Dad starts asking questions, at this point I can honestly say that as far as I know, Lily hasn't done anything illegal tonight."

"Like he'd even care," says Lily, coming up behind her. "Did you see that blond he was talking to at dinner? Bet he brings her back to the room tonight."

"Shut up," Hilary says with real anger. No, not just anger—panic. "Just shut up, Lily."

"They're our friends," Lily says, waving her hand around the hot tub. "We can be honest in front of them. Our dad cheats on our mom," she tell us all.

Hilary grabs her shoulder and swings her around so they're nose to nose. "Shut the fuck up."

"Fine, fine." Lily suddenly kisses Hilary on the cheek. "Whatever you want, babe. I love you."

Hilary shoves her away. "God, I can't wait until she comes down."

"I thought you didn't even know she was high," Oscar says.

"You can shut up too." With an almost violent jerk, Hilary undoes the knot at her waist and tosses the fabric onto a lounge chair. She plunges into the tub. I look at her with sympathy. Tonight hasn't been any more fun for her than it has for me.

"Aren't you coming in?" Finn calls over to Lily,

who's still standing on the deck. "This whole thing was your idea."

"Mm-hmm," she says noncommittally.

"Go back to your room and put on a bathing suit."

"I don't think she should wander around the hotel by herself," I tell Finn quietly. "Someone should go with her."

He nods. "Yeah." He stands up in the center of the hot tub. Water streams off his shoulders. They're so much broader than they used to be. Much good it does me now. But I still look. I can't seem to stop. His torso narrows down to a waist so slender that his board shorts sit low on his hips and you can see the bones jutting out above them. "I'll go up with you. Keep you company."

Lily wags her finger at him. "You'd like that, wouldn't you? Get me all alone up there? Help me take off my clothes?"

Phoebe snickers. Finn crosses his arms and glares at Lily. "Do you want to put on a bathing suit or not?"

"Nah. Too much work." She suddenly plunges into the hot tub.

"Your clothes are all getting soaked!" Hilary says, horrified.

"I'm really worried about that." She ducks down, so her head is completely underwater. She stands up quickly with a yelp and wipes her hair out of her eyes. "Man, that's hot!"

"What the hell's wrong with you?" her sister hisses. "You just ruined that top—and it cost a fortune."

"It's not ruined."

"It's leather," Hilary says. "It's *ruined*."

Lily shakes her head like a dog, spraying us all. "Who cares?" she says. "Who cares about anything? Just relax for once, Hil. Or don't. Doesn't matter to me." She turns to Finn and throws herself against him.

"Ugh," he says, peeling off her arms and moving away from her. "Wet leather."

She looks around the tub. Phoebe and Eric are cuddling together with Phoebe's head on his shoulder. Lily suddenly sends a big splash of water right at them. It hits Phoebe in the eyes, and she springs upright.

"Oh my god, Lily! Why are you being so annoying!"

"Why are you?"

"What have *I* done?"

"Look at yourself," says Lily. "Just look at yourself." She giggles.

"I'm going back to the room," Phoebe says, rising to her feet and tugging Eric up. "This stopped being fun." They wade out of the hot tub. "Oh, great—no towels," she spits out angrily. She drags on her terrycloth bathrobe and uses its belt to wipe off Eric a little before he puts on his T-shirt, and then they head back into the hotel.

"Nicely done," Hilary says to her sister. "Really. You're charming tonight."

Lily sends another splash her way, then puts both her hands in the water and starts churning it up. "It's a whirlpool!" she cries.

"I think Phoebe had the right idea." Oscar glides onto his feet. "Who wants to ride up in the elevator with me? We can press all the buttons before we get out."

"I do, I do." I follow him out of the tub.

"Let's all go up," Finn says. He rises and holds out his hand to Lily. "Come on. This didn't turn out to be as relaxing as we'd all hoped."

Lily lets him pull her up. Her clothing is so water-logged that she has to struggle her way out of the tub. "I want to swim in the pool first," she says as the water pours off of her. "A quick dip."

"You can't swim in those clothes," Finn says. "They're too heavy."

"People jump in pools in their clothes all the time. Haven't you ever seen a teen movie? You go to a party, you jump in a pool. Or get pushed in. Hil, you want to come with me?"

"You've got to be kidding," Hilary says. She has the hot tub all to herself now. She leans her head back and closes her eyes. "It's freezing out. I'm going to soak for five more minutes and then go to bed."

"One quick dive and one lap," Lily says to Finn. Her wet jeans stick to every curve of her narrow legs. She looks unearthly with her wet black hair, smudged dark makeup, and the sagging leather corset, like some sort of bedraggled modern-day witch. She turns toward the pool.

Finn grabs at her arm. "Don't," he says. He's shivering in the cold air, still wearing only his wet board shorts. He has his T-shirt in his hand, but he's too busy dealing with Lily to put it on. I wrap my bathrobe around myself and wait for Oscar to finish drying himself off with the towel he (and he alone) had the foresight to bring down from the boys' room.

Lily breaks away from Finn. "I'll be fast," she says, and trots toward the pool. "Watch me—I'm going to dive."

"The sign says not to." Finn points to a poster on the side of a wall. "Seriously, Lily—it's really shallow."

"Who cares?" she says, right before leaping up at the edge and—as Finn shouts at her with rising panic—curving forward in a swift and messy swan dive. She disappears under the water as Finn shouts again. He races over, still calling her name, and Oscar and I are right behind him. We all crouch at the edge of the pool, peering in, and I'm wondering why she's taking so long to come back up—she's not moving or swimming, she's just lying facedown in the water. It's Lily, so she's probably teasing us. She's probably holding her breath and will pop up in a second, laughing at us.

Only she doesn't.

We're all shouting her name now, and I don't care if she comes up laughing at us for being worried, I just want her to *come up*, but her head's still not rising. She's sinking, if anything. The dark mass of her body twisting away from us. So Finn slides in feetfirst—and we can see how shallow the pool is now, because his feet touch and he's standing with the water around his waist and that's bad, very bad—she dove in, and it's that shallow—and he's dragging her up by what turns out to be her arm, and then he's got her shoulders and he's struggling to get her out of the water. She's not helping him—she's not moving at all—she's deadweight, her head flopping back—and Oscar and I are trying to help, catching at whatever part of her we can, the two of us pulling and hauling as Finn pushes her up toward us, until we've got her completely out of the pool. Even with three of us, it's a struggle. Her wet clothes are so heavy, and she's so floppy.

Oscar and I roll her onto her back, but her eyes aren't open—she's not responding at all. Finn hauls himself out of the pool and kneels down next to us.

I keep waiting for her to look up and smile and tell us she's joking, and I'm going to be so mad at her when she does because I'm scared right now. Really scared. And she shouldn't make me feel this scared.

I feel someone at my shoulder and look up. Hilary's standing over me, dripping water. She's saying "Is she okay?" over and over again.

I look back down at Lily again. There's a trickle of water coming out of the corner of her mouth and that scares me so much I want to start screaming and never stop, but the other part knows I can't do that and is thinking about what we should do because we have to do something. I manage to say, "Who's got a phone?" and I'm surprised at how normal my voice sounds because I feel like I should be shrieking. No one does. "Run inside and get them to call 911," I tell Hilary. I have to repeat the direction, but it sinks in and she dashes—still in her bikini and soaking wet—toward the lobby doors.

"What do we do?" Oscar's voice is so hoarse, I can barely make out what he's saying.

"I think we should turn her on her side," I say. "If she swallowed water, it's better for her to be on her side." I took a junior lifeguarding class a million years ago. That one bit of information seems to be the only thing I remember from it.

"She's breathing, right?" Finn is looking at me like I should know.

Actually, though, I do—I can see her chest moving. "Yeah, I think so." As we carefully turn her on her side, I can see streaks of something darker in the pink-bleached strands at the bottom of her hair. I touch them and look at my fingers. "Her head's bleeding," I say.

Oscar makes a choking, gasping sound.

"I told her not to dive," Finn says. "I should have held on to her. If I hadn't let go—"

"It's not your fault," I say. "She pulled away."

Hilary's back at the pool gate. She opens it and runs across the courtyard toward us, followed by a pudgy middle-aged man in a suit and tie.

"The ambulance is on its way," he says as they get to us. He's panting from the short run. Or maybe from panic. "Is she breathing?"

"I think so," I say. "But she hasn't opened her eyes."

"Don't try to move her."

"We just put her on her side—so she couldn't choke if she vomited water. That's okay, right?" I'm suddenly terrified I did the wrong thing, but he just stares at me blankly.

"Is she going to be all right?" Oscar asks him.

"God, I hope so," he says. "I'm not a doctor—I just work for the hotel. What happened?" He stoops over, peering at her. "Is that blood? Holy shit. Sorry. Why is she bleeding?"

"She dove into the pool."

"Headfirst?" the guy says with horror. "Are you all crazy? That pool is only four feet deep—there are No Diving signs everywhere."

"We told her to stop," Finn says. His voice is so uncertain and high that he sounds like a little kid. We probably all do right now. I know I *feel* like one—like a scared, stupid little kid. I want some adult to take over and take care of Lily and make everything okay again—but I need an adult who knows more than I do, and I don't think this guy does. "She didn't listen. She just kept going."

"Was she drunk?" he asks. His eyes are hard as he glares around at each of us. Hard and weary. I know what he's thinking. He doesn't like teenagers in his hotel: they make his job harder, and they do stupid things like this.

I shake my head but don't elaborate.

Hilary says, "I have to tell my dad. But I don't have my phone." I look up at her. She's visibly shivering and clutching herself, still in that wet bikini, her eyes wild and unfocused. "What should I do, Anna? I can't leave her. But I have to call my dad."

"Is your father here?" asks the hotel guy.

"He's probably still at the music festival. I don't know. We have to tell him. But he'll kill me. Is she going to be all right? What if she's not? Why isn't she moving?" Her words are turning into a wail.

I'm still squatting down, so I grab hold of her ankle and squeeze it firmly. I tilt my head back so I can look up at her. "Hil. We just have to deal right now, okay?

You can fall apart later. Go upstairs and put on some dry clothes and get your phone and wallet so you can go to the hospital. You can tell your dad to meet us there once we know which one it is. Okay?"

"I don't want to leave her."

"That's why you have to get changed. You can't go to the hospital like that, and you need to stay with her." I turn to Oscar, who's still kneeling next to me. "Will you take Hilary upstairs and help her get ready and bring her back down? You should get changed too. Finn and I will stay with Lily for now, and then we'll get changed once you're back. Right?" I look at Finn, who seems stunned but manages to nod.

Oscar stands up and takes Hilary by the elbow and steers her toward the lobby. "Pack up some stuff for Lily," I call after them. "Some clothes and whatever else she might need." Oscar raises his hand in an *I got you* gesture. But Hilary's head just sags forward. No response. They disappear into the lobby.

Then we wait for a while. The hotel guy, Finn, and me. All of us crouching over Lily's body, not doing anything to or with it, because what can we do? She's on her side, breathing but unconscious, her pants sodden, her mouth still leaking dark-looking water, her hair sticky with blood. I don't have the guts or knowledge to start poking around to see how bad the wound is.

It occurs to me that I'm very cold, my bathrobe

soaked through from my wet bathing suit, the night air freezing. But it's like my body is far away from me, and I note how I'm shivering with an almost clinical detachment. It doesn't matter. The only thing that matters is that Lily needs to open her eyes and make us all angry at her for scaring us so much.

"I shouldn't have let go of her," Finn mutters, almost to himself, after we've waited there in silence for a minute.

"I should have kept the pool gate locked while the music festival was in town," the hotel guy says morosely. "I should have known something like this would happen."

Hil and Oscar reappear just as we hear the sirens of the arriving ambulance. Lucy and Phoebe and Eric are with them, dressed in sweatpants and hoodies. I don't waste time talking to them, just jump to my feet and haul Finn up next to me.

"Come on," I say. "We need to get changed so we can go to the hospital with everyone else." I tug him toward the lobby, and at first he seems reluctant to walk away—keeps twisting around like he needs to keep an eye on Lily—but then he suddenly seems to get that there's time pressure and speeds up and runs into the lobby and then I say, "Let's take the stairs—it'll be faster," so we find the door to the stairs and run up and then I open the girls' room with my key—it's lucky I already put on my bathrobe, since it's in the pocket—and that's when he realizes he doesn't have his, that it's still with his T-shirt down by the pool. He hits himself angrily in the head, but I remind him that our rooms connect and he can get in that way, so he follows me inside. Once the door closes behind us, he stops for a moment and just stands there.

"Anna," he says, and I look at him and I see how his face is screwing up like a little kid's who's been hurt, so even though we don't have time for it, I put my arms around his neck and he buries his face in my shoulder and just shakes for a while. I don't know if he's crying or just shuddering, but I give him about ten seconds and then I gently push him away and say, "We have to get ready, or the ambulance will leave without us."

"Right," he says, without meeting my eyes, and races into the other room, where I'm guessing he's doing what I'm doing, which is tearing off my bathing suit without any concern about whether or not he might see, because right now I care a lot more about speed than modesty. My suit's off within seconds, and it takes about one minute longer for me to throw my clothes back on. I stick my feet in my flip-flops, grab my purse and key, and call over to Finn, who calls back that he's just about ready. He reappears in the doorway in jeans and a sweatshirt, and I say, "Let's go."

We race out the door and back down the stairs. It's a

good thing we rushed: they're already lifting a stretcher with Lily on it into the back of the ambulance. She's encased in one of those neck-immobilizing braces. The others are all grouped a few feet away, clutching one another and watching. Hilary sees me and grabs my arm. "They'll only take two of us in the ambulance—one in back and one in front. What should we do, Anna?"

"You should ride in the back with Lily—oh, did you reach your father?"

She nods. "He's meeting us there."

"Finn should ride in front." I figure he'll want to get there as soon as possible. "The rest of us will get a cab. Eric, go ask the front desk to call for a cab to get here as soon as possible." He races off obediently. "Do you guys know which hospital?"

They all shake their heads, but fortunately the EMT guy overhears me and gives me the hospital name, and then he helps Hilary up into the back, settling her into a seat at Lily's side. She stares at me imploringly as he closes the door. I have no idea what it is she wants me to do. Make it all go away, I guess.

Finn goes to the front of the ambulance and gets in as the driver takes his own place, and they're off in a second, sirens blaring.

"What did they say?" I ask the others. "Is she going to be okay?"

Lucy says, "They didn't tell us anything. Just put

that thing around her neck and an oxygen mask on her and an IV. But they didn't say *anything*." She digs her fingers into my forearm. "What if she's not okay, Anna?" There's no answer to that question. I just shake my head. Lucy shakes my wrist hard. "What happened? Why did you guys let her dive?"

"We didn't. Finn tried to stop her. She wouldn't listen to him."

"What if she broke her neck?" Phoebe asks in a tiny voice. "What if she's crippled for life? I read an article once—"

I cut her off quickly. I don't want to hear about some girl who was paralyzed for life. "Her head was bleeding, so it's probably not her neck."

"It could be both," says Eric, who has returned in time to contribute that helpful possibility. "Our cab will be here in five minutes."

I tell the others that if they need wallets or phones or to change their clothing they should take care of that before the cab comes, and everyone races back inside except for me and Oscar.

We look at each other.

"This is so unbelievably awful," he says. I don't think I've ever heard Oscar sound so serious and so sad. "I keep seeing that moment over and over again—Finn shouting at her to stop and her diving . . . And then . . . her arm rising up in the water . . ." He stops.

"She'll be okay," I say. "She has to be okay." And for the first time—now that it's all quiet and I don't have to figure out what to do next anymore—I burst into tears.

Oscar holds out his arms, and I move into them. He hugs me close. "If she is okay, it's thanks to you," he says. "You were the only one of us who was thinking clearly. I didn't know you were so good in a crisis."

"Me neither," I whimper into his neck. "I wish I still didn't."

eighteen

By the time our cab leaves us at the ER entrance, Lily's already been taken into a treatment room, and Finn is sitting alone in the small, deserted waiting room. He jumps up from a metal chair as soon as he sees us.

"Her dad got here a few minutes ago," he says. In the fluorescent light, his face is pale and slightly green. "They only let family members go back."

"You okay?" I ask.

"Not really. You?"

"Not really."

We all find seats. I sit down next to Oscar and then Finn takes the chair on my other side. He keeps glancing at me. Like he's waiting for something. Forgiveness? Consolation? Punishment?

It doesn't matter. I can't give him anything right now. I'm exhausted.

No one feels like talking. We pull out our cell phones and stare at them.

"Everyone's asleep back home," Phoebe says, after a little while. "No one's answering my texts."

"It's almost two," Lucy says with a huge yawn. "Of course they're asleep."

"Why do things like this always happen late at night?" Eric asks.

"Probably because people are drunk or stoned late at night," Phoebe says.

Eventually Hilary and her father emerge from the back area. We jump up and rush at them, all of us asking if she's okay.

Mr. Diamond puts up his hands, holding us off, shushing us. "They don't know yet. She's definitely had a concussion. The good news is her spine's okay. But they're doing a CT scan now to make sure there isn't any bleeding around her brain."

"That's what that actress died of," Hilary adds in a wavering voice. "The *Parent Trap* mom. She hit her head, and they thought she was okay, and then she died." She starts crying. I expect her dad to take her in his arms, but he doesn't. He crosses them instead.

"I'm really disappointed in all of you," he says. "No—horrified by you. What you did tonight verged on criminal." His angry glare turns toward the sobbing daughter at his side. "Especially you. That you could just stand there and let her do something so dangerous—"

"It's not Hilary's fault. It's mine." Finn steps forward. He pauses, and I can see the muscles in his throat working, but when he speaks, his voice is clear. "I was closest to her. I saw where she was heading. I should have tackled her or something. But I didn't. Hilary was too far to do anything about it. I wasn't."

"Remind me who you are again," says the twins' father, giving him one of those up-and-down looks that make you want to run and hide.

Finn holds his ground and says his full name.

Mr. Diamond nods slowly. "Well, Finn, if that's true—if you stood there without doing a thing while my daughter dove into a shallow pool—then you may be criminally liable for failure to act. And even if I decide not to press charges, just know that for the rest of your life, you'll have to live with the fact that my daughter's life was put at risk by your negligence."

Finn doesn't argue. He just hangs his head and takes it. Maybe he thinks he deserves the abuse.

But I don't. I step toward Mr. Diamond, my chest pounding with anger. "Stop blaming everyone! I'm sorry Lily's hurt—we all are—we love her—but it's her own fault." I realize I've balled my hands into fists at my sides. "If you're upset that she's hurt, be upset that she's hurt—don't start attacking the people who care about her."

He looks at me like I've just crawled out from under a rock and he doesn't want me to get on his shoe. "I'm simply being honest. You all let her down."

"No," I say. "She let *us* down. She should have listened to Finn when he told her to stop."

There's so much anger in his face, I'm afraid of him, and it's hard for me to keep my chin up.

Lucy's all about defusing tense situations, so she speaks up now. "What about the blood on her head?" she asks him. "How bad is the wound?"

He slowly swivels away from me and toward her, passing his hand wearily over his forehead. "It's not too bad," he says. "It's a long but shallow cut. She'll need a few stitches. They're not sure what she hit down there—maybe just the pool floor, but there's a chance there was something metal like a rung, so she needs a tetanus shot to be safe—but the actual cut isn't the problem. It's the possibility of internal bleeding from the trauma. It's not good that she's still unconscious."

"What can we do?" Lucy asks.

"Nothing. Go back to the hotel and get some sleep." He turns to Hilary. "You too."

She shakes her head vehemently. "I'm staying. I wouldn't be able to sleep anyway. And if she wakes up, I want to be here." Then she gasps a little and says, "*When. When* she wakes up."

"Couldn't we all wait here?" Lucy asks. "We'd rather."

"The last thing Lily needs right now is people crowding in on her. Hilary will let you all know how she's doing. Do you need money for a cab back?" He's already reaching for his wallet when a small figure comes flying in from the street entrance, calling out to us.

"Where is she? Is she okay? Where's my baby?" It's Yuri Lee, the twins' mother.

No dangling silver bracelets and necklaces tonight— she's wearing yoga pants and a hooded jacket over a tank top. No makeup either, and under the artfully cut black hair, her face looks haggard.

Hilary runs to her, and her mother manages to crush her to her chest despite the fact that Hilary is a few inches taller.

"They're doing a scan now," her husband says. "They'll come get us as soon as she's done."

She glares at her husband above Hilary's bent head. "I can't believe I let you take them here. I blame myself. I know better than to trust you to be responsible."

He flushes a dark red under his baseball cap. "I wasn't even there."

She practically spits her response. "Of course you weren't."

"The girls are seventeen! And they were together.

Was I supposed to push them around in a stroller?"

"All I know," says Yuri Lee, "is that my daughter left town with her father, and now I'm visiting her in the emergency room, where we still don't know the extent of the damage. That's all I know."

He stares at her a moment, then turns and walks to the far side of the waiting room and throws himself in a chair.

Lucy touches my arm. "We should go," she murmurs, and I nod.

Lucy, Phoebe, and I all slip over to Hilary and give her quick hugs. Poor Hil—her face is swollen, her eyes are red, and terror radiates off her in waves. I wish I could do more than just hug her and tell her I love her, but that's all any of us can do.

We leave the waiting room and stand in front of the hospital entrance. Oscar's the only one who remembers the cab company's name, so he calls and they promise to send out a car. It's dark and cold, and we all huddle together—as much for comfort as warmth.

"I can't believe it's still the same night," says Phoebe. She's pressed against Eric's side, his arm slung around her neck like a scarf. "It feels like days have gone by since the sun went down."

"Weeks," Oscar says.

I'm standing near Finn, who's still very quiet. I nudge his arm gently with mine, and he flashes me a wan smile.

It's funny: I've felt so far away from him this year, and just a few hours ago, I thought maybe we weren't even friends, but now it feels right to slip my hand into his and give his fingers a comforting squeeze. "It wasn't your fault at all," I say. "Her father was wrong. He wasn't there. He didn't see what happened."

He curls his fingers around mine. "I just want her to be okay."

"Me too."

An ambulance comes roaring up and pulls into the driveway that ends at the ER entrance. From where we're standing on the curb, I can't see the person they take out on the stretcher, but I can hear one EMT's grim comment to the other: "Second teenager of the night. That music festival's going to be the gift that keeps on giving." They disappear into the hospital.

I wonder who's on the stretcher. *Please don't let it be anyone we know. Please let whoever it is be okay. Please let Lily be okay. Please please please.*

nineteen

Back at the hotel, we leave the connecting doors open. Phoebe and Eric curl up together in a double bed in the boys' room, and Oscar, Lucy, and I all squish together in one bed in the girls' room. Finn ends up by himself in the bed next to ours. I feel bad he's alone, but it would be too weird for me to crawl in next to him. Instead I lie on my side and surreptitiously watch him as he stares up at the ceiling in the dim light. The sun is just starting to come up.

I guess I doze a little, because bright daylight is leaking around the edges of the curtains when I open my eyes again, and I can easily see that Finn is sitting up in bed, reading a text. "Who is it?" I ask, propping myself up on an elbow. "What is it? Is it news?"

"It's Hilary. Good news. Really good news. Lily's conscious."

"Oh my god." I sit up, and that wakes Lucy, who's next to me.

"What's going on?" she says groggily. Oscar pops up next to her, instantly alert. "How's Lily?"

I tell them. "What else does Hilary say?" I ask Finn, who's thumbing a response into the phone.

"Not a lot. Lily's still pretty confused, but at least she knew who they were. She doesn't remember anything about last night."

"But she's okay?" Lucy says.

"The scan was clean, and she's conscious—"

"Thank god."

"—but they still have to keep her there a while longer just to be safe, make sure they haven't missed anything."

"Still," I say. "It's *good*."

He lets his head sag back against the pillow and closes his eyes. It occurs to me that he probably didn't sleep at all. "Yeah" is all he says.

We all snuggle back down into the beds.

Lucy whispers to me, "I want to go home."

"Me too," I say. "Unless the twins need us here."

"Right," she says sleepily. "Unless they need us here."

We all get a chance to talk to Hilary on the phone later that morning. She says that Lily's still very shaky and incoherent; her short-term memory is all wonky, and she can't say more than a few words at a time. She's very emotional and keeps bursting into tears. But she's okay. That's what Hilary keeps repeating over and over to each of us: "She's okay."

"They said she's had a severe concussion, and that takes time to recover from," Hilary tells me when I'm on with her. "So they want her to stay in the hospital for another forty-eight hours. But Anna, she's going to be all right! The nurse started telling us stories of patients they've seen who broke their necks in shallow swimming pools. . . . I wish she hadn't. I feel queasy just thinking about it. And grateful that nothing like that happened to Lucy." She lowers her voice to a whisper. "Except now that it looks like she's going to be fine, I sort of want to kill her. You get that, right?"

"Totally," I say. "I sort of want to kill her too. Let's both kill her once she's all better."

When it's Lucy's turn to talk to Hilary, she tells her that we're over the music festival. "We just want to see you guys and go home."

In the end we just go home without seeing them. Hilary's parents don't want us to come by the hospital and they tell Hilary to tell us that Lily needs absolute quiet.

Her father sends the van to pick us up.

Finn takes the seat next to me. He doesn't talk much at first, just sticks in his earbuds as the van drives away from the hotel and listens to music with his eyes closed. Lucy and Oscar are together in front of us, Phoebe and Eric behind us.

Too many empty seats.

We're pretty subdued. No one talks much. Mostly we doze.

At one point Finn checks a text and nudges my arm, then angles the phone toward me so I can see. It's a photo from Hilary of Lily sitting up in bed smiling, which makes it pretty much the most wonderful photo I've ever seen. I look at Finn and see the relief in his face. And something else too. Something that makes him look away from me before I can figure out what it is. Confusion maybe? He turns back to the window and curls up with his phone again.

I sit for a few minutes, which turns into dozing for a few minutes, which turns into groggy waking up for a few minutes, and then I decide I should do something more useful with this time. I reach down and pull out the sketch pad from the bag at my feet.

"Hey," Finn says, taking out his earbuds. "What happened with those sketches you were doing on the drive down? The ones of all of us. How did those come out? Can I see them?"

I quickly leaf through the pages, checking to see if my drawings are better than I remembered. But they're not.

I close the pad. "No—they suck. I don't like any of them."

"I doubt they suck."

"Thanks. I don't feel very talented at the moment." I touch the sketch pad. "None of these feel right to me. Sometimes when I work on something, it just feels right in a way I can't explain. Even if it's only partially done or I know there's stuff I have to fix . . . I just get a feeling that it's working. It feels satisfying. And none of these give me that feeling. They just sit on the page. They don't have any soul."

"You said you needed to do a portrait? Why's that?"

"I can put together a portfolio for my applications without one, but it's better to show some range." I keep folding and unfolding a tiny triangle at the corner of the sketch-pad cover. "I guess my choice is to include a technically decent but emotionally soulless portrait or to not include it and hope they appreciate what I *can* do without worrying about what I can't."

"What does your gut say?"

"My gut?" I think for a moment. "I guess my gut says to not submit anything I'm not really proud of. But Oresco's been through the application process a lot more times than my gut."

"You want to hear my completely ignorant and therefore entirely discountable opinion?" Finn asks.

"Always," I say, and mean it.

"Put in only what you love, and if they ask you why all your work has a similar feel to it, tell them it's because that's the work that excites and interests you right now as an artist. Tell them it might change someday, but for now this is the art you're making." He shrugs. "Maybe some admissions people will worry you can't do anything else, but I bet most of them will admire you for having a vision."

"Huh." I think about it. "I can't tell if I actually think you're right or if I'm just so relieved at the thought of not having to do a decent sketch that I'm convincing myself I think you're right."

"In either case . . . can I please see the sketches?"

"Only if you promise to agree that they suck." He reaches for the pad, but I move it away from him. "I'm serious, Finn. Don't tell me they're good—I hate phony praise."

"I promise to adequately convey any disgust I feel," he says. He takes the sketchbook out of my hands and leafs through it, flipping the pages up and over as he finishes with them. He doesn't say anything, just studies them thoughtfully. He lingers for a while on the one of Lily. I drew her with her head leaning back against the van headrest—she's smiling up at nothing in particular. To me, there's something too static about it. It looks like her, but I didn't capture her energy and restlessness.

The last one is of him. I drew him turning to show

Lily a photo on his phone. (She's not actually in the drawing, though, and neither is the phone.) I made him look too young in the drawing, more like a fourteen-year-old than a seventeen-year-old.

I didn't do it on purpose.

Finn gazes at that one for a little while without saying anything, then closes the sketchbook and holds it out. "Please don't make me say they suck."

I snatch it away from him. "Is that how you keep your promises?"

"It's either break a promise or lie. Which is more dishonorable?"

I glare at him.

"Fine." He holds up his hands in mock surrender. "The one of Hilary—that wasn't as good as the others."

"That's better. A tiny scrap of honesty."

"But that's all I'm saying. Unless I'm allowed to compliment you."

I shake my head.

He taps the sketchbook. "Seriously, Anna, I think any art school is going to want you, whether you include one of these or not. You're really talented."

I feel a kind of warm glow in my face and chest. "Thanks."

"I mean it." There's a pause. He and I are just sitting there, looking at each other. And then he leans back suddenly. "Text," he says, and pulls out his phone. I'm so close to him right now, I can read what's on the screen.

Lily wants you to come visit as soon as we get home.

I can also read Finn's response, which he quickly punches in:

I'll drive back to the hospital tonight if your dad will let me.

I stare at the seat in front of me and start thinking about how, one night before my parents got divorced, I woke up to the sound of my mother going downstairs at two in the morning. I could hear her pacing around down there, so I came down to see what was wrong, and she said, "Your father's not home, and he's not answering his phone." I asked her if she was worried that he'd been in an accident, and she snarled, "Terrified. Because if that son of a bitch cripples himself, I'll be stuck taking care of him for the rest of my life, like Ethan Frome's wife." I didn't know who Ethan Frome was, and I didn't want to think too much about the point she was making, but when I was older, I figured it all out: Mom was already thinking about leaving him and knew that her conscience and the world's opinion wouldn't let her walk away if Dad got badly injured. (He was fine, by the way—just on a work trip. There had been a breakdown in communication between the two of them. There was always a breakdown in communication.)

If my mother—who ultimately had no problem walking out on her husband and kids—felt that an injury changes everything, forces you to be loyal and present, that means Finn must be feeling completely committed to Lily after last night. Maybe he was feeling that way, anyway (but *was* he? He had seemed so fed up with her last night before the accident—even before this trip, come to think of it), but now their attachment is written in stone.

I move over in my seat, shifting away from him. I rest my head against the window, close my eyes, and pretend I'm going back to sleep.

twenty

get dropped off with Lucy at her house. Neither of us wants to be alone—we're still pretty shaken up. And I know her parents will make me feel more like I've come home than my own father will. Sure enough, they give us both warm, reassuring hugs, ask lots of concerned questions about Lily, and insist on plying us with tons of food. I realize I'm starving—we haven't eaten since the night before, and now that all of Hilary's texts are reassuring, I don't feel sick to my stomach anymore.

We go up to Lucy's room to do homework but make the mistake of working on her bed, and at some point we both drift off to sleep.

By the time I wake up, it's dark outside, and I have some new texts. I sit up to look at them.

Meet up somewhere? We're heading to the South Stage but could change plans.

I text Wade back.

Sorry—we left. A friend had an accident.

He texts me back instantly.

Wait—was she the one who hit her head? Everyone's talking about that.

Yeah. She's still in the hospital. But prob ok.

Wow. Talk when we get back?

definitely.

I also have a text from Hilary.

If nothing changes, we can bring Lil home tomorrow. You know a guy named James Baskille?

He go to our school?

no, St. Francis. Anyway, he's here too—alcohol poisoning.

he ok?

they pumped his stomach. Lily says she's glad she's not the only stupid one.

Lucy rolls over and sees me looking at my phone. "That Hil?"

"Yeah."

"How's Lily?"

"Making jokes—seems like a good sign."

Lucy curls into a ball. "It all feels unreal, doesn't it? Maybe we just fell asleep here after school on Friday and dreamed the rest."

"Would you ever dream that part where Connor wanted to make out with you?"

"Ew, no. Even my worst nightmares are classier than that."

I stretch out my legs. "It all happened. But it could have been so much worse."

"I know," Lucy says. "I keep thinking about if she had hit her neck wrong—"

"Don't," I say. "Don't think about that." We're both silent for a second, then I say, "Something smells good. I think your mom's cooking dinner."

We go down to investigate. She's making chicken breasts with some kind of apricot sauce and some incredible rice thing with pine nuts. I love Lucy's mom.

Lucy drives me home after dinner. Dad's not there. I check the garage, and his car is gone. Well, it *is* Saturday night. He's probably gone out for dinner with friends. I go up to my room and work on an English essay.

I'm surprised at how happy I am to hear the garage door open a couple of hours later. Normally I'm fine being home by myself, but I'm still feeling freaked out and sad, and I actually want to know someone else is in the house. I fly down the stairs and into the kitchen just as he comes in from the garage.

Laughing. And talking to Ginny Clay, who's all dressed up in a tight, blue, shiny dress and spiky high heels. Her hair is down tonight, and she's not wearing the glasses. She looks pretty. And a little trashy.

Okay, I might be editorializing with that.

My father spots me and comes to an abrupt halt in the doorway. "Anna? What are you doing home? I thought you were supposed to be gone until tomorrow."

"One of my friends got hurt and ended up in the ER, so we came home early."

"Oh my god," Ginny says, clutching her hand to her chest. "Who got hurt?"

"Lily Diamond."

"The pretty little Asian one? The twin? Is she okay? What happened?"

"She dove into a pool that was shallower than she realized and got a concussion." It sounds so innocent the way I describe it. "It was really scary at first, because she lost consciousness. But she's doing better. She's still in the hospital, though, so the rest of us came home."

"Her poor parents," Ginny says.

Okay—my turn to ask some questions. "So, um . . . what are you two up to?"

"We just had dinner." Ginny glances over at my father. "I can't even remember how we ended up making plans—"

"You called me," Dad says. "This afternoon."

"And then you said you were all alone for the entire weekend." She smiles at him. She's wearing bright red lipstick—must have just reapplied it in the car, because it looks fresh and glossy. "I took pity on you."

"Ha," Dad says without any actual mirth. "We had an amazing dinner," he tells me. "At Jocasta. They had this swordfish special that was unbelievable. There was a crust made out of tapenade and bread crumbs—it wasn't like anything I've had before. All salty and crisp . . . I couldn't get Ginny to try it, though."

"I had quinoa," she says. "Which was delicious."

"Quinoa," my father says, shaking his head. "Glorified animal feed."

"It was delicious," she says again.

"And now here you are," I say. "Continuing the fun?"

Dad clears his throat uncomfortably. "I happened to mention the Hockney lithograph in my office. Ginny hadn't seen it, so . . ."

"You sure it isn't an etching?" I say sweetly.

They both pretend they didn't hear that. "So now that we're here, let's make our way into the office," Dad says to Ginny.

"Yes, and then I should probably go. It's getting late, and I don't want to impose."

There's a pause, which Dad should probably fill with "The night is still young" or something of that sort, but doesn't.

"You kids do whatever you want," I say, flapping my hand airily. "I'm going to bed."

Back in my room, I wonder what would have

happened if I hadn't been home. Dad would probably have poured them both a drink. They would have sat somewhere in this big, empty house sipping wine or whiskey and talking about . . . what? I'm not sure. Dad would have talked about work or food or wine or something that interests him, and Ginny would have nodded and listened and licked her red lips.

Sometimes I forget that Dad's a man. He's dated women but never in any way that's affected my life. He usually goes out somewhere with them and doesn't bring them back to our house. So I never think about whether he has the kind of dates that lead to sex. It's not something you want to think about your father, anyway. But Dad's handsome and in good shape—and let's not forget that he makes a decent income, because I'm guessing Ginny hasn't—and even though he's not the most introspective or sensitive guy in the world, he has decent social skills. He can be gallant. He's not a Neanderthal. Or a loser. He's just . . .

Self-centered. Conceited. Distracted. Obsessed with food and exercise.

I wouldn't want to go out with someone like him. Not in a million years. I've never once in my life thought, Gee, I wish I could find a boy who's just like my dad. Pretty much the opposite. But Ginny Clay seems to like him. Maybe it's a tougher dating world out there for annoying young women than I realized. Maybe Dad's an easy target, and she wants a sugar daddy. Or maybe she really likes him.

That last possibility makes me sit up straight. Right there on my bed in my red footsie pajamas. (Lucy gave them to me last Christmas—she has a matching pair.)

Could Ginny actually *like* Dad?

Could he actually like her?

Because that might change the way I look at the whole thing.

I mean, if Ginny's just some kind of desperate gold digger who figures she'll get a bunch of expensive (vegetarian) meals and maybe some jewelry out of Dad—or even, if all goes well, a lifetime of alimony—I definitely don't want her around.

But what if she's just a girl who likes a guy? I may question her taste—and his too, if he likes her back—but do I have the right to condemn her for it?

Not really. No more than Wally's parents had a right to order Molly out of their house. People should love whoever they want to love.

Even if they're both annoying.

Especially if they're both annoying. Because then they're lucky to have found each other.

I figure I'll keep my eyes on ol' Ginny. If she's faking all this interest in my father just to squeeze some cash out of him, I'll make life difficult for her. But if I think she and Dad actually like each other, I'll leave them alone. They're adults.

I feel virtuous and evolved and at peace . . . for an entire three minutes, right until I hear a Ginny-giggle float upstairs and kind of want to vomit.

Honestly? I can't stand her.

I put the pillow over my head and block out her voice. No one ever said it was easy to be open-minded.

twenty-one

Word travels quickly. Every kid at school on Monday wants to know the details about what happened to Lily.

"What have you been telling people?" Phoebe asks me as we walk into Spanish together on Monday morning.

"Just that she miscalculated the depth of the pool. You?"

"Same. But people keep asking me if she was drunk or stoned or on Ecstasy or anything. I've just been shrugging and changing the subject, but by not saying no, I feel like I'm kind of saying yes."

"I know," I say as we both settle down wearily at desks next to each other. "Same thing here."

I'm happy to see Hilary in line at the cafeteria, especially since she looks a thousand times better than she did the last time I saw her. I ask her how Lily's doing, and she says, "Much better now that she's at home," but then asks me to wait for more details until we're all gathered at the table, so she doesn't have to keep repeating the same information.

By the time we've both gotten our food, Lucy and Finn and Oscar are already eating at our usual table. I sit down next to Oscar, which puts me across from Finn. Our eyes meet, and while the others are talking, I ask him quietly how he's doing.

"Okay." He looks exhausted.

"You sleeping?"

He shakes his head and says in a low voice, "Every time I close my eyes, I see her diving again. It's like those nightmares where you try to stop something from happening and can't—except this really happened."

"But it's all okay now."

"Doesn't make that image go away."

Phoebe and Eric join us at the table, and I turn to Hilary. "*Now* can we ask you all our questions?"

She takes a sip of Diet Coke. "Fire away."

"When will Lily be able to come back?" Lucy asks.

"The doctors say one more week of rest."

"And she's fine?" asks Finn.

"I think so." She hesitates. "Except . . . It's really weird, guys. She can't remember much about that night. And she has these dizzy spells when she can't even stand up. And she gets these bad headaches. And sometimes she uses the wrong word—like just this morning, she said something about my suitcase when she meant backpack. It freaks my mother—she's convinced Lily's brain damaged. But the doctors keep saying all this is pretty normal after a concussion, and she should get better."

"Oh god," says Finn. I look at him. His face is white.

"The doctors say it's normal," I remind him.

"Right," he says tonelessly.

"Is she going crazy having to stay at home?" Phoebe asks Hilary. "I can't picture Lily sitting still for two minutes, let alone a week."

"Okay, that's the other weird thing." Hilary opens up her sandwich and starts scraping the mayonnaise off the bread. "She's been really quiet since the accident. And calm."

"Calm?" Phoebe repeats. "You sure you brought Lily home and not someone else?"

"It's definitely her," Hilary says. "Once she was feeling better, she made friends with everyone in the hospital—the nurses, the doctors, those bedpan guys— oh, and especially that kid they brought in with alcohol poisoning."

"Oh, right, you mentioned him," I say. "How's he doing?"

"He left late last night, right around the same time we did. He and Lily totally bonded while they were in the hospital. They're constantly texting each other."

"Aw, that's kind of sweet," Oscar says. "Fellow sufferers."

"Fellow idiots."

"That's harsh," says Lucy.

"Sorry," Hilary says. "But you know what I mean. I'm glad Lily's going to be okay, but if she hadn't been, it would have been her own fault."

It's kind of a relief to hear Hilary sounding like her old self—if she can dig into Lily again, then she can't be too worried anymore.

I touch Finn's arm as we're all walking out of the cafeteria, and he stops and turns to look at me. "Hilary's not scared anymore," I say. "You don't have to be either."

"I'm working on it. I'll feel better when I actually see her."

"We all will." I'm turning away when he says my name. I turn back.

"I just . . ." He stops. He runs his fingers through his hair and shifts from one foot to the other. Then he says, "I just want to say . . . You've been kind of amazing, Anna. After Lily got hurt, you were the only one who knew what we should do. We were all panicking, and you—"

"You were the one who jumped in after her. That's what made the biggest difference. If you hadn't moved so quickly . . ."

He shakes his head. "That was physical instinct. I wasn't thinking at all. But you kept telling us what to do, and that's what got her to the hospital as quickly as possible, and if she's okay, it's because of you. And you've been great since then too. You've made me feel better—not that I have any right to—"

"I'm not just saying stuff to make you feel better. It really isn't your fault, Finn. You have to see that."

There's a pause, and then he says in a low voice, "I tried to stop her, Anna. But she wouldn't listen to me. You saw that, right?"

"Lily never listens to anyone," I say.

"I know. I thought that was kind of cool. . . ." He stares down at the floor. I follow his gaze, but there's nothing to look at. Just gray-white linoleum with flecks of crimson.

The bell rings. "We'd better run," I say, although part of me—a big part of me—wants to stay there with him. Because something's changed. He's definitely my friend again. Even the way he looks at me . . . it's like he sees me. He's not looking past me anymore, not avoiding my eyes. He sees me.

"Hold on. I wanted to show you something." He pulls out his phone. His voice speeds up. "I saw this photo, and I thought it would be good for one of your paintings. You know how you were looking to do something a little bit different maybe? This is a little bit different.

But it also fits with the other ones. It's a landscape. It's just not like your other landscapes." He flicks through some photos and shows me the one he's talking about. "It was taken near a river in Peru. How incredible are these trees?" There's a long shot of several dense rows of some kind of low tree with crazy, curling branches of leaves—the branches curl so much and the trees are so close to one another that it's hard to see which branches belong to which trees.

He's right—I've never drawn anything like it. I tend to go for more barren landscapes. But this . . . this could be cool. I could outline the leaves in ink and use watercolors to fill them out—no, not watercolors, acrylics, because I want something dense and heavily pigmented; there's a green I love in one of Oresco's sets. I'd use it undiluted in any way for the darkest, shiniest leaves at the bottom, in the shade, but I'd add in a bit of yellow for the ones at the edges and then for the ones all the way at the top, I'd—

Finn's finger shifts on the phone, and I remember where I am.

"Will you email it to me?" I say. "And the name of the website?"

"Yeah." He puts his phone back in his pocket. He stands there a moment, looking at me.

"Thanks," I say. I should move—we're going to be late for our classes—but I don't.

"Sure." A pause. He reaches out his hand for a moment, like he's going to touch my arm or something. But he doesn't. He just lets it drop. Awkwardly. Then says, "Anyway. Bye." And he heads in the opposite direction without another look back.

When school's over, Lucy and I find Hilary and ask her if we can go see Lily.

She says, "I'll let you know as soon as my parents say it's okay. They're being really strict about visitors. Finn drove all the way back to Santa Ynez to see Lily at the hospital yesterday, but Dad only let him say hi and then told him Lily needed to rest up for the ride home. But they've been talking and texting."

No wonder Finn looks so tired—he's probably been talking to Lily all night long. She's stuck in bed, bored, no difference to her between day and night. And he's going to make himself available whenever she wants him, because he feels guilty and sorry for her.

And maybe because he's in love with her. Maybe for that reason too.

Although . . . I'm not as sure about that as I was a couple of weeks ago. Even before the accident, you could tell that she was getting on his nerves more and more.

But it doesn't matter. No matter what, he has to be there for her, for as long as she wants him. Because she's hurt and alone now, and a guy like Finn—who once showed up at school covered with scratches from a sick and hungry feral cat that he had coaxed into eating and then wrestled into a box to take to a shelter—would never abandon someone who's hurt and alone and who needs him. And that's part of why I like him as much as I do and why no other guy has even come close to comparing to him—not back in ninth grade and not since.

I have unexpected visitors that night. Wade and Connor come knocking on our front door around nine.

"Hey," I say when I open the door and find them standing there. "You guys!"

"Us guys!" Wade agrees cheerfully. He kisses me on the cheek—like a cousin, not like a boyfriend.

We made out at the festival, but that feels like a lifetime ago. And in a different universe.

He says, "We came to see how your friend was doing. And to make sure you're okay. Sounds like you had a brutal couple of days."

"It was bad. But it looks like she's going to be fine, which is all that matters. You guys want to come in?"

"Yeah, but only if it's a good time for you. We promise not to stay long."

I lead them into the kitchen and offer them something

to drink. Wade declines, but Connor accepts a glass of orange juice.

"Anyone else home?" Wade asks as we watch Connor drink his juice.

"Just me. I'm not sure where my dad is." I ask them some questions about the rest of the music festival. They say it was basically like that first night: a few great bands but a lot of mediocre ones.

"It's no Coachella," Wade says, and I'm glad Hilary isn't here to hear that.

We're talking about the kid who went to the hospital with alcohol poisoning—James Baskille—and Connor says he knows him a little. "We played on the same AYSO team when we were, like, ten. I see him at parties sometimes. He's a total animal."

"And if *you* say that . . ." Wade gives me a comical raised-eyebrow look. He's sitting on the stool next to me. He sits up straight. "Oh, hey, guess what, Anna? I just sent in my Stanford EA application."

"Cool. Good luck."

"Thanks. It's kind of terrifying." He nudges my arm lightly. "So . . . I was wondering . . . Could you do me a really big favor?"

"What's that?"

"Ask your dad to make a call for me? To the admissions office there? Or write a letter, if that's easier."

I hesitate, and he says quickly, "No worries if he doesn't want to. I figured it couldn't hurt to ask."

"I'm honestly not sure what he'd say. He doesn't really know you."

"He could get to know me! Just say the word, and I'll move right in with you. This house has lots of bedrooms, right?"

I laugh.

"And you can vouch for me, can't you? Tell him I'm only moderately horrible?"

"Sure. I'll do what I can." It's not the kind of thing my dad tends to do, but Wade is a relative. Sort of.

He swivels in the stool so he can nudge my knee with his. "Thanks."

"Oh, right," Connor says, looking up. There are flecks of orange pulp in the corners of his mouth. "Wade told me your dad is super-connected at Stanford. Can he help me too?"

"Ignore him," Wade says, rolling his eyes.

Connor shoots him a look. "Hey, man, if you can stalk her because of her connections, so can I."

"Stalk me?" I repeat.

He nods. "Yeah, Wade's totally obsessed with finding people who can help him get into Stanford. He's been online-stalking you and your dad for months."

"Not true," Wade says hastily, shaking his head emphatically. "Anna and I met by accident at a

Starbucks a few weeks ago."

Connor rolls his eyes. "But you already knew who she was. Come on, man, just admit it. You were obsessed with tracking them down. Anna doesn't mind, right, Anna? I mean, it's about getting into college. We're *all* obsessed."

I nod absently, because I'm thinking furiously. About how Wade occasionally goes through the motions of acting like he's interested in me . . . but doesn't actually seem all that interested in me. The only time he made a move was when he was stoned. Sober, he says the right things but doesn't show any real signs of wanting to, like, touch me or anything. And when he dropped by my house that other time, he seemed more excited to spend time with my father than to be alone with me. In fact, he *left* once he had talked to Dad, even though we had a chance to be alone then.

So . . . what does that mean?

That he's been using me to get to my father, I guess. And it sounds like he's using my father to get into Stanford—or would if he could.

Suddenly I like Wade a lot less than I did a few minutes ago. And, oddly, I like Connor a lot *more*. He may be annoying, but at least what you see is what you get. With Wade, clearly there's a lot that's hidden. You might even say underhanded.

Or slimy.

I feel stupid and a little bruised around the ego. For all he knew, I could have been falling in love with him. The fact that I wasn't . . . well, if I'm being honest, it's because I've had Finn around to compare him to. And Wade doesn't come close. I mean, he didn't come close even *before* I knew he was manipulative and dishonest. Now he's miles away.

But I guess Wade and I are even in one respect: I was also just going through the motions of being romantically interested. The truth was that I liked the idea of getting swept away by someone, since Finn and Lily were becoming a couple—which is probably why I ended up kissing Wade right after the two of them started making out in front of me. And maybe that's not as self-serving as wanting a letter of recommendation for college, but it still wasn't entirely sincere, and I'm not convinced I have a strong moral upper hand here. So there's no point in getting angry.

Well, maybe there's a little point.

And maybe there's also a little point in stringing Wade on for a while. I mean, it's kind of funny that he's been trying to charm a letter of recommendation out of me. Why not let him keep trying? He's not getting one, not now that I realize what's been going on—but *he* doesn't know that.

"There is so much freakin' pulp in here," Connor says now, squinting at his juice, oblivious to the sudden tension in the room. "Do you have any that's pulp-free? This is like drinking something that's"—he searches for the right phrase and lands on—"that's not a real liquid."

"We're out of here," Wade says, rising to his feet abruptly. "Crazy amounts of homework." He's assessing me out of the corner of his eye. I assume he's trying to gauge whether or not I completely absorbed what Connor was saying and what it means about our friendship.

I give him a big, fake smile. "Yeah, me too."

At the door he says, "So you'll ask your father? About the Stanford thing?" He just can't let go of that.

My smile broadens. "Why wouldn't I?"

twenty-two

Hilary invites Lucy and me to visit Lily on Thursday night. She won't be back in school until Monday, but her parents are finally willing to let her have a quick visit from her closest friends.

When Lorena leads us into the family room, Hilary's already in there with Lily, who's sharing the sofa with a strange guy about our age. He's sitting at one end, and she's reclining full-length like an old-fashioned consumptive heroine—although her tight Lululemon workout pants and matching tank top ruin the effect a little. She's not wearing makeup, and she looks pale and there are dark circles under her eyes, but she smiles happily as we enter and holds her arms out to us. Lucy and I run over and hug her.

"You scared us," I whisper as I press my cheek against hers. "Don't ever do anything like that again."

"I won't," she promises. As we step back, she gestures to the kid sitting at the other end of the sofa. "Do you guys know James?"

He raises his hand in greeting. He's got longish hair and eyebrows that are shaped like steep hills, and he's small and slim. Basically he looks like an elf.

"James and I were in the hospital together," Lily says. "We bonded over the horrible food and the crazy nurses."

"And the fact we had both done really stupid things to get there," he adds.

"Especially that." They smile at each other. A private smile that excludes the rest of us.

"I don't actually remember much about that night." She turns back to us as Lucy and I both perch on the arms of the big upholstered chair near her. "Isn't that weird? I remember getting to the hotel and going to the music festival, but then it all gets fuzzy. You ran into a friend, right, Anna? A guy? With red hair?"

"There was a redheaded guy," I say. "But the one who was my friend has dark hair. He's my cousin, remember?"

She shakes her head with a rueful smile. "It's so weird. I get freaked out when I try to remember and can't, so I try not to think about that night too much."

I wonder if she remembers making out with Finn.

Weird to think she might not. Even weirder for him. I wonder why he's not here tonight—and that other guy is.

"Hil's filled me in on what I've forgotten," she says. "Or at least whatever she was there for—I guess we split up for a while?" Lucy and I glance at each other but just nod silently. "I know I dove into the . . . um . . . you know—the—not the hot tub—the—" She looks at James.

"The pool," he says gently.

She nods. "Right. The pool." She sees the expressions on our faces and laughs a little. "Don't worry, guys. I do this all the time. It's a retrieval thing—the doctor says it'll get better soon. Anyway, I know I dove in after you guys told me not to. And sometimes I almost remember doing it, but I think it's a . . . you know . . . false memory. I only remember because people have told me about it." There's something different about how she talks. She's not as rapid-fire, not as confident. She stops between every few words, searching for what she wants to say next. It's her voice but with someone else's rhythm.

"What about you?" Lucy asks James. "Why were you in the hospital?"

"Someone dared me to drink a bottle of whiskey in five minutes." He smiles weakly. "I'm sure you'll all be happy to know I succeeded."

"And almost died of alcohol poisoning," Lily says.

"But didn't."

"Which is a very good thing." Because she's lying on the sofa and he's sitting at the end, her bare feet are near his leg. She flexes her right foot so her toes lightly brush against the outside of his thigh.

I stare at her foot. What's that about?

"We both hit bottom," Lily says. "I mean, I *literally* hit bottom with the pool, but metaphorically too. James and I kept talking in the hospital about how we felt like we'd both been on this *path*, and then suddenly we were thrown off of it and could see how stupid it was."

"Is this, like, a sobriety thing?" Lucy asks, her forehead wrinkled.

Lily shakes her head. "Nothing that obvious or clichéd. I don't even know how to describe it. . . ." She looks over at James.

He puts his hand on her ankle, gently squeezing it. "We both realized we'd been pushing ourselves to do crazier and crazier things because we thought that would make life more intense and interesting. But if you don't let yourself feel what's actually going on at any given moment—if you're always looking for the next rush— you get numb and stop feeling anything. And that just makes you look for the next excitement in the hope it will break through the numbness. You get on this bad spiral." His eyes burn with intensity as he gazes at Lily. "What we both went through—it was like a reminder to stop. To slow down. To take each moment as it comes. I know it sounds like new-age crap when I try to put it into words, but it feels true to me."

"To me too," Lily says softly. And her toes brush his thigh again.

Hilary's mom buzzes down on the intercom. "Time to say good-bye, girls," says her disembodied voice. "Lily needs to save her strength for school."

Lucy and I say our good-byes and stand up, but James stays where he is. He and Lily are talking in voices too low for us to hear as we walk out of the room.

"Well, the good news is Lily finally has something to write her college essay about," I whisper to Lucy.

"No joke," she says. "I bet it really will be about how the accident changed her life."

Hilary follows us to the door. I shake the car key invitingly and say, "Boba run, guys?"

"Definitely," says Hilary. "I've got to get out of here. My parents aren't talking to each other, and Lily's either with James or talking to him."

"Sounds good to me," says Lucy. "But we can't take too long. I have a ton of homework."

"So what's the story with this guy?" I ask, once we're settled in my car. I'm driving, Lucy's riding shotgun, and Hilary's in the back. "He and Lily seemed awfully cozy."

"Yeah, I was wondering about that too," Lucy says.

"Okay, so it's not just me," Hilary says. "They feel like more than friends, right?"

"What about Finn?" Lucy asks.

"Yeah," I say, wondering if I sound too eager. "What about Finn?"

Hilary leans forward and rests her elbows on the edge of our seat backs. "Good question. My parents finally agreed to let him come over last night, but Lily invited James too, so they were both there. And Lily and James kept talking about the hospital and how different they feel now—and Finn just sat there. And then left. James stayed much later."

"Poor Finn," Lucy says. "After that make-out session—"

"Wait, what?" Hilary says. "What make-out session?"

"Oh, right. You weren't there. She wasn't there," Lucy says to me.

"When we split up at the music festival," I say to Hil's reflection in the rearview mirror. "Remember? Finn and Lily and Lucy and I went to see that other band, and then we ran into my cousin and his friend, and then we all got a little stoned, and then—"

"Everyone started swapping spit but me and that

other guy," Lucy interrupts. "And that loser actually thought he had a chance—"

"Not the point right now," I say.

"I don't think Lily remembers anything about that," Hilary says. "She's never said anything about it to me, and she's forgotten most of what happened that night. She always says she doesn't remember much other than arriving at the festival. And eating kale chips—for some reason she remembers the kale chips."

"That's so weird," I say. A little giddily. Because if Lily doesn't remember that she and Finn had gotten physical with each other that night, and if she really likes this guy James (and her foot certainly seems to), then—

I stop myself. Then what? Even if she doesn't like Finn anymore, that doesn't mean that he's stopped liking *her*. Or has started liking me again. All that stuff he said about her being brave and my being a coward—none of that goes away just because Lily has a new crush.

"I'm pretty sure Finn remembers making out with *her*," Lucy says lightly. Then, more seriously: "Did you see his face when she was unconscious? He looked like he'd been shot."

"I know," Hil says. "And he was constantly texting me to see how she was doing."

"Tell Lily to let him down easy," I say. Because I

don't want Finn to be hurt again by a girl. Once was too many times.

"You could comfort him," Lucy says. For a second I think she's talking to me, and I freeze, embarrassed to be read so easily, but then I realize she's looking over her shoulder at Hilary. "I mean, if he's available now, why not? You've always had a thing for him."

Hilary shakes her head. "Not if he already made out with Lily. That's gross. There are rules."

"There are?" Lucy says. She appeals to me. "There are?"

"Not that I know about. But I've never been attracted to the kind of guys"—I correct myself—"the kind of *people* my sisters like. So it hasn't ever come up with us."

"Maybe it's a twin thing," Hilary says. "The idea of kissing someone Lily's already kissed . . . Bleah. Anyway, I gave up on him a long time ago. Maybe it's sour grapes, but I have issues with someone who'd choose Lily over me. You know what I mean?"

"Yeah," Lucy says. "That's definitely sour grapes."

"Shut up," Hilary says. "It's not. It's a matter of taste."

I want to ask them if they really really really think Lily's over Finn, but there's no way to ask without sounding like it matters to me, and I don't want them to know it matters to me. Because even if she's over him, he could still be in love with her, and even if he's over her, she could still be in love with him, and even if they're both over each other, he might still not be interested in me, and anyway the conversation's moved on, and I'm mostly relieved that it has.

twenty-three

The next day, Friday, I check my texts after school and see one from Wade.

You talked to your father yet? I could come talk to him myself, if that's better

No, I'll deal with it

Great. Like I said, I already sent in my EA application

Cool

I'm deliberately missing his point—that there's a rush on this. My goal is to drive him a little crazy, by letting him think he's got a shot at getting a letter out of my dad but never actually making it happen. I'm enjoying the thought of him staring at his phone, trying to figure out how to get me to move faster on this without alienating me altogether. He's going to tie himself in knots trying . . . and then it will be too late, and I'll blithely tell him I never bothered to ask Dad for the letter.

It's a small, petty revenge, but I'm enjoying it. He should have picked a different alum's daughter to target.

I'm on my way to the art room, but I come to a halt in the mostly empty hallway when I see Finn leaning against his locker. He's staring somberly at something on his own phone.

"Hey," I say, and he looks up. "Everything okay?"

He holds out the phone to me without a word. I take it and read the text. It's from Lily.

I'll always think you're great. But a lot's changed for me.

"Oh." I hand the phone back to him, trying to read his expression. He looks unhappy. Well, why wouldn't he be? Lily's broken up with him. I can't be equally sad about that, but I can be sympathetic. "That doesn't sound good. I'm sorry."

"Did you hear about this James guy?" he asks.

"I met him."

"Me too. She told me they connect on some deep, emotional level."

"I guess being in the hospital at the same time turned them into soul mates."

"Did you know she liked him this much?"

I shake my head. "Only that they had bonded. Not that she was going to . . . do *that*." I gesture at his phone. "Are you okay?"

He rams his phone into his pocket and stands there biting his lip for a second before taking a deep breath. "If I tell you something, will you promise not to hate me?"

"Easiest promise I've ever made," I say lightly. But I mean it.

"I feel so guilty right now. Not just because of the accident—"

"Which wasn't your fault."

He waves that off. "I could have prevented it. I should have. Anyway, that's just part of it. Mostly I feel guilty because just now, when I got that text from Lily, I was *relieved*."

"Relieved?" I repeat. That's not what I expected him to say.

But I like hearing it.

He nods and leans back against the lockers. Some kids walk by, and he gives them a chin-jerk nod as they pass. "That night at the festival . . . she was driving me crazy. She wouldn't listen to anything I said. She was totally out of control."

"I thought you liked that she was so impulsive. I mean up until the pool thing—"

"I liked it at first. Then I tolerated it. But even before we left town, I was starting to feel like maybe I couldn't tolerate it much longer. I kept trying to convince myself it was a good thing that she always did just what she wanted at any given moment, but it was seeming less and less good—especially the night of the festival. If she hadn't gotten hurt, I was going to try to pull back. But then, after the accident . . ." He trails off.

"I don't know," I say slowly. "You looked like you were enjoying her company plenty that night . . . when we were all sitting in that circle . . ."

He flushes and looks away. "I was caught up in the moment."

"Yes. Yes, you were."

"What about you?" He wheels around with sudden energy. "That guy you were inhaling—"

"Inhaling?"

"Practically."

"I was caught up in the moment?"

"Seriously—"

"Seriously. In the light of day, he's kind of a jerk. Long story. And that night, we were both a little stoned, and it was just the thing to do at the moment. . . . But you and Lily—I mean, you told me you thought she was brave."

"I still think she's brave," he says. "But also irresponsible."

"That's not what you were saying to me when we were waiting for the Molten Pops."

"I know. I'm sorry. I was sort of trying to make

a point. But I was pretty sure we were doomed as a couple."

"You sure you're not just saying that because she likes someone else now?"

He gestures at himself with a grin. "Do I *look* heartbroken?"

Actually, no. He looks kind of happy. But he hadn't when I first came upon him in the hallway. The smile just appeared.

Roughly around the time I said Wade was a jerk.

That realization makes my heart speed up. I tell myself not to get too excited by this whole conversation. The past hasn't changed. The past never does. Still . . .

I say abruptly, "Come with me to the art room. I want to show you what I've been working on."

He hesitates. "I was supposed to meet Oscar five minutes ago."

"Oh." So I was right: nothing's changed, and I read too much into one quick smile.

But then he says, "Just give me a second to text him."

Oh. Okay.

He sends his text, and then we move down the hallway side by side, falling into step together without trying.

Mr. Oresco is organizing some supplies in the artroom cabinet. He looks over his shoulder when we enter. "Anna! Come to finish that painting?"

"I was thinking about it. Is that okay?"

"Fine. I'm leaving in two minutes, though. Do you mind locking up when you go? You know the drill, right?"

"Yep. No problem." I retrieve my painting from the drying rack and spread it out on one of the tables, beckoning to Finn to come see.

He joins me at the table, leans over and studies it, then looks up again. "You used the photo I sent you!"

I nod. I painted those thick, curly, leaf-laden trees with the shiniest, most intense greens I could find. The branches intertwine so much, you can't tell which belongs to which trunk, just like in the original photo.

"I want to go there," Finn says, gazing down at it. "It's so beautiful. Except . . . there's something hidden, right? There's always something hidden. Ah, there you go." He's spotted the little figures I've drawn off to one side. "What are they? They look . . . rusty."

"They might be made of metal," is all I say. I like to keep things a little vague with my art. I have my own ideas about what's going on, but it's fun to me when people come up with different ones.

"It's not a good world for someone who's made out of metal," Finn says, staring at it thoughtfully. "All that greenery—it must rain a lot."

I nod. "Maybe they're far from home. Or aren't supposed to go outside."

"I wonder how they got there."

"There might have been a spaceship crash," I say.

"Or a wormhole?"

"Or maybe there's a guy who lives in an old, crumbling mansion just outside this forest who makes his own metal slaves, and a couple of them escaped."

"That one," Finn says. "I like that one."

"Me too." It's how I imagined it.

Mr. Oresco calls out a cheerful "Good-bye! See you tomorrow, Anna," and the door shuts after him, leaving us alone.

Finn studies the painting some more. "There's fruit on the tree they're standing under. I didn't see it before."

"Just on that one."

"Oh my god." He stands up straight, and he's shaking his head and laughing a little. "One of them has its little robot hand on a piece of fruit! But the other's backing away. It's Adam and Eve, isn't it?"

I'm so pleased he got it that I bounce up on my toes like a little kid.

"So the one reaching for the fruit—that's a female?" he says.

"I don't know. Maybe they don't have genders."

"It's *Eve*," Finn says. "She has to be a female. She

knows she shouldn't eat the fruit, but she does it, anyway. *Because* she shouldn't. Which makes her a total girl, and I'm allowed to say that because I'm a card-carrying feminist."

"But the other one gives in, which makes him just as guilty." I point at the painting, and we both peer down at it again. "He's scared, but he's not leaving. The second she offers him a bite, he's going to take it."

"Maybe he'll distract her. Offer her a Snickers bar or something."

I shake my head. "That's not how the story goes. They *have* to eat the fruit. Adam and Eve always have to eat the fruit, or we'd still all be in the Garden of Eden."

"It's possible," Finn says, turning his head to look at me, "that that would be a boring place to be." We both stand all the way up, still looking at each other. He says, "I think—" and stops.

"What?"

"It's just . . . I've been thinking." He stops again.

"What about?"

"About you," he says, and my pulse jumps. "The thing is," he says slowly, not quite meeting my eyes, "not many people can do *this*." He gestures at the painting. "And the fact that you just do it, quietly, on your own, not shoving anything in anyone's face, not dancing all over the place saying *Look at me, I'm so creative and wild and free* . . . You just make art because you can. And that's cool, Anna. Genuinely cool. Not forced or fake cool. The real thing."

My cheeks are flushing with pleasure. Even my nose feels warm.

I've gotten used to feeling overlooked and dismissed. Especially by him. This feels so good, I don't know what to do with it.

I struggle for a response that will let him know how much his praise means to me without making myself look needy. "Thanks. And just so you know, every photo you've ever shown me . . . they've all inspired me. *You've* inspired me." I quickly add, "Don't feel weird about that or anything. It's just that you have good taste in photos. That's all."

He laughs a little, and I realize how stupid that sounded, and I laugh too, sheepishly. My embarrassed smile freezes on my lips, because he leans forward and hesitates, his face near mine, his eyes scanning mine uncertainly.

Like he's thinking about kissing me but isn't sure I'll want him to.

And I do. I do want him to. More than anything else in the world. So I tilt my face up toward his. Then panic. What if that wasn't what he meant at all? I start to pull back, wondering if he noticed how eager I looked, wondering how I can cover this stupid stupid mistake of thinking he wanted to kiss me when he was probably just shifting his feet—

And then his mouth comes down on mine.

So it wasn't a mistake.

Maybe I'm done making mistakes. Or at least ones that concern Finn Westbrook.

That would be nice.

twenty-four

Once upon a time, Finn Westbrook and I kissed each other a lot. But that was years ago.

Now his lips are on mine again. Again *and* for the very first time.

His mouth touches mine, lightly at first, then, as I lean up into the kiss, more confidently. For a while that's enough, just that awesome warmth against my mouth and the sense that his body's close to mine.

I've been wanting this so much, missing it so badly.

I grow hungrier, and I guess he does too, because he pulls me firmly against his chest as our mouths linger and explore and remember. He's a lot taller than he was the last time we held each other this close. I like the way his shoulders feel under my tightening fingers. I like that they're so much broader than his waist. I like that now I have to arch my neck up to reach him.

But I also like that his hair feels the way it used

to—thick and alive under my twining fingers—and that he tastes the same, a heady mixture of peppermint and something warm and earthy and unique. He's definitely the same Finn, the one I've missed so much these last few years. The layer of familiarity under all this discovery—it's like having a wild, exciting adventure and then finding your childhood blanket waiting for you when you make camp. Everything's new and wonderful, but there's comfort and safety here too.

I don't want to stop kissing him. Not ever. He starts to pull away, and I grab on to his waist, almost panicking, but he just wants to whisper something.

"I'm kind of glad Eve ate that fruit."

I express my wholehearted agreement with that sentiment by rising up on my toes and seeking out his lips again.

This has to go on forever. I don't ever want to do anything else. I can't think of a single thing that's more important than being held tight against Finn's chest. I would happily wave away any and all college offers if it meant I could spend the next four years in this room alone with him.

He doesn't seem to be in any rush to move along either.

I'm planning to stay there with him until the building falls down around our ears sometime during some intergalactic planetary war in the far distant future, but the plan is ruined by the stupid door, which bangs loudly open.

"Well, what have we got here?" says a delighted voice.

We aren't doing anything wrong—I'd say we're finally getting something right—but we jump apart guiltily, anyway.

Ginny Clay regards us from the doorway, her arms folded, her narrow face alight with sly amusement. She wags her finger at me and sings out, "Busted!"

Life is funny: one moment I'm in pure bliss, the next I want to commit murder.

I should have locked the door. Oresco told me to lock the door. Why didn't I lock the door?

Finn touches my arm and, when I look at him, says softly, "I should go. I totally forgot about Oscar. He's waiting for me."

"Go?" I repeat forlornly. How can he go? We just found each other again.

He laughs at my expression. "I know where you live," he says. "Expect to see me soon."

"How soon?"

He leans his head toward me, his eyes so close, I can see the outline of his contacts around the irises. "I'll come over tonight. Promise."

I nod, and he heads toward the door. I feel stunned as I watch him walk away. He's mine again. He was and then he wasn't and now he is. Somehow I got back the thing I missed so deeply and wanted so badly. I'm not sure how. But I did.

He slips out the door with a polite nod in Ginny's direction as he passes her.

"Well, well, well," Ginny says, once we're alone, tilting her head to the side with a little wink. "Looks like someone's made the art room her very own little love nest."

I'm sure she thinks she's teasing me the way a big sister would. And she's not wrong. Lizzie would probably be just as annoying in this situation.

"I was finishing up some work," I say, and pointedly turn back to my painting. I still have to fill in the sky. I want it to be very sunny right above the tree, with ominous clouds hovering way off in the distance. Streaks of dark purple in the coming storm.

"Don't worry," Ginny says, coming closer. "I was joking about busting you. I won't say a word to your father. Not if you don't want me to."

"Do whatever you want." I move over to the paint cabinet and consider my options.

Ginny leans against the counter, watching me. "Don't pretend to be working, Anna. You can't possibly focus after *that*. Let's talk about it! That was Finn Westbrook, right? The kid who left school and came back? He's very cute. A lot of the girls on the volleyball team have crushes on him. Well done!"

I try to imagine a universe in which Ginny's approval of my love life would mean something to me, but I can't. I bring some tubes of paint, a few brushes, and a palette back to the worktable and sit down on the stool. "I really need to focus," I say.

She comes closer and looks over my shoulder, studying the picture for a few minutes before saying, "I don't get it. The landscape is beautiful—but why the weird little creatures?"

"It's what I do."

She shakes her head. "But wasn't the point for you to stretch yourself? Why not just do a pretty landscape for once? Prove that you've got the basic skills covered and that you're not a psychopath. Not that *I'm* saying you're a psychopath, of course—"

"Nice save."

"Just that the school might *think* you are with all your creepy hidden little drawings. You don't want admissions people to worry that they're letting in a serial killer, Anna. They'll be looking for reasons to turn kids away, anyway—why hand them one?"

"Mmm." Noncommittal sounds may be the way to go with Ginny.

She waits for more, but I keep prepping my paints in silence. I really want to be alone to think about what just happened with Finn, but she won't leave.

"I'm serious about not telling your dad," she says, after a moment. "About Finn, I mean. You can trust me, Anna."

"Do you honestly think my dad would care?"

She waves her hands around in the air. "Of course. I mean, he's not a prude or anything—I mean, I *assume* he's not, I don't know—but you're his little girl, and it can be uncomfortable sometimes for a father—"

"The thing is," I say, cutting her off, "Dad and I? We leave each other's personal lives alone. He doesn't criticize my choices, and I don't criticize his. And that's a good thing, don't you think?" I fix her with a long, innocent stare.

She takes a step back. "I guess," she says. And tells me she's late for practice and has to run. Leaving me blissfully alone to paint my sky and think about Finn.

In the middle of everything that's making me happy is one small thing that's making me worried, so instead of driving home after I'm done painting, I head to the twins' house.

Lorena lets me in as usual and tells me she didn't know I was coming. "Neither did I," I say. "Are the twins home?"

"Hilary has Krav Maga. But Lily is here. She has a friend over. They're up in her room."

"Can I go up?"

"Yes. I think so." But she seems oddly hesitant. "Just, maybe . . . knock first. If the door's closed."

"Of course," I say, and head up the curved, enormous stairway that rises from the front foyer up to the second story. I prefer the smaller, straight stairway in the back of the house, but this is the fastest way to Lily's bedroom. At least her parents aren't around—I really don't want to have to make small talk with them. I want to see Lily and leave as quickly as possible.

I make my way along the carpeted hallway, which goes on for longer than you'd think an upstairs hallway could go, and find Lily's room. Her door *is* closed, so I knock.

"Who is it?" Lily's voice calls out. A little breathlessly.

"It's Anna," I tell the door. It's white, but the panels are outlined in silver paint. Gilding the Lily, I think every time I see it. It's one of my mother's favorite phrases and one of the few things about her that's stuck to me. "I should have texted, but I was already in my car and had a question for you. Can I come in?"

"Yeah—wait—one sec." There are sounds of shifting and moving, and then she's standing in the suddenly open doorway. She hugs me. "Hi! I'm glad you came by. You know James, right?"

I look past her. James is sitting on her bed. His shoes are off. He waves at me.

"Hi again," I say, and I almost burst out laughing,

because I realize I already have the answer to my question. But I'm here now. "I need her for one second," I tell James. "We'll be right back." I grab Lily and pull her across the hallway into Hilary's room and shut the door behind us, then turn to her. "How much do you like James?"

She raises her eyebrows. "*That's* what you wanted to ask me?"

"Sort of. I mean, I came here to ask you how you were feeling about Finn these days, but I feel like they're related. Not the guys. The questions. You know what I mean."

She crosses her arms and studies me. Her hair is slightly rumpled, especially in back. She's wearing just a tank top and yoga pants. Her mascara is slightly smeared.

I definitely interrupted something.

"Why are you asking?" she says. "Do you like Finn?"

I look down at the carpet. Hilary picked it out, so it's very practical: dark blue with an abstract gray design that couldn't show dirt if it tried. The carpet in Lily's room is white with neon-green polka dots.

"Yeah," I say. "But I needed to talk to you before anything happened." Okay, that's a little dishonest, since it implied nothing has happened yet. "Before anything really serious happened," I amend it to, which is slightly more truthful.

"Oh, for god's sake," Lily says. I look up at her. She's rolling her eyes. "If you like him and he likes you, then to hell with me or anyone else who gets in your way. That's how it *should* be."

"You're not helping," I say. "I don't want it to be like that."

"Did he tell you I already basically broke up with him?"

"Yeah. It's the 'basically' that worries me."

She breathes out sharply, impatiently. "I couldn't *really* break up with him because we weren't really going out."

"Still—"

"Anna," Lily says, cutting me off impatiently. "Finn's a nice guy, but—" She shrugs. "He can't compare to James. Not for me. Sorry."

"Don't be sorry," I say, and I start laughing, mostly because I'm so relieved, but also a little bit because it's so funny to me that anyone could like that guy—that slightly ridiculous, mildly pompous elf—more than Finn. But I know that's how this romantic stuff works: one girl's perfect guy is another girl's reject. And right now I'm glad of it. Lily's welcome to James. Hallelujah for James!

Lily goes back to her elf, and I go home to shower

and change and dry my hair and fool around with my makeup. And even though "singing" isn't on the agenda, I end up doing a lot of that too while I'm doing all that other stuff.

twenty-five

Early that evening I hear a car pull up in front of our house, and I look out the window. It's Finn's Volt. I run downstairs and fling open the door. Then I step back, shy suddenly and a little scared that he's going to say something like, *We both know what happened today was a mistake, right?*

He peers at my face. "Everything okay?"

He looks anxious, and I realize that my hesitation is making him wonder if *I* have doubts, and that we could go on passing our anxiety back and forth for a while, each of us wondering if the other regrets what happened until we're completely dysfunctional . . . and that seems like a waste of a potentially awesome evening.

So I reach out, grab him by the sleeve—he's put on a light blue hoodie since I last saw him and changed from contacts to glasses—and drag him over the threshold. "Get in here," I say, and throw my arms around him.

That's clearly all he was waiting for. He clutches me so hard that we stumble over our own feet and almost fall over but laughingly manage to catch ourselves in time. We wind up safely propped against the door, locked in a kiss that lasts for a good long time. His glasses bump into my temple at some point, and I pull my head back.

"Sorry," he says. "I should have left my contacts in."

"No. I like these. They make you look like old Finn."

"Do you like old Finn better than new Finn?"

"I like seeing that he's still in there."

"I haven't changed all that much," he says. "I still like the same girl I did in ninth grade."

"Not still," I correct him. "Again."

He shakes his head. "I never stopped. I tried to but couldn't." I'm curious about that, but he's distracted, glancing around the foyer. "I probably should have asked this before, but is anyone else home?"

"Not right now. But my dad could show up any minute. Want to go up to my room just to be safe?"

He raises his eyebrows. "You move fast."

I heave an exaggerated sigh. "Finn, I've known you for, like, four years. There was a break in the middle, but all things considered, I'd say we've moved pretty slowly. Anyway, my room is just the easiest place for us to hang out in. It's not a brothel."

"Well, that's a relief," he says disappointedly.

"Don't worry—it's not a temple of purity either. Follow me." I lead him up the stairs and into my room. "Oops. I probably should have cleaned it first." I cringe as I survey it with the eyes of a stranger: dirty clothes overflow my wicker hamper and make cloth puddles on the floor all around it; schoolbooks and my laptop lie in a circle on my unmade bed, since that's where I was doing homework before Finn arrived; and my desk is covered with its usual mixture of art supplies, CDs, and old dishes. I eat in my room a lot, since I eat alone a lot. "I'll clear some space for us."

I start stacking up the books and papers on my bed.

"I'll help you," Finn says.

"You don't have to clean my room."

"I like organizing." He starts moving swiftly around the room, making neat piles of CDs and putting books back onto my shelves. He stacks up the dirty dishes and carries them all down to the kitchen for me. By the time he's back, I've picked up my laundry off the floor, made the now uncluttered bed, and even arranged the pillows at the head in the way they're supposed to be and haven't been since the day I first bought the matching bedding when we moved into this house ten years ago.

Finn stands in the doorway, surveying our work.

"Much better," he says.

"You're weird."

"What makes you say that?"

"A girl invites you up to her room, and you clean it."

"Are you questioning my masculinity?" He lunges at me, literally sweeps me up in his arms, then deposits me on top of the bed on my back. He looms over me.

I grin up at him. "Not questioning it anymore. Just enjoying it."

"Much better." He looks around. "Now where *did* I put my feather duster?"

"Shut up," I say, and pull him down on top of me. We have a lot of catching up to do.

Eventually the making out gives way to talking—because we have a lot of catching up there too, and I still want to know what he meant when he said he never stopped liking me. Which seems equally wonderful and impossible.

He's on his back, and I'm curled up against him, my head pillowed on his shoulder, his arm wrapped around mine. Maybe there are better places in the world to be. Maybe there are people happier than me right now. But I'd need a lot of proof before I'd believe it.

"I thought I'd blown it with you forever," I tell him, lacing my fingers through his and rubbing my cheek against his T-shirted chest. (When did his hoodie come off? Oh, right. I tore it off him—it was getting in my way.)

"I thought you had too," he says. "All that time I was

away . . . you became like this monster. The Girl Who Humiliated Me. I thought that when I actually saw you again for real, you'd look all twisted and evil and ugly, that my eyes would finally be open to your true appearance. And there you were, just as pretty as ever. Prettier. With your quiet smile and that little mischievous glint in your eye—"

"I have a mischievous glint?"

"It's your finest quality."

"So you don't like anything else about me?"

He gives me a punitive little shake. "You're not getting any more compliments out of me, so stop trying. Anyway, it was very disturbing to see you again. You weren't supposed to be cute. You were supposed to have fangs and horns and a unibrow."

"I'm sorry I disappointed you. Did you really hate me that much?"

"Only when I wasn't with you." He brushes his lips against my hair—so softly, I can hardly feel it. "I tried hard to hate you full-time—"

"It felt like you succeeded. You were cold, Westbrook."

He shakes his head. "Just an act. When I was around you, it was work to remember that I hated you. I tried to hold on to the image of you as this spoiled, self-satisfied crowd-follower, but all I ever saw was this sweet, cute girl who still made me want to slay dragons just to get her attention. Or save her from mad dogs, at least."

"Yes, you did do that, didn't you?" I sling my arm across his chest. "You totally rescued me from Mad Dog Fang. Even if you were too busy falling all over Lily afterward to let me thank you."

"I wasn't falling over her."

"You so were. You guys were inseparable that night."

"Well, you weren't an option. I had decided that. And Lily was easy to like. She was cute and funny and smart, and I could tell she would never let anyone tell her who to date. Or who not to."

Even though I'm lying safely inside the circle of his arm, I feel a sick thud when he says that. He may have forgiven me for it, but I still did something hateful to him. And I'd give anything not to have.

"I am so sorry for what I did that night," I say, hiding my face against his chest so my words are muffled. "I wanted so badly to be able to take it back, to get you to forgive me, but you wouldn't let me. And then you were just so totally gone . . ."

He nuzzles my temple. "It's okay, Anna. You were fifteen—so was I—and we both acted pretty stupidly. You shouldn't have blown me off, but I should have given you a chance to apologize."

"What I did was worse than anything you did. And you know it wasn't just that night." I swallow hard. I want everything out in the open. So I can be completely forgiven. I just can't look at him while I put it out there. "I should have told the whole world how much I liked you right from the beginning. And instead I kept it a secret. I don't even know why. I guess I was scared that if my friends knew and didn't approve, I'd have to choose between them and you. But afterward I realized that not being with you was a thousand times worse than having to stand up to them would have ever been."

"When did you figure that out?"

"The second I didn't get to be with you anymore." I push my face even harder against his shoulder. "I mean it, Finn. I missed you so much, and I only had myself to blame, which didn't exactly make it better."

"You know, my family would have moved away even if we'd kept going out."

"I know. But we would have stayed close. We would have texted and talked and seen each other whenever we could." I lift my head to look at him. "Like when we go to college next year. We may end up far away, but—" I stop, worried I'm being presumptuous. Maybe he doesn't think this is something that will last until next fall.

But all he says is, "You're right. Being geographically separated isn't the same as being *apart*."

"And you admit that I was way more stupid and at fault than you were?"

"Okay," he says with a grin that I can only see from

the side but is all the cuter for being lopsided from this angle. "I'll admit that. And I'll admit something else too, while you've got me pinned down and unable to escape—"

I raise my arm off his chest. "Hardly!"

He pulls it back down across his body. "I like it there. Anyway, do you want to hear my confession?"

"Of course."

"That night at the music festival . . . I was incredibly jealous of that guy who was kissing you. I mean, there I was with Lily, who is by all objective counts a total babe—"

"Prettier than me."

He shakes his head and says vehemently, "No! I don't agree with that at all. But anyone who saw me with her would definitely say I was the lucky one of the two. Anyway, my point is that instead of appreciating my luck and enjoying myself, I kept looking around to see what was happening with you and that Wade guy and thinking about how he was kissing you and how I used to get to do that and how much I wished I still could. I kept wondering if you still had that little gap next to your front incisor. . . ."

"Do I?" I try to feel if it's there with my tongue, but it just feels like the inside of my mouth.

He hits his forehead with the palm of his free hand. "Can you believe it? I forgot to check."

"Too late now," I say regretfully.

"I think you're wrong about that," he says, and rears up over me, pulling my upper body up to meet his as his mouth descends on mine.

"The gap is gone," he murmurs in my ear a few minutes later. "I used to be able to stick the tip of my tongue in there."

"Are you disappointed?"

"Not sure yet. Let me see."

I'm working on convincing him it's not a major loss—that kissing me can still be moderately pleasurable—and I feel I'm making some real progress in that direction when I hear voices coming from downstairs.

"My dad's home." I sit up so I can listen more intently. "And I'm pretty sure he's got Ginny with him."

"Ginny? Who's that?"

"The volleyball coach—the one who came into the art room today."

"Oh, her. What's her connection to your father? Are they going out?"

"I don't know," I say. "Sort of? But it's weird. She's my sister's friend. She's like a quarter of a century younger than he is. Also? She's incredibly annoying."

"Yeah," Finn says. "I got that in the thirty seconds I spent with her today."

"It's her superpower."

"Do we have to go down and say hi to them?"

I flop back down next to him. "I don't want to. Do you?"

"Why would I want to?"

"Wade would have." I explain to him how Wade was using me to get to my father's Stanford connections.

"I knew I didn't like him," Finn says.

"Shh," I say, because there are voices on the stairs and whispers going past my room. Fortunately my door is closed. Fortunately for all of us, I guess, because the only place Dad and Ginny can be heading right now is toward the master bedroom.

A door shuts.

"Um," Finn says. "I think your father just brought a girl up to his room."

"He could just be showing her his art collection." I put up my hand. "Don't dignify that with a response."

"Don't worry. I'm not touching it." He points up at the ceiling. "You ever think of putting solar panels on your roof? Your house is made for it."

"I'll mention it to my dad," I say. "But maybe not right this second."

"Does it bother you?" he asks, sitting up and leaning back against the headboard. "That your dad's in there with her?"

"I don't want to *think* about it, but otherwise it doesn't bother me. They're both grown-ups. I just wish he had better taste in women."

"She did seem kind of awful."

"You have no idea. You don't think there's any possible future where I might have to call her 'Mommy,' do you?"

"I'm pretty sure this is how 'Cinderella' started."

"Yeah, or 'Snow White.' It's more—" I stop. "Who's that?" A car has stopped in front of our house. I get on my knees and push back the shade over the window so I can peer out. Someone gets out of the car. "Oh my god, it's *Lizzie*. What's she doing home?"

"Lizzie? The one who used to drive me?"

I look over my shoulder at him. "Excited to see her again?"

"Excited's not the right word. Are you sure you're from the same family? You're like two different species."

"Maybe I was adopted?" I sigh. "Nah, I look too much like my mother."

"Come on," he says, scuttling off the bed. "I want to see your sister."

"Really? Why?"

"I want to see if she's changed. Also, if she can help me get into Berkeley."

"You'd better be joking," I say, and he just grins at me and holds out his hand to help me off the bed.

Lizzie's already inside the house by the time we make it to the bottom of the stairs.

"Oh, hi," she says, dropping an enormous suitcase

down onto the floor. "I didn't think anyone was home. It was so quiet." She narrows her eyes at Finn. "Who are you?"

"I'm Finn. I rode in the back of your car for an entire year."

"Oh, right! You were that little guy. Wow, you've changed."

"So have you. You cut your hair."

She rolls her eyes. "Yeah, like a hundred times since then."

"And I'm sure you looked lovelier with each trim," he says soberly.

Lizzie stares at him with the suspicious uncertainty of someone who's not sure if she's being teased or not.

"Why are you home?" I ask, and she turns to me.

"My Monday class was canceled and I had a ton of laundry." She gestures to the ginormous bag. "And my roommate invited some friend of hers to stay all weekend long, and they're both into musicals, and they wouldn't stop playing *Cats* and *A Chorus Line*, and I thought I'd probably kill them both if I didn't get out of there. And then this girl I know said she was driving to LA and back this weekend, so I had a free ride. Except just now she asked me to chip in for gas, which doesn't seem fair, given the fact she was going to make the trip whether I went with her or not." She glances around. "Is Dad home?"

340

I glance at Finn and hesitate just a moment before saying, "Yeah. I think he's up in his room."

She pushes the suitcase to the side with her foot. "I'd better go say hi. He sounded kind of sad the last time we talked. He doesn't do well when I'm not here."

"He sobs into his pillow every night. I can hear him from my room."

"Don't be obnoxious," she says, and heads up the stairs. Finn and I follow close behind.

"You should stop her," he whispers. "Or at least warn her."

I'm tempted to stay quiet and see what happens, but I know he's right (and I want him to think I'm as nice a person as he is), so I call after her, and she turns around at the top of the stairs. "What?" she says.

"I think someone might be in there with Dad. We heard a woman's voice."

"You mean like a date?"

"Maybe. I don't know. We didn't actually see them."

"Weird," she says. "He usually tells me if he's dating someone. Are you sure you didn't just hear the TV?" She knocks on his door. "Dad?" she calls. "It's me! Surprise! Can I come in?" Then she opens the door and steps inside. We can only see her from the back, but we can still hear her. First she says, "Oh god—I'm sorry." Then she says, "Wait—Ginny? *Ginny?* What are you doing here?"

Ginny steps forward and I can see her through the open doorway. She's buttoning her blouse with one hand and holding up the other hand in a placating gesture. "Everything's cool, Lizzie. Relax."

"What the hell, Ginny? I mean, *what the hell*?"

"Why are you freaking out?"

"Are you seriously asking me that?"

"Yes, I'm seriously asking you that!"

Their voices are almost identical, high-pitched and outraged.

Well, Lizzie's may be just a touch shriller. "He's my father! That's so incredibly— Do you ever think about anyone other than yourself? Ever?"

Ginny tucks in her shirt and smooths her hair. "I just don't see what the problem is." She spots me and Finn hovering in the shadows and beckons to us. "Help me out here, Anna. Anna's known about me and your dad for a long time," she informs Lizzie. "And she's completely cool with it, aren't you, Anna?"

"Oh, Ginny," I say kindly but sadly. Not for any special reason—I've just wanted to *oh, Ginny* her for a while.

I'm saved from saying anything more—which is good, since I have nothing more to say—by my father's appearance behind her, fully clothed and not a hair out of place. Either things hadn't progressed far, or he can pull himself together quickly. He steps past Ginny and puts his hand on Lizzie's arm. "I'm so sorry," he says. "I don't know what happened." He passes his hand over his forehead. "I think I had too much wine at dinner."

Ginny stares at him openmouthed. "You're *sorry*?"

He avoids her eyes as he strokes Lizzie's shoulder reassuringly. "This is very awkward for us all," he says gently.

I hear a little cough from Finn, and I glance over. I see how the edges of his mouth are twitching and our eyes meet, and then he has to cough again. He's desperately trying to stifle a laugh. That starts me off. I have to press my hand against my mouth to keep from giggling audibly. We press our shoulders against each other, shaking with repressed laughter.

"I came home just to see you, Daddy," Lizzie says in a little-girl voice. "I missed you. I didn't know *she'd* be here."

"Do you want her to go?" Dad says. She nods, and he musses her hair a little. "All right." He turns to Ginny. "I think it would be best."

"You have got to be kidding me," she says. "I mean, *seriously*?" She shakes her head vehemently. "You have *got* to be kidding me."

"Let's take a short time-out," he says. "That's all we need. Just a little time. Everything is fine. We're all good here. We just need some time. . . ." His eyes flicker around desperately and settle on me. "Anna? Can you give Ginny a ride home?" He nods at Finn. "Hello there, young man. I assume you're a friend of Anna's? Welcome." Trust Dad to keep his company manners even in this situation.

Finn introduces himself, and I say, "We can drive Ginny home."

Ginny straightens her shoulders and raises her chin. Her breasts are kind of magnificent when she stands like that. "Are you sure?" she says to my father in a coldly dignified tone. "I may not come back."

"Just go," Lizzie snarls from the safety of my father's arms.

twenty-six

Ginny dissolves into tears on the way to her house. "I thought he was different," she moans from the backseat. "I thought, here's a nice guy. A decent guy. Someone who can take care of me. I mean, he takes care of all of *you*, right?" And then she wails, "My father never took care of me—he was an alcoholic, and I always had to take care of hi-im!"

My phone buzzes. At the next red light I check the text. It's from Finn:

well that explains it, right? The father thing?

I glance over at him and nod, pressing my lips together hard and biting the inside of my cheek so I don't laugh out loud.

"I thought Lizzie was my friend," Ginny says a little while later. She's stopped crying, but her nose sounds stuffed now. "How could she act like that?"

"I think she was just surprised," I say.

"Even so . . . she didn't have to be mean."

When we reach her apartment building, she opens her car door then turns back to us. "Tell your dad—" She stops. "Never mind," she says. "If he wants to apologize, he knows my number."

Finn and I wish her a good night and watch her walk up the path to the front door of her building. It's one of those ugly little apartment buildings you find all over the west side of LA: squat and stuccoed and no different from a dozen others on the same block.

I say slowly, "If you had told me six hours ago that I might feel sorry for Ginny Clay . . ."

"I don't understand your father. He didn't even put up a fight."

I'm silent for a moment. Then I say, "If he really does like her, he's just made a terrible mistake. And he's going to regret it. A lot."

"Yeah? How would you know?"

I glance over at him. He tilts his head at me, his eyes aware and slightly amused.

"Some of us learn from our mistakes," I say.

He reaches out for my hand and takes it. He presses each finger gently between his thumb and index finger. It's the lightest touch, but it still makes me breathe in with sudden sharpness.

"Let's go somewhere," he says.

"Anywhere," I say, and I mean it.

* * *

We end up back at the bluffs. As we hold hands and look at the dark water below us, I tell him again that I'm sorry, that I knew I was hurting him when I said I wouldn't go to the dance, and that I've never seen the ocean since then without regretting it.

"Not even the Atlantic?" he teases.

"Not even a Great Lake," I say. "A glass of water makes me feel bad. . . ." I shake my head. "I'm serious, Finn. Well, not about the glass of water. But about feeling bad."

He's silent for a moment, then he shifts and says, "Don't."

"Don't what?"

"Be all regretful." His voice speeds up. "I mean, look at where we are, right now, today. Would we be this happy and this relieved and this thankful to be together if all that hadn't happened? So many other things might have gone wrong along the way. But we're standing here, looking at the ocean, happy to be together, and it couldn't be any better. So don't waste time with regrets. Okay?"

"Okay" is all I say, but I think, *So this is what bliss feels like.*

After the bluffs and some shave ice and a walk through the Santa Monica Promenade, which is crowded and noisy because it's Friday night, Finn takes me home and we have a long, lingering good-bye, which only ends so we can get some sleep before we meet up again as early as possible tomorrow morning.

I text Lucy on my way upstairs.

If youre awake call me.

The phone rings as soon as I'm inside my room.

"It's about time," she says when I answer.

"About time for what?"

"That you told me about you and Finn. I can't believe you told the twins before you told me."

Right. My visit to Lily. News travels fast.

"It's been like five minutes," I say. "And I only told Lily first because . . . you know . . . it felt weird not checking in with her. And that was before I was sure about anything."

"It's fine," she says. "I'm not really mad. I might have been if you hadn't texted tonight, but you did, so we're good. So . . . seriously? You and Finn?"

"Yep."

"Cool. Weird, but cool. And you don't have to worry about Lily at all. I talked to her, and she's really happy for you guys. I think she felt guilty about dumping Finn for James, and this took that all away." She pauses. "It's funny, though, you know?"

"What?"

"That you wouldn't even dance with him back in ninth grade. I guess people change."

348

"Yeah," I say. "They grow up and stop acting like idiots."

"That's half true."

"Are you saying I'm still an idiot?"

"I'm saying we all are." And then she talks for a while about Jackson and how he says he wants to see her but never has time. I listen and say all the right things, but mostly what I'm thinking is that any girl who likes anyone other than Finn is crazy.

Lily texts me on Sunday.

Well?

Well, what?

You and Finn?

I'm with him right now.

We're drinking hot chocolate at Starbucks and supposedly doing homework. Our books are open in front of us, but we're not actually looking at them. Finn was just telling me about this trip his family took to Scandinavia a couple of years ago and how the sun pretty much never went down and how he and his brother and his parents walked back to their hotel through the streets of Finland at 2:00 a.m. one day and he felt like he was dreaming. He's excited, and he's speaking quickly, and he's shoving his hair out of his eyes as he's talking, and he keeps pushing his glasses up his nose, and he's so incredibly and adorably the Finn I've always known that I could explode with happiness.

It's hysterical how you both felt like you had to come see me on Friday.

What do you mean both of us?

GTG

Lily always ends a conversation when she's ready to, which isn't always when other people are ready.

I look up from the phone. "Did you go see Lily before you came over to my house Friday night?"

He looks down at his empty mug. "Yeah. I should have said something, but I didn't know how you'd feel about it. It wasn't like I needed her permission or anything. I just knew I'd feel better if I told her how I felt about you. Just so everything was out in the open."

I laugh. "I did the exact same thing. I'm surprised we didn't run into each other there."

"Really?" He laughs too. "Well, that explains why she didn't seem surprised to see me. I thought she was just distracted because James was there—"

"He was there when I came by. Either you and I just missed each other, or he's always there. Or both." I glance at him sideways. "Were you okay that she was there with him?"

"Totally," he says. Then he hesitates. "Except—"

"What?" It comes out more sharply than I intend.

350

"She could do better. He's kind of a pretentious douche bag."

"Yeah," I say. "I thought so too when I met him. But are you sure you're not just saying that because you're jealous of him? Maybe just a little bit?"

"Anna," he says, and reaches for my hand, "I'm the guy the rest of the world should be jealous of right now."

I squeeze his hand. "What would you have done if Lily had said she wasn't comfortable with our going out?"

"I knew she'd be okay with it."

"But if you knew, then why bother?"

"You went to talk to her too!" he says accusingly. "What were *you* thinking?"

"Exactly the same as you," I admit. "That I didn't *need* her to say it was okay, but I *wanted* her to. I have no idea what I would have done if she'd said she didn't want us to date. Argued her down, I guess. Or told her I was sorry, but—" I stop.

"But what?"

"But I wasn't going to give you up. I couldn't."

"And if everyone else had been mad at us because of her?"

"I wouldn't care what they think. I've learned my lesson, Finn."

"Good," he says. And if he sounds a tiny bit smug, I can't really blame him.

We spend the rest of the afternoon together, but he's supposed to see his grandparents that night, so I go home alone around dinnertime. Lizzie's gone back to school, which is a relief. She spent the weekend acting like she'd been injured in some way. Somehow she convinced Dad he owed it to her to take her to her favorite restaurants and even shopping at Fred Segal. I don't know why he fell for her "poor little me" routine—he was the one who was barged in on—but I don't care. While they were racing around spending money, I was hanging out with Finn.

Dad's in the kitchen when I arrive, hunched over a plastic take-out container of sushi, some sort of legal-looking document next to it that he's marking with a pen. He's a small and solitary figure in our big kitchen, and I almost feel sorry for him, but his first comment—"Oh, it's you. I was hoping Lizzie hadn't left yet"—kills my budding sympathy.

"She's gone," I say.

"That's too bad." He glances around. "The house feels very quiet tonight."

"You could call Ginny."

He shakes his head. "Oh, no. That whole thing was a mistake."

"Why do you say that?"

He seems surprised by the question. "Isn't it obvious?

Didn't you see Lizzie's reaction?"

"Does Lizzie's reaction matter? She doesn't even live here anymore."

"This is still her home. And I care what my daughter thinks. What all my daughters think," he adds. He skillfully and delicately picks up the last piece of sushi with chopsticks, pops it into his mouth, and pushes the empty container away. He chews and swallows and says, "It's unfortunate that Lizzie didn't call before coming this weekend. Always remember, Anna, that surprises are a bad idea. More often than not, the person who's giving the surprise ends up getting one."

"True enough in this case. Lizzie was definitely surprised."

"Painfully awkward for everyone . . . But maybe it was for the best. In fact, I'm sure it was. Sometimes we get swept up in other people's plans and lose sight of our own, and I'm afraid that in spite of all my education and experience, I'm as susceptible as the next man."

He must be making a point under all that verbosity. I try to figure out what it is. "Are you saying Ginny liked you more than you liked her, and you were just going along with what she wanted?"

He shifts uncomfortably. "I can't speak to her emotions. I do think she was more focused on creating some kind of forward momentum than I was."

Why can't he just say things normally? I'm still

confused. "You could 'speak to' your own emotions, Dad. What were they? What are they?" I really want to know the answer to this. Does he like her? Is he embarrassed by the idea of going out with her? Is he worried he's too old? Was he already getting sick of her? If Lizzie had been in favor of the whole thing, would he have been relieved? Or was he relieved that she tossed Ginny out? He must feel *something* about all this, right?

If he does, I'll never know. He gives a little awkward laugh and says, "I'm just glad I didn't make even more of a fool of myself. I don't know what I was thinking."

"But didn't you like her?"

"I'm too old for this kind of conversation, Anna. Don't you have homework to do?" He bends back down over the brief he was editing.

Maybe if Lizzie hadn't shown up when she did, Ginny and Dad could have enjoyed each other's company for a while, or maybe they'd have grown tired of each other pretty quickly. I guess it doesn't matter. She's gone.

And will apparently not be publicly mourned.

twenty-seven

I t's good to walk into the cafeteria at lunch on Monday and see Lily sitting there, laughing and talking, part of the group again.

But I still feel like something's different about her now, and that feeling grows as we all talk. She listens more, speaks less. She doesn't fidget or jump up or grab at things or insist that everyone's attention be on her most of the time.

Maybe the blow to her head affected her brain—Hilary told me a couple of days ago that the doctors had said it wasn't unusual for someone with a concussion to come out of recovery with some personality changes. So maybe it's that. Or maybe her close call with serious injury just made such a profound impression on her that it's changed the way she thinks and acts.

She's dressed simply again today, in an old pair of jeans and a cotton sweater. She hasn't done anything special with her hair—it just hangs, the bottoms still light from where she bleached them, all the color washed out. If she's wearing makeup, I can't tell. She looks younger, prettier, more vulnerable than the old costumey Lily. And much more tired.

Finn is the last one to arrive at the cafeteria. "You're back!" he says to her happily, and puts down his tray so he can give her a hug. When he lets go, he glances over at me, and even though the hug was a little tough to watch, it's okay because his glance says that he knows I might need reassurance and that I don't have to worry about anything. When he sits down across from me, his foot finds mine and presses against it, repeating the message.

"So how does it feel to be back?" he asks Lily.

"Strange. Nice, but strange. James said when he went back to school last week, he felt like he was underwater. Like he could see everything and everyone, but there was this . . . *thickness* in the air all around him. And that's exactly how I feel." She gazes at each of us in turn with her expressive eyes, like she wants to impress upon us just how in sync she and James are. "Underwater."

"Did you have to choose that particular metaphor?" her sister asks, wrinkling her nose.

"Yeah," Finn says. "I'm not entirely comfortable with it either."

Hilary turns to glare at him and then at me. "I'm pissed at you guys," she says. "I had to hear about you from Lily."

"Hear about them?" Oscar repeats. He squints and waggles his finger back and forth between Finn and me. "You two?"

"Kinda sorta," I say.

"Your enthusiasm is overwhelming," Finn says to me.

"Here." I put a plate on his tray. "You can have my brownie. If that's not a sign of true devotion, I don't know what is."

"I made brownies once," Lily said. "They were great."

"No, they weren't," Lucy says.

"No, they weren't," she agrees.

"Well, no one told *me* anything," Phoebe says. "But I approve, anyway. Anna and Finn make a lot more sense than Finn and Lily ever did."

"What's that supposed to mean?" Lily says. "I mean, I approve too, but still—what's that supposed to mean?"

Phoebe shrugs. "Finn has this whole nerdy intellectual side that doesn't fit with you—no offense," she adds to Finn, who shakes his head and says, "None taken."

"I can be intellectual," Lily says with some of her old sass.

No one responds.

"Screw you all," she says. "Intellect is overrated, anyway."

"Yes, you'd have to think that, wouldn't you?" Hilary says sweetly, and her sister throws a roll at her.

"Well, this is just great," Oscar says glumly. "There's Phoebe and Eric—"

"Just call us Pheeb-ric," Eric puts in.

"And now Finn and Anna—"

"Fanna?" Finn suggests.

I say, "That's just . . . No."

"This isn't a friend group anymore," Oscar says. "It's Match-dot-com."

"It's a friends-with-benefits group," Phoebe says.

"Only for some of us." Hilary slumps in her chair. "Seriously, this is getting ridiculous. Lucy has Jackson, and Lily has James. I'm like the only person here who's alone."

"Ahem," says Oscar. "Ahem."

"This is all your fault," Hilary tells him. "If you were straight, we could go out and then we'd all line up perfectly."

"You're assuming he'd be into you," Lily says.

"I would be," Oscar says.

"Yeah, right."

"Let's go out, anyway," Oscar says to Hilary, ignoring Lily. "Gay guys make the best boyfriends. I actually like to go clothes shopping."

"Oscar's already got more potential than Jackson," Lucy says. "Jackson and I *talk* about dating, but we almost never actually go out."

"You're right, Oscar's better," Hilary says.

"Just don't call me your 'gay boyfriend,'" Oscar says. "I hate when girls do that."

"What *should* I call you?"

"A hunka hunka burning love."

I laugh with everyone else, only I think I laugh harder. Not because I think it's all so funny, but because I'm so happy that we're basically all back to normal except that this time I'm the one with Finn.

After school he and I walk over to our old haunt—the frozen-yogurt shop—which I've spent the last two years avoiding but am willing to go back to now that I can go with Finn again. Over a shared bowl of four different flavors and about eight toppings (I'm a brownie and chocolate chip kind of girl, but Finn is all about fruit), Finn says, "Hey, whatever happened with your sister and that girl? Do you know?"

I nod. "I just IM'd with Molly yesterday."

"And?"

"They had started to see each other again, and Molly was thinking maybe she'd been unfair, but then Wally's family came to town for family weekend. Molly ran into them and waited to see what Wally would do. And Wally just let them ignore her again. Didn't try to make them say hi to her or acknowledge her in any way." I lean forward. "Some people don't appreciate it when they get a second chance." I push my knee against his. "Some do."

"Two's all you get," he warns me. Joking. But not entirely.

"I only needed one and a half," I say.

epilogue

five months later

"Now I know how movie stars feel on the red carpet," Lucy says as we swivel obediently toward one camera after another.

"Get closer together," her mother orders as she squints at her cell phone. "Anna, smush right up against Phoebe, and you two twins come forward at the ends. Lucy, smooth out your skirt. Okay, that's better." More clicking.

"Now one with the boys," Yuri Lee says.

"Not yet," Phoebe's mother says. "They keep looking in different directions. I need one shot with all the girls looking at me." She waves her hand in the air, and we all obediently turn toward her. "Smile and say *prom*, girls!"

Phoebe groans with embarrassment, but the rest of us laugh and say, "Prom." I glance at Molly, and we roll our eyes at each other, but she's grinning. She's right in the middle of all the parents. She drove down from school for the weekend because she knew that if she didn't, I'd be the only kid without a family member clucking over me tonight. Dad didn't take photos of her or Lizzie on their prom nights, so it seemed unlikely he'd start with me. I didn't think I cared all that much about having my photo taken, but I have to admit it's kind of nice to gaze out at the sea of middle-aged faces all focusing on their own children and see someone who's looking at *me*.

Molly got home late last night, and this morning we drove out to Glendale to see Marta, our old nanny. She hugged us to her chest, tears in her eyes, because she said we had both changed since the last time she'd seen us and that we were too beautiful for her to believe. In the car on the way home, Molly said to me, "Do you ever think of how screwed up we might have been if Marta hadn't been around to take care of us when we were little?"

I didn't have to respond to that. We both knew the answer.

"Okay, now with the boys!" Phoebe's mom says, and we beckon to our dates, whose parents were taking some shots of them over by the pool while the girls were getting the paparazzi treatment over near the deck.

We're in Hil and Lil's backyard. They invited everyone

over to give our parents a chance to take their fill of photos before we all share a limo to the hotel. Not that the parents seem like they'll ever have enough shots— they've taken what feels like a million, and they're still going strong.

We rearrange ourselves into girl/boy couples. Well, not entirely girl/boy: Oscar's date is named Matthew. He has black hair and wide green eyes and is almost exactly Oscar's height. The two of them look pretty adorable in matching tuxes. Matthew goes to James's school; Lily met him at some party a couple of months ago and instantly got him and Oscar to FaceTime each other. They had their first date ten days later and have officially been a couple for well over a month. Oscar likes him a lot but, being Oscar, continually frets about whether or not it will last and whether or not it *should* last and whether or not they're really in love or just think they are because their choices are so limited.

Finn comes over to stand behind me. I swivel so I can look at him. I know I'm biased, but he's the cutest guy here today. He's combed back his hair, and he's wearing his contacts and looks totally killer in a slim black tux. I wouldn't want him to look like this all the time—his slightly scruffy everyday self is just fine with me, and most of the time I actually prefer him in glasses because it makes me think of the old Finn—but it's definitely fun to see him all fancy for a night.

I guess the feeling's mutual, because he touches my bare shoulder and says, "It's a good thing girls don't dress up like this all the time. Guys would lose the ability to speak coherently."

"You seem to manage."

"It's a struggle."

I *am* pretty pleased with my dress. I found it at a small store in Venice. It's pale green with a tight, strapless bodice that flows into a long, full skirt. I had my hair professionally curled, and when I move my head, I can feel the ringlets tickling my naked upper back. My shoes are very delicate—just a couple of narrow, gold-leather straps on spike heels.

Phoebe and Eric are posing next to us. She's wearing a short, tight, electric-blue dress that gives her curves she doesn't normally have. Her hair is swept up in a French knot, and she had her makeup professionally done so for once she looks glamorous instead of like she's ready to go for a jog. She helped Eric pick out his tux, and the vest matches her dress.

I swear Eric's face is going to break into two halves if his grin gets any broader. He still can't believe he gets to go out with Phoebe, even after over six months. She's told me more than once that she might break up with him before leaving for college, and I'd be worried for him, except that I don't believe she'll actually do it—I've seen how much she depends on his support when she falls apart, like when she got rejected by her first-choice college. He dropped everything to hold her through an entire weekend of weeping and despair (only the one weekend though, because she found out she was accepted at UCLA that following Monday and decided that was just as much her first choice as Pitzer had ever been). Anyway, I don't think she'd last a week without running back to him. She needs him. She just doesn't know it yet.

Lucy's standing next to Phoebe and Eric, in front of her date, Flynn Flexner. "Hate the name, love the guy," I said when she told me he had asked her to the prom and she'd said yes. Over the years Flynn's been in a bunch of my classes, and even though we've never been close, we've always been friendly. He's tall and skinny, and his hair looks like someone attached it to his head wrong—it's bunched up on one side, flat on the other— and he has a great laugh and is really smart. What's not to like? Other than his name, I mean.

Mostly I'm relieved Lucy's finally over her crush on Jackson. All it took was one week of them really dating for her to realize it wasn't going to work. Lacrosse season had ended, and he finally had time for her, but after they'd spent about three solid hours together, she was complaining that they had nothing to say to each other, and after five, she was trying to figure out how to break it off. I'd say it's a lesson in "be careful what you wish for," except *I* wished for something and was very happy to get it, so I guess you just should be careful that what you wish for is *worth* wishing for.

She's not actually going out with Flynn. They're just friends. Although I've noticed the way he keeps looking at her in her strapless, black-lace minidress, and I have a feeling that, before tonight's over, Lucy will either have to kiss him or break his heart. It could go either way, but I doubt anything between them will last long, since they're going to colleges on opposite coasts. He's heading off to Berkeley in the fall, and she's going to Yale, just like she'd hoped.

The twins are standing next to each other on the other side of Lucy. They're doing something tonight I've never seen them do before, not once in the three years I've known them: they're wearing matching outfits. I was stunned when I walked in and saw them in their identical, long, clingy navy gowns. Even their hair looks the same: Lily's had a geometric, chin-length bob for the last few weeks, and Hilary pinned hers underneath so it looks like it's the same length. They're wearing identical makeup too: smoky eyes, dark red lips, and barely noticeable blush.

I asked them why they decided to dress the same tonight, and Hilary said, "It was Lily's idea. Since we're going to different colleges, she said this was our last chance to have fun with the whole idea of being twins."

Lily added, "We've always tried so hard to make every-one see us as two different people—but now that you all do, we wanted to mess with your heads."

What's funny is that I've always assumed the two girls would be almost indistinguishable if you took away their different haircuts and style and all that, but now that they're dressed exactly alike, I can see how different their features really *are*—maybe not from a distance (they're hard to tell apart from across the yard), and maybe not to people who don't know them well (Finn's mother keeps asking them, "Which one are you again?"), but it's surprisingly easy for me to tell who's who. Hilary's face is longer and thinner, and her eyes are slightly smaller, her nose more tipped up. Lily's got a rounder face and looks younger because her eyes are so big. I never noticed the smaller differences before because I never needed to. There were always easier ways to tell them apart.

Lily and James are still going strong as a couple. He's here tonight in a hipster tuxedo that's designed to fit tight and short—you can see an inch of neon green socks above his black-and-white leather shoes. They're both heading off to the University of Miami in the fall.

Hilary thinks this is a huge mistake. "What if one of them wants to break up, and the other doesn't?" she keeps saying to me when they're not around. "Then they're stuck in the same place for four more years."

But they certainly show no signs of breaking up anytime soon. Besides, as I've pointed out to Hilary, it's a big school. They can avoid each other if they have to.

Hilary's going to Tufts—she really wanted to be in the Boston area, and this was the school that worked out for her. She's looking forward to being somewhere new and different, but I think she's going to miss Lily more than she realizes. For all that her sister could drive her nuts, they've moved through the world side by side. This will be the first time she's going to face something new all by herself.

Hil's date tonight is a good friend of James's, a guy named Wilson something (I never did catch his last name), who goes to high school in the Valley. The date was basically a setup by Lily and James, but Hilary met him and approved. Right now he's good-naturedly and willingly putting his arms around her for the couples photos, so I'm guessing he's also happy with the setup.

"Which direction are we supposed to be looking in?" Finn murmurs in my ear. His arms are warm around my shoulders, the fabric of his tux scratchy on my bare skin.

"I'm trying to focus on Molly and your mom," I whisper back. "I figure theirs will be the photos that matter."

"The twins' mother is so loud, I keep looking at her unintentionally."

"I know. How can someone so tiny have such a loud voice?"

The cameras and phones whirr and pop, and my cheeks are hurting from smiling for too long. Phoebe finally steps forward and says, "Enough with the photos. Mom, please stop."

The cameras lower, and we all gratefully move apart. Yuri Lee invites the other parents to enjoy the hors d'oeuvres that Lorena's put out on a table in the shade. The limo isn't due to arrive for another ten minutes.

Finn's mother comes over to us. She's a small woman with a brutally short haircut and round, wire-rim glasses that make her look like an owl. She's wearing what I've come to realize is practically a uniform for her: khakis, a cardigan sweater, and loafers.

"Look at you," she says to her son, running her hand over the front of his jacket. "You look like James Bond."

"Yeah, no one has ever said that to a guy in a tuxedo before," Finn says.

"Be nice to your mother," I say. "Let her enjoy seeing you all cleaned up for once."

"See?" she says to Finn. "Anna appreciates me, even if you don't."

The funny thing is, she's right: I *do* appreciate her. She works long hours and is maybe a little absent-minded and distracted, but she always makes me feel welcome in their home and has told me several times that she's never seen Finn happier than since he and I started dating.

Finn's dad totally scares me. He's not usually around much, but the one time he and I were both at their house for dinner, he turned to me and asked me what I would do about the Israeli-Palestinian situation if I were secretary of state. Apparently that's his idea of making small talk. I panicked and said I hadn't really thought about it, and then to my relief Finn cut in and said, "Let her eat in peace, Dad," and his father said, "I apologize if an intellectual discussion feels onerous to your friend. Perhaps you'd prefer it if I stick to observations about the weather?" "Actually, yeah," said Finn. "We both would."

At least Mr. Westbrook makes me appreciate my own father, who's always gracious and polite to Finn. He's taken us out to dinner a couple of times, and Finn proved to me—not for the first time—that he can talk about anything with anyone. It's incredible. My dad said something about how much he likes wood-fired pizza, and Finn was instantly able to tell him all about the temperature the ovens get to and how it affects the crust and the cheese and stuff like that. Which is why Dad now thinks he's totally brilliant.

Finn's never really warmed up to Lizzie—probably because of his carpool memories—but he likes Molly a lot. She's an abnormal psychology major, and one night back in January I sat and just listened as the two of them discussed everything from autism to schizophrenia to rage disorder. Molly's smart, and she's graduating with all these honors and going right into a graduate program at NYU next fall, but even so, Finn kept up with her, and, after he left that night, Molly said, "He's a good guy, Anna." Since she's never been exactly gushy, I took that as a pretty major compliment.

I look around for her now and spot her talking to Oscar and his boyfriend over by the pool. When I told her he was bringing another boy to prom, she had said, "Tell him he's my hero." I did, but it looks like she's repeating the message herself right now.

Phoebe's mother calls my name, and I turn toward her. She's wearing a silk wrap-dress with a heavy gold necklace today, even though most of the other parents are dressed casually, and her hair has clearly been professionally styled into an updo. I'd like to believe she's going out to a fancy dinner after this, but I have a feeling that she's dressed up to feel like she's sharing in Phoebe's prom experience.

"Wait, wait," she says anxiously. "I haven't gotten a photo with you and Finn yet. I need one."

Finn's mother glances over at her with a slightly baffled expression. She clearly doesn't understand why someone she barely knows would want to take a photo of her son and his date. But I'm not surprised—Phoebe's mother has made it clear she wants to record every single moment of her daughter's high school career, and that includes keeping track of her friends and who they date.

"Now remind me," she says, lowering her camera once Finn has obligingly put his arms around me again and she's taken several shots. "You're both going to be in Rhode Island next year, right? That worked out nicely. I assume you planned it?"

"Well, Anna got into RISD, which is amazing—" Finn says.

"And Finn had his choice of schools, which is even more amazing," I add.

"He really did," his mother says with a small sigh. She had hoped Finn would choose MIT or Stanford, but he didn't. He claims he chose Brown because it was his top choice—and that it was only a coincidence that it was practically within walking distance of where I'm going to be for the next four years.

That's what he claims.

I've been floating ever since we made our decisions, ridiculously happy. I'm going to be studying art at one of the best schools in the country, and Finn will be in the same city. And Molly's going to be in New York, so we'll be able to visit each other easily.

I know that plenty of things might go wrong over the

next year or so. I could trip going up to get my diploma at graduation and break my nose or my hip or my leg. I could get a horrible roommate and spend freshman year fleeing from my own dorm room. I could hate Providence and miss Los Angeles. I could get lost in a snowstorm and get hypothermia. Finn could fall in love with someone else and we could split up. *I* could fall in love with someone else and have to break his heart—

No, that one won't happen. Maybe those other things, but not that last one.

Anyway, there's no point in thinking about what could go wrong. I'm here, right now, basking in the early evening spring sun with my closest friends, waiting for a big-ass limo to take us to the prom that we've been thinking about and planning for and making fun of for the last three and a half years.

And Finn is here, at my side, when he so easily might not have been.

The two mothers move off, and Finn and I look at each other, laughing a little at their essential momness and at this whole ridiculously formal, overly photographed event that we've willingly committed ourselves to.

"The limo will be here soon," I say.

He nods and then says, "Oh, wait! I just remembered—I saw the coolest photo this morning. It's this flower called a monkey orchid. The blossoms look like little dancing men. Little purple dancing men. Here, I saved it for you—" He reaches into his pocket and pulls out his phone.

"Show me," I say, moving right up close to him so I can peer over his arm at the screen. "Show me."

Will Elise's love life be an
epic win or an epic fail?

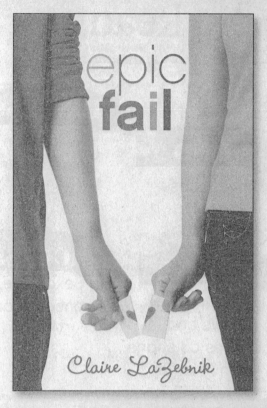

epic
fail

Claire LaZebnik

At Coral Tree Prep in Los Angeles, who your parents are
can make or break you. As the daughter of the new principal,
Elise Benton doesn't have a lot to bank on—until her sister
catches the eye of a guy whose best friend, the gorgeous
Derek, is Hollywood royalty. Now Elise gets to spend a lot
of time with Derek, whether she likes it or not.

And she doesn't. But pride and prejudice can only
get in the way of true love for so long . . .

HARPER TEEN
An Imprint of HarperCollinsPublishers

www.epicreads.com